THE CORPSE IN THE BOG

A GALWAY MURDER MYSTERY

DEREK FEE

Copyright © 2022 by Derek Fee

All rights reserved.

No part of this book may be reproduced in any form or by any electronic or mechanical means, including information storage and retrieval systems, without written permission from the author, except for the use of brief quotations in a book review.

Publisher's Note: This is a work of fiction. Names, characters, places, and incidents are a product of the author's imagination. Locales and public names are sometimes used for atmospheric purposes. Any resemblance to actual people, living or dead, or to businesses, companies, events, institutions, or locales is completely coincidental.

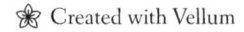

❀ Created with Vellum

For Johnny McDonagh for making me write this book

Behind every great fortune lies a great crime

Honoré de Balzac

CHAPTER ONE

Fiona Madden entered the small church in Glenmore and was surprised that she wasn't struck by a thunderbolt from above. She had last entered this church twenty-three years before and her visits to church had been limited to attendance at the funerals of deceased police colleagues. The church was packed and Fiona was aware of the stares of the congregation as she stood at the rear beside her partner, Aisling McGurk. She was dressed for the occasion in black trousers and a long black coat over a black roll-neck pullover. All three items had been purchased by Aisling on a trip to Galway following the announcement by the hospice of the death of Fiona's father, Conor Madden. Fiona walked forward uncertainly. The past three days had been a whirlwind and a nightmare combined. Fiona and her mother had been launched into organising a funeral. The local priest, Father Flanagan, had been a vital asset in assisting them. The death had been expected. Her father had already received his death sentence in the US and had come home to Ireland to die. By some miracle, he had lasted more than six months and had spent the last month of his life receiving palliative care. As Fiona moved along the nave, it looked like the entire population of Glenmore was in attendance. There's a strange relationship between the Irish and funerals. Maybe it was truer to say that there was a deep relationship between the Irish and the process of putting the dead to rest. Conor Madden was brought home to the house of the woman that he had deserted but never divorced and displayed in his coffin while the denizens of Glenmore sat around in shifts drinking tea and eating sandwiches. Fiona had been obliged to attend for some of these sessions already dressed in his new shop-bought gear. Then came the removal, where Fiona stood beside her mother while several hundred people viewed the body and expressed their condolences. Most of those attending had never met Conor Madden but there was no need to allow that to interfere with a potential social occasion. Fiona passed along the pews trying to avoid the stares of her former neighbours. There were no smiling faces aside from Sean Tracy, her partner from Galway CID, who sat at the end of a pew and nodded at her as she passed. Fiona knew she didn't have many friends in Glenmore. She had burned her bridges when she had solved the murder of a young pregnant girl and sent all the adult members of a family to jail. She searched for a seat in a pew near the rear but every seat was taken. She looked at Aisling who kept her moving along until they reached the pew at the front where her mother sat as the principal mourner. Aisling shouldered her into the pew and let her sit beside her mother before sitting beside her. Fiona glanced across the nave at her father's family, who occupied the other front pew. They were strangers to her. Between them was the pine box that contained the remains of her father, the man she idolised as a child and grew to hate. On the coffin sat a photo of him as a young man. It bore no relation to the skeletal form in the coffin. Thankfully, the top had been screwed down and she wouldn't have to view the shrunken body and the thin face again. Her partner was a clinical psychologist who was identified by her continual asking of the question, 'How do you feel?'

At the moment, Fiona would answer that she wanted to be anywhere but in that church. She hadn't cried since she'd learned of her father's death. Even after six months of visiting him as he disintegrated, he was still a stranger to her. They had tried to connect but too much water had flowed under the bridge. She pitied him but the love she had felt as a twelve-year-old never returned.

Father Flanagan moved to centre stage and the mass began.

Fiona knelt with the rest of the congregation and prayed for someone to get her out of there. The mass was interminable and she stood ready to leave when the priest intoned, 'The mass is ended go in peace.'

But it wasn't over. Uileann pipes struck up a lament from the rear of the church and she waited while the undertaker's men entered and prepared the coffin for its final journey. Her mother grasped her hand and started to weep. They held hands as they followed the coffin from the church. Outside, the priest indicated that Fiona and her mother stand with him at the exit. The congregation filed past, each member shaking hands and intoning the same Gaelic phrase, 'Tá brón orm faoi do thrioblóid.' *I'm sorry for your trouble.*

This whole process was excruciating for Fiona. These people hated her guts and didn't give a damn about her trouble, which in fact didn't exist. Tracy exited and did the necessary, expressing his condolences with sensitivity before moving away and joining Aisling on a grassy knoll. Eventually, the church emptied, and everyone followed the coffin to the small graveyard beside the church.

FIONA STOOD beside her mother at the graveside. The rest of the mourners had already left and made their way to Tigh Jimmy, where drinks and sandwiches would be served, and the wake could be properly held. The grave had been temporarily covered with a swath of artificial turf and two men stood nearby with shovels at the ready to complete the process by filling in the grave.

Maire Madden held on tight to her daughter's hand. 'He wasn't a bad man.' She dabbed at her eyes with a handkerchief.

Fiona had her own opinion on that subject, but she decided to keep it to herself. She could not forget the abandonment and the feelings of betrayal her father had generated. She steered her mother away from the grave. Before they had gone any distance, the quiet of the graveyard was disturbed by the sound of shovelfuls of earth hitting the coffin. She led her mother across the road to Tigh Jimmy, pushed open the door and let her enter. She had been obliged to suffer the stares and whispered remarks of the congregation in the church, but there was no way she was going to repeat the indignity in the pub.

Aisling stood close to her. 'Not going in?'

Fiona shook her head. 'Not my scene. I need to get out of here.'

They went to the low wall on one side of the pub and sat.

Aisling put her arm around her partner. 'It's over. You did well.'

Fiona tapped her head. 'It'll never be over in here.' She looked around. 'Where's Tracy?'

'Inside.'

'Not drinking, I hope.'

Aisling laughed. 'You're not his mother. He's having a coffee and being chatted up by a couple of young women. There are a lot of women who envy you being around a handsome guy like that.'

'He'll soon be on his way. His face is going to be his fortune.' The area surrounding the church and the pub was packed with parked cars. She noticed a car struggling to find a free spot and realised that she recognised detective Garda Brophy as the driver. 'What the hell is he doing here?'

'Who?'

'A colleague from Mill Street.' Fiona continued to watch Brophy manoeuvring until the car stopped. 'He's the one who's generally sent to represent CID when a colleague's relative is being laid to rest. If he intended to attend the funeral, he's a bit late.'

Fiona's phone rang. She glanced at the caller ID. 'Now, there a coincidence.' She took the call. 'Sir.'

'Sorry I couldn't make it to the funeral. I sent Brophy along.'

DI Horgan's attempt at sensitivity fell woefully short of the mark. 'He's just arrived and the funeral's over. We're on to the wake. You realise that I'm on a day off. An official day off for the interment of my father.'

Horgan cleared his throat. 'I know, but something's come up and it's right beside where you are. I thought you might take a look.'

'What about Brophy? Couldn't he deal with this something that has come up?'

'This requires the involvement of a senior officer. You'll be needing to travel a bit and I wasn't sure whether you and Tracy might have started on the grog.'

She would have liked to have already started on the grog. In fact, it had been her intention to put away the maximum amount of grog that her body would take. 'You'll be pleased to hear that neither Tracy nor I have started on the grog, as you put it. What's so bloody important that we have to give up our day off? My father was put into a hole in the ground ten minutes ago.' There was a silence on the phone.

Fiona had been working with Horgan for almost two years and she knew her man. Her boss had the sensitivity of a stone and, in her opinion, a brain to match. She could just imagine him groping for something to say that would display that he actually felt an emotion. She decided to relieve his distress. 'What have we got?'

'A man working on a bog, close to where you are, has called in and says that he's found parts of a body.'

Fiona had planned a long white-wine filled lunch with Aisling and a restful afternoon. But she and Tracy hadn't had a decent case for a while and there was no way she was going to join the crowd in the pub. She supposed that in a way she was glad that Horgan was providing her with a means of escape. 'Man or woman?'

'He wasn't sure. There's only an arm showing. Apparently, he was footing turf close by when the so-called arm popped out at him. It might not even be a body. Could be some kind of animal. We need an experienced detective to take a look at it. And you're just around the corner.'

'How far around the corner?'

'It's in a place called Béal an Daingin.'

Horgan was from Cork city and his idea of around the corner didn't match with hers. 'I know it and it's not just around the corner and I'm dressed for a funeral, not for rambling around a bog.'

'Brophy has some scene suits and overshoes in the car. I'll make the day up to you and Tracy.'

Fiona had heard that one before. 'Can we have that in writing?'

There was silence on the line. 'Get back to me when you have some news.' The line went dead.

Fiona looked at Aisling. 'Will you go inside and get Tracy for me? Even if you have to drag him away from his admirers.'

CHAPTER TWO

Béal a Daingin is a small village in south Connemara whose infrastructure consists of a pub, a post office and a school. The name in Gaeilge means the mouth of the ford and the anglicized name is Bealadangan.

Brophy piloted the police car through the village and continued west before turning onto a narrow road. 'Thanks be to God for the Satnav,' he said. 'I'd never have found this place without it.'

Tracy was riding shotgun while Fiona sat in the rear wearing her glum face. They travelled less than a mile when they saw a man on the top of a small hill waving in their direction. Brophy stopped.

Tracy looked out at the uneven scrubland potted here and there with pools of water. 'This is my best suit. Sorry, let me rephrase that, it's my only suit.'

Fiona opened that passenger door. 'Just be careful where you put your feet. Brophy has scene suits and overshoes in the boot.'

Brophy put on a puzzled look.

Fiona stared at him. 'I am not going on that bog in my good clothes.'

Brophy smiled broadly. 'Only kidding, sergeant. I brought the gear.'

Fiona and Tracy suited up and trekked through the bog until they reached the small hill on which the man was standing.

'Thart ar an am a tháinig sibh' *It's about time you came.* The speaker was a big man over six feet and broad-shouldered. He was leaning on a slean, the traditional tool for cutting sods from the bog. He was in his fifties with a full head of curly dark hair and a broad, weather-beaten Irish face.

Fiona introduced herself and Tracy. 'We'll speak English and I've just come from my father's funeral, so keep a civil tongue in your mouth. Who might you be?'

The man bowed his head. 'I'm Johnny O'Toole. I live just outside the village. I heard the announcement of your father's death on Radio na Gaeltachta. I'm sorry for your trouble.' He extended his hand and Fiona took it. O'Toole indicated two young boys eighty metres away. 'Those are my sons Donal and Michael.'

She noticed that O'Toole was shuffling nervously, but she thought nothing of it. The normal citizen has an inbuilt reaction to both doctors and policemen. The doctors call it *white coat syndrome,* but the police don't have a name for it.

'Where's the body?' Fiona said. She hoped there was still time to salvage the lunch with Aisling, but it would be a late lunch.

O'Toole pointed in the direction of the two boys. 'They're more or less standing on the spot where we found the hand. I was starting a new cut on the bog, and I was only a few feet down when we found it. At first I thought it was just the scraw, but then I saw the hand and I stopped cutting and called nine-nine-nine. They said that someone would be right out, but that was three hours ago. I don't get as much time on the bog and I don't like to miss the day.'

Fiona looked at where the boys were standing and then at

her new girly shoes inside the white plastic overshoes. O'Toole was standing beside her and his wellington boots were covered in muck. There was no way her shoes were going to make it. She looked at Tracy and his sullen face told her that he had made the same assessment about his footwear.

O'Toole started out across the bog, moving nimbly between the pools of oozing black liquid. Fiona kept her eyes on his feet and tried as best she good to use his footsteps. She had almost reached the boys when her right foot slipped and she went up to her shin in bog water. She steadied herself on her left foot and pulled her foot out, making a sucking noise in the process. She looked down at her shoe. Remedial action would be required.

When they arrived at the two boys, Fiona let out a sigh of relief and cursed Horgan in the same breath. She welcomed the possibility of an investigation, but not today and not a body in a bog

O'Toole introduced his two sons who were aged twelve and ten, respectively. Ten metres away on a dry patch of ground, there was a rick of sods under construction and beside it was an old wooden wheelbarrow used for hauling the sods.

'Over here.' O'Toole jumped off a ledge where two rows of sods had already been cut and landed three feet below.

He held out his hands to Fiona. Normally, she wouldn't have taken them but given the circumstance and the potential for further destruction of her footwear she allowed two hands the size of baseball catcher's mitts to ease her gently to the ground.

Tracy was left to his own devices and landed on the ground beside her, accompanied by a squelching sound.

O'Toole released his grip on her and pointed at the face of the cut. 'There.'

Fiona stared at the spot. There was what could be a bare hand covered in brown slime. She had seen some bodies that had been buried in normal ground and they showed significant decomposition after only a few days. The hand that stuck out of the cut section was well preserved. There was a section of arm behind the hand and beyond that only God knew. It was entirely possible that the hand and wrist could be the only body part that existed, or they could be connected to a complete or incomplete corpse. It would be a delicate operation to find out, and it would have to be managed by the Garda Technical Bureau. She took out her phone, but there was no signal.

She turned to O'Toole. 'Has your family always worked this bog?'

O'Toole nodded. 'All the way back to my great-great-grandfather. And with the grace of God, my children will work it when I'm no longer able.' He looked over to the wooden wheelbarrow. 'Mikey is the fourth generation who has handled that barrow. And I hope he won't be the last. But you know as well as me that the young people are leaving in droves.'

Fiona nodded her agreement. She turned and looked towards the sea. The bog extended away inland as far as the eye could see. It was a Neolithic sight. The ground on which she stood had once been the estuary of a great river. The landscape had been altered when the ice retreated and revealed what had lain underwater for eons. If someone had buried a body here, they had chosen well. The question was, how long had the body been in situ? 'Has anyone ever gone missing in the parish?'

'Not in my time, and I never heard my father speak of one. People have gone, but their relatives generally know where.'

'I've got some bad news for you. You won't be working this section of bog until we find out if there's a body connected to the hand.' She turned to Tracy, who had bent to examine the body part. 'Get back to Brophy and see if he has any crime scene tape. I guess the techs will be on site tomorrow and they'll begin excavating. Then we'll have to wait and see what they find.'

O'Toole went to his sons to give them the bad news.

Tracy stood, looked at her and then looked at his feet.

'Don't even think about it,' she said. 'It's as bad as it's going to be.'

'It's all right for you, but I don't have a man mountain to lift me around as though I'm breakable.'

'Do you have a fiver?'

Tracy checked the contents of his pocket. 'Yes.'

'Young Michael looks like he could make the trip to Brophy and back easily enough.'

Tracy held the five euros in his hand and called Michael.

After the transaction had been completed, he re-joined Fiona. 'They're always finding bodies in bogs but they've usually been buried for hundreds or thousands of years. The bog is a great place for preserving bodies.'

Fiona was staring at him. 'There no more for us to do here. As soon as you've affixed some crime scene tape, we're out of here.'

Tracy looked on as O'Toole assisted Fiona to climb back to ground level.

She looked back at Tracy and smiled. Sometimes it paid to be a woman and to look like one.

Mickey arrived with the crime scene tape and helped Tracy string it around the area where the hand was exposed.

Fiona followed O'Toole to the edge of the bog. 'This one looks like it's been in the ground a while,' she said. 'But the techs will be able to tell us. In the meantime, spread the word that the bog is a crime scene and anybody found up here will be prosecuted. Okay? And thanks for taking care of me.'

O'Toole nodded. 'I buried my own father last year. I don't think I'm over it yet.' He teared up and wiped his eyes with his hand.

She didn't expect such gentleness from a man who could audition for the part of Shrek.

Tracy joined her, they ditched their oversuits, saluted the two boys, and Brophy drove back to the main road. As soon as they hit the tarmac, Fiona's phone beeped, indicating that she could get a signal. She punched in the station number and asked for Horgan's extension.

'What do you think?' Horgan asked.

'I think you owe me a new pair of shoes, but I doubt I'll ever see the money. As far as the corpse in the bog is concerned, I have no idea. There's a hand sticking out of a cut and there's a pretty good chance that there's a body attached.'

'The question is: do we need to do something?'

She'd never met Horgan's wife, but she'd learned to pity her by proxy. 'Let's put it this way. I don't think he lay down for a sleep and the bog grew over him. In general, bodies in bogs got there through some crime or other, usually murder. But that conclusion will have to wait until we disinter the remains.'

'Shite, I'll put in a call to the Technical Bureau.'

Horgan was always quick to take on the arduous tasks like calling in the techs. 'We've staked out the area with crime scene tape and I've told the man who was working the bog to keep it on the lowdown, but I guess it's already common knowledge locally.'

'How big is this Béal an Daingin place?' Horgan asked.

'One horse village.'

'No worries then. You and Tracy can handle the follow-up. Keep me posted.'

THE WAKE WAS in full swing when Brophy dropped Fiona back to Glenmore. Thirty or more men had left the pub and spilled out onto the road, smoking and drinking. Fiona and her mother had put five hundred Euros behind the bar, but that had probably been consumed an hour earlier. Fiona exited the car and Brophy was about to drive away when Tracy held his arm. 'Not yet.'

Fiona looked at the crowd. Aisling was nowhere in sight, and there was no way that Fiona was going inside. She turned back and saw that the car was idling and Brophy and Tracy were staring at her. A beer bottle landed at her feet and the shattered glass sprayed her ruined shoes. She turned back and faced the crowd of men.

'Fucking lesbian,' one of them shouted.

Another chimed in. 'Fucking cop bitch.'

The crowd mumbled among themselves, and the mood was turning ugly. She heard a car door open behind her and then Tracy and Brophy were at her side. Another man in the crowd threw a pint glass and Fiona had to duck.

'Time to get out of here.' Tracy took Fiona by the arm.

She resisted. There was no way a crowd of drunken louts was going to intimidate her. All she needed was for one of them to try his hand at assaulting either her or her colleagues. The first one to lift his hand would pay the price for those who thought she was easy meat.

'What the hell is going on here?' Jimmy, the owner of the pub, had exited his establishment and stood in front of the men. 'This woman buried her father this morning. You should be ashamed of yourselves. The next man that tosses a glass will never drink in my pub again.'

Aisling pulled up in her car beside them. 'Fiona,' she shouted. 'Get in before a full scale riot starts and somebody gets hurt.'

Fiona could feel the pressure of Tracy's grip increasing, but she wanted to stand her ground. She didn't want a drunken mob to dictate what she should do.

Jimmy turned and faced her. He didn't speak, but the message was clear on his face—get out of here.

She allowed Tracy to lead her to Aisling's car and open the passenger door.

'They're drunk,' he said. 'And they're not worth the effort. Go home and forget about them.'

She climbed into the car and Aisling immediately put it in gear. As they sped away, the crowd cheered and there were lots of finger signs.

'Home?' Aisling asked.

'Pub, I'm going to get pissed.'

'That won't help. Tracy and that other policeman are behind us. I suppose they're afraid that we might be followed.'

Fiona felt her body sag and she realised her fists had been clenched. 'I wish someone had followed us. I really need to have an aggressive drunk to beat the shit out of.'

'I thought you had done all these exercises to control your aggressive instincts.'

Fiona forced herself to smile and she could feel the tension easing out of her. 'They don't appear to be working today.'

They reached the main road to Galway without incident and Brophy overtook them and sped towards Galway.

'They forced me out of my own village,' Fiona said. 'Why do they hate me so much?'

'You did your job and three members of the same family went to jail. They were their neighbours and they resent you for that.'

'I should have left the murderers of the Joyce girl go free?'

'In the past, it would have been swept under the carpet. You handled the funeral really well. Let's find somewhere for a nice lunch and then we can go home.'

Fiona suddenly felt very tired and pouring alcohol down her throat until she passed out didn't appear as appealing as when she stepped into the car. 'You win, professor. Take me to lunch and then home.'

CHAPTER THREE

When Fiona and Tracy arrived at the bog, two Technical Bureau vans were already parked on the narrow dirt road. Tracy parked up directly behind one of the vans.

Fiona never enjoyed being a spare wheel. The techs were milling about, taking photographs and preparing their gear to ease whatever was on the end of the arm out of the bog. They had already set up the ground penetrating radar, so they had some idea of what they would find. They had a job to do, whereas she and Tracy were bystanders.

Fiona didn't recognise any of the crew and she supposed they were a specialised unit. Removing a body from under three feet of peat bog would be a delicate operation. She and Tracy walked over to the tech who was giving the orders and introduced themselves.

'They said you'd be by.' He extended his hand. 'Detective sergeant Rory O'Donnell, I'm in change of this crew.'

'How long will it take to get the body out?' Fiona asked. She reckoned that O'Donnell was in his mid-thirties. He was slightly built, spoke with a Northern accent and was red-headed. She would have bet a month's pay that he hailed from

Donegal. His designer glasses were tinted and disguised the colour of his eyes, but he had a pleasant face.

'How long is a piece of string?' He looked towards the section of bog where two techs wearing scene suits were fiddling with what looked like a commercial vacuum cleaner. 'We're setting up the GPR and I reckon we'll have some idea of what's ahead within the hour. We have some tea in the van and you're welcome to a cup.' He looked out at the Atlantic. 'That's some view. I've never been to Connemara before.' He turned to Fiona. 'I hear you're a local.'

'Born and bred,' she said. 'This area is known locally as Na h'Oileann, which means the Islands.'

'I know what it means,' O'Donnell said. 'I'm from Glenties.'

Fiona would have won the bet with herself about Donegal. 'The series of small islands stretch out into the Atlantic and are connected by bridges.' She pointed at a large landmass directly to the west. 'The biggest one is Letter Mullen, and it has the most residents.'

'Looks beautiful,' O'Donnell said.

'You're catching it on a good day. You wouldn't fancy it when the wind is howling and the rain is horizontal.'

There was a shout from the techs with the radar machine.

O'Donnell waved. 'We're ready to do a few passes. I'll get back to you when we've got an interesting trace. In the meantime, why don't the two of you have a cup of tea?'

'Do you mind if I watch?' Tracy said.

'Be my guest.' O'Donnell headed in the direction of the GPR, closely followed by Tracy.

THE TEA WAS in a series of thermoses and was piping hot. Fiona poured herself a cup, added milk and sugar, and sat in the car with the door open. Away to her left, she could see the activity was concentrated on the GPR. Although she tried to concentrate on what was happening around her, she kept returning to the sight of the wizened old man lying in the coffin. In her mind, Conor Madden had died twice, but had only been buried once. Aisling constantly asked whether she had been able to cry, and she replied with the truth that she hadn't. Her thirty-five-year-old self hadn't cried, but the twelve-year-old girl had wet her pillow with tears for months after her father's departure. Perhaps the sanguine manner in which she had accepted her father's actual death was unnatural. But she didn't think so. She finished her tea, leaned back in her seat, and closed her eyes.

She came awake when she heard her name being called. She had been dreaming, and it had been her father calling her from afar. A tear was sliding down her cheek and she wondered whether that constituted crying for her father.

'They've got some preliminary traces.' Tracy was standing by the passenger side open door. 'O'Donnell says you should come and have a look.'

Fiona slid from the seat and followed Tracy to the rear of the front van.

O'Donnell and one of the techs were staring at a series of computer screens.

Fiona came up behind them and looked over O'Donnell's shoulder. The screen was a mass of wavey lines. 'What are we looking at?'

'The traces of a pass over the edge of the bog with the protruding hand.' He moved his finger along the trace. 'It looks like we have a mass that could be a body.'

Fiona followed O'Donnell's finger. 'I don't see it.'

O'Donnell pointed to a discontinuity in one of the lines. 'That's it.'

Tracy leaned over the other tech's shoulder. 'I thought we'd see something like a skeleton.'

O'Donnell moved back from the screen. 'We use sound waves. A skeleton would show up on X-rays but they only penetrate soil to a depth of a foot or so. But we've got a bit of news for you. We ran a couple of traces over the area. I think there are two bodies down there, not one. They're lying side by side.'

'Will they be easy to get at?' Fiona asked.

'You'll want the bodies in the best possible condition, I suppose,' O'Donnell said.

'Absolutely.'

'Then we'll have to proceed with care.'

'How long?'

'We should have the first one up by this evening and the second soon after. There's nothing more you can do here. I'll give you a call when we're close.'

Fiona toyed with the idea of leaving Tracy, but O'Donnell was right, there was nothing they could do until the bodies were disinterred. 'Okay, but I want to be on site before they're bagged and shipped to the Regional Hospital.'

O'Donnell nodded. 'We'll do a couple more traces with the GPR to verify the situation. Then we'll start the process of recovering the bodies.'

'Any idea how long they've been down there?' Fiona asked.

'That's way beyond our capabilities. But they're shallow. I don't think you'll be using carbon dating to work it out.'

'Call me,' Fiona headed towards the car with Tracy in tow.

'Two bodies,' Tracy said as he took his place behind the wheel. 'Maybe it was a suicide pact.'

Fiona closed her eyes. It never rains but it pours.

CHAPTER FOUR

DI Horgan's brow furrowed. 'Two bodies, you say? I hope to God they've been down there for centuries. But given your luck, Madden, they were only laid there last week.'

Fiona and Tracy were sitting facing their boss in his office. 'I think you're okay there, boss,' Fiona said. 'They'd be more fresh if it was only last week. The arm looked like it's been down there for a good while.'

'Nothing for us to do, then.' Horgan smiled as he leaned back in his chair. 'The technical team will bag them up and we can arrange for them to be laid to rest with a corresponding Christian ceremony.'

'What if they were Jewish?' Tracy said.

Horgan shot forward. 'Are you trying to be funny, Tracy?'

'No, boss,' Tracy said quickly.

Fiona decided to defuse the situation. It was her job to poke fun at Horgan, but lately Tracy was getting in on the act. She wasn't sure how Horgan had reached the exalted rank of detective inspector, but there had to be a story. Maybe there was another Horgan who was a competent detective and a good manager and one of the lads in the Phoenix Park had stuck the pin in the wrong one. 'The chief tech, a detective sergeant Rory O'Donnell, thinks that they may have one of the bodies out by this evening. Garda Tracy has a point, though. Depending on the age of the corpses, we should attempt to identify them. There may be relatives still living. We should give them a chance to lay their own people to rest.'

'True, true.' Horgan stroked his chin. It was his thinking tell. 'I don't think there's any need to bother the chief or the Park with this. It'll probably turn out to be a damp squib. Follow up with the tech team.'

Fiona stood. 'In the meantime, I'll ask detective Garda Brophy to run a search on any missing persons in the area. We'll be a little ahead in the game if they turn out to be more recent deposits.'

'I'm not happy that you're continually co-opting Brophy,' Horgan said. 'I already warned you about empire building.'

'He's more proficient than Tracy in terms of research. Of course, if he's otherwise engaged.' She knew that Brophy was downstairs twiddling his thumbs, or more likely playing a computer game.

Horgan picked up a file and opened it. 'I suppose there's no harm in letting him look into the missing persons angle. Just in case we need it in the future.'

'Good thinking, boss,' Tracy said as he followed Fiona out the door.

'Are you trying to get yourself fired?' Fiona said as they descended the stairs.

'I'm a bit tetchy today. And quite honestly, I don't give a damn whether I'm fired or not.'

'And why is that?' They reached the squad room, but Fiona didn't open the door. This wasn't the Tracy she was getting to know so well. She smelled girlfriend trouble.

'I'm wondering whether this is the right job for me,' Tracy said.

Fiona smiled. There wasn't a policeman alive that didn't question whether the job was really for them. It generally had something to do with dealing with the dark side of life. Or sometimes it was about the disintegration of family life or substance abuse. Police detective is not a job for the faint-hearted. 'Is it only now that you starting wondering? I started considering whether I was in the right job the day after I passed out at Templemore. If you want my opinion, I think that you'll make a damn fine copper. Of course, if you quote me, I'll deny I ever said that. Are you sure there's not something else?'

'Nothing I'm willing to share.' He opened the door.

Fiona went to Brophy, who quickly terminated his game of solitaire. She gave him her theory that the bodies in the bog might be missing persons from the area, which included not only the mainland at Béal an Daingin but also the islands. Brophy wrote the details and seemed grateful to have something like police work to do.

She went to her own desk and looked at her in-tray. There was a single white envelope with the logo of the Director of Public Prosocutions on it. She could already guess the contents. She and Tracy had been fully occupied with preparing evidence for the upcoming trial of Charles Grealish. Her heart wasn't in the prosecution and she had left most of the donkey work to Tracy. Perhaps that was one of the reasons for his current bout of ennui. Maybe the bodies in the bog would give him a lift. She picked up the envelope and slid her chair over to Tracy.

'Another letter from the DPP. Probably a load more questions to be answered.'

Tracy took the envelope. 'No, I think it's just an official notice that the trial has been put back another six months. One of the DPP's assistants gave me a head's up this morning. Nobody wants this trial. But Grealish murdered a man.'

'Is that what's bothering you?'

He shook his head. 'I suppose you're going to probe away at me until I tell you. My father's been diagnosed with prostate cancer. I have to go home at the weekend and discuss the prognosis and the possible treatment with my parents. They need me there because we're seeing that switch they talked about in college. The child becomes the parent and the parent becomes the child.'

'It's not a death sentence these days.'

Tracy had a face that didn't do glum well. 'The oncologist is optimistic. Luckily, my father went to his GP for a check-up and he was sent to the specialist immediately. I know it'll probably be alright but it brings the whole question of mortality to the fore.'

Fiona laughed. 'Our job is to look at dead people who have been the subject of violent deaths. I would have thought that you'd already reflected on the fact that we are joined to this life by a thread that is thinner than a stand of a spider's web.'

Tracy didn't look her in the eye. 'There's another aspect of the diagnosis.'

'What?'

'Prostate cancer is hereditary. It's very likely that I'll have it too. Not right now, but sometime in the future. It's like a time bomb ticking away down below, waiting to go off.'

Fiona got a sudden rush of mothering. The desire to enfold Tracy in her arms and tell him that everything was going to be alright was almost overwhelming. It shocked her to think that there was a mother inside her somewhere ready to come to the fore. 'Think about the positive side. If and when that time comes, you'll have to face it, but now that you know you'll be able to prepare. Talk to the oncologist. Don't worry until you have something to worry about. It may never happen.' She suppressed the desire to hug him. She'd never seen him as vulnerable. He was too young to have the thought of future illness already planted in his head.

Her desk phone rang and she scooted across and lifted the handset. 'Okay, we're on the way.' She turned to Tracy. 'That was O'Donnell. They're ahead of schedule. One of the bodies is already out.'

CHAPTER FIVE

The fifty-minute drive from central Galway to the bog outside Béal an Daingin took place in silence. Tracy turned on the radio as soon as they left the outskirts of the city and Fiona closed her eyes. She hadn't slept well the previous night and she attributed it to her reflection on the past few months and her vain attempts to reconnect with her father. She had visited him at least once a week and their short conversations resembled those of two strangers meeting for the first time in a pub. Their collective lives together had ended twenty-three years earlier and she had no interest to hear of his life in the US. She noted that her mother had infinitely more patience than her and was more deserving of her respect. Her father began every meeting with an apology. After the second meeting, this opening gambit had little effect on Fiona. The constant regrets did nothing to mend the broken heart of the twelve-year-old abandoned girl, nor did it assuage the fear and guilt of the sixteen-year-old rape victim who was forced to bear her child. Regrets did nothing for the eighteen-year-old self-harmer who couldn't sleep without the help of alcohol or drugs. The attempt at reconciliation turned out to be an exercise in futility. Fiona was coming to realise that the hurt was too deep. The positive outcome was that her mother and her were becoming closer.

The car left the road just beyond Béal an Daingin and bumped onto the rough bog road.

'We're here,' Tracy announced.

Fiona stirred and sat up straight. Ahead they could see the two Technical Bureau vans parked on the road and beyond them a white plastic tent fluttered in the wind. She noted that work had stopped on the disinterment. Tracy parked behind the vans, they exited, suited up, and headed for the tent.

Fiona pulled the flap of the tent open and entered. Three techs were bent over an object lying on a trestle table set up in the centre of the tent. She coughed.

O'Donnell turned. 'Come in. It's a bit of a crush, but we don't see something like this every day of the week.'

Fiona pushed forward and the techs tried to make room for her. Tracy was obliged to remain at the entrance. 'What have we got?'

'Take a look,' O'Donnell moved aside.

Fiona took his place and stared at the brown mass lying on the table. The body was curled into the foetal position with the knees bent up towards the upper torso. The arms, legs and hands were discernible and she could see the head clearly at the top of the mass.

'I'm not sure of the sex,' O'Donnell said. 'You'll have to wait for a post-mortem for that. If I were to hazard a guess, I don't think the body has been down there too long. Even in a bog, decomposition begins after three days, but bodies found after centuries still have the skin and organs preserved. The combined action of highly acidic water, low temperature, and a lack of oxygen preserves but severely tans their skin. The man, or woman, was crouched when he or she was laid in the bog.'

Fiona leaned over and examined the body. She removed her face mask. The smell was more fetid vegetation than decomposing flesh. A layer of brown slime had attached itself to the body. She looked for wounds but realised that she was wasting her time. 'I'm not going to ask you how he or she died. That's not your area of expertise.' Fiona stood aside to allow Tracy to move forward so that he could view the body.

'We found a couple of interesting items buried with the body.' O'Donnell moved to the table, picked up a thin, heavily-rusted semi-circular piece of metal and handed it to Fiona. 'We found this underneath the body.'

Fiona held the metal in the centre of her palm. It was the size of a large coin. The top was straight and about an inch and a half long. The piece beneath was an approximate half-moon shape and was slightly convex. There were three holes punched in it, two on each corner of the top and one at the bottom at the centre of the half moon. She rubbed her fingers over it and although rusted she found it was tactile. 'What is it?'

'Never seen anything like it,' O'Donnell said. 'We've been trying to work that out. Without success, but it was right underneath the body and I suppose it was buried at the same time the body was.' He took the metal back from her. 'If you run your fingers over the surface on the bevelled side, you can just about feel the marks of an etching.' He slid his fingers along the outer side. 'There, I can just about feel it.' He handed the metal object back to Fiona.

She slid the tips of her fingers along the outer surface and felt the small indentations. 'Is there a way we can recover the etchings?'

'We can get rid of the rust easily enough, but we might have to use more sophisticated methods to unveil the writing. We also found these.' O'Donnell handed her six small rusted circular objects. 'I'm not sure, but I think they may be buttons. I've also bagged what remained of the clothing, which wasn't much.'

Fiona held the metal objects in her palm. She would have drawn the same conclusion as O'Donnell. They were covered in rust, but they had the shape of buttons. There was a faint decoration on the top. 'Can you get rid of some of the rust from these?'

O'Donnell smiled and held up what looked like a spray can. 'Funny you should ask. I just happen to have a can of rust remover. All this stuff might turn out to be evidence, so we've been waiting for you to make the decision on removing at least some of the rust.'

She tossed him a button. 'Let's see what the rust remover does to that. If the spray destroys it, we still have five.'

O'Donnell caught the small object, laid a cloth on the table beside the corpse, and sprayed it. He then enveloped it in the cloth and began to rub gently. After two minutes, he opened the cloth and exposed the object. Both he and Fiona had concluded correctly. It was a button. He held the cloth out for Fiona and Tracy to see. The button was a faded gold colour, and the decoration was eroded, but still clear.

Fiona examined the top of the button. 'It's an anchor connected to a chain.'

'That's exactly what it is,' O'Donnell said. 'So perhaps our friend was a mariner?'

'He could have been washed ashore,' Tracy said.

Fiona noticed that the body was now assumed to be male. 'The sea is a half a mile away,' she said. 'How did he get into a bog hole? If he had washed up, the body would have been found on the coast. There's nothing to suggest he was a seaman. Lots of men wear those peacoats. A gilded button with an anchor and chain motif might be just a button.' She took out her mobile phone. 'It's time to call Brophy to organise transport for the corpse to the morgue, and DS O'Donnell needs to get these metal bits to the lab.' She had a feeling that DI Horgan's conclusion that this case had nothing to do with them would prove to be erroneous. She looked at Tracy. 'Take some photographs of the corpse, that metal object and the button.'

Tracy took out his mobile phone and circled the table, taking photos as he went. Then he placed the metal objects on the table and took close-up photos of them. 'All done,' he said as he put his phone back in his pocket.

Fiona turned to O'Donnell. 'How long before the next body is up?'

'Some time tomorrow. We'll get what we have to the lab. I thought this was going to be straightforward, but I'm getting that tingle that says we're looking at something unusual here.'

Fiona turned for the exit. 'I'm getting that same tingle.'

CHAPTER SIX

Fiona looked at her watch as soon as they were settled in the car. They wouldn't get back to Galway before closing time. She looked at Tracy, who appeared lost in thought as he had been most of the day. 'Are you in a hurry to get back to Galway?'

'Not particularly. What do you have in mind?'

'Glenmore is nearly on the way home.'

'We're going to get the bastard that threw the bottle at you? The drink will have worn off and he might be regretting his actions.'

She had no intention of searching for the bottle-thrower. 'Not worth the effort. I want to see how my mother is getting on. She's just buried her husband.'

Tracy looked at her but didn't speak. He turned on the ignition and they moved down the bog road. 'What do you think about the body in the bog?'

'We don't have enough information to form an opinion. But like I said to Horgan, I don't think he lay down in a bog hole, went asleep and didn't wake up. We'll have to wait until we know more about him and how he ended up where he did.'

'So you think he was murdered?'

'I don't know. We'll have a hell of a job proving that he was and given that he's been in that bog for a good number of years, we'll have an even more difficult job finding the killer. Someone might just have pulled off the perfect crime. Let's see what Brophy comes up with on the missing persons.'

'I put the picture of the button out on the Net. Somebody might get back to me.' He turned left at Casla and they were on their way to Glenmore.

As soon as they turned, Fiona was regretting her decision to visit her mother. The little devil on her right shoulder was saying that her mother had made a mistake and everyone makes mistakes. You need a mother and someone to trust. Meanwhile, the little devil on her left shoulder was saying: *how did trusting her the last time work out for you?* She decided to stop listening to the devils and play the cards as they fell.

Twenty minutes later, they arrived at the Madden residence in Glenmore and Tracy parked directly outside.

'You can come in,' Fiona said when Tracy switched the car off.

'I'm not intruding?'

'It's a friendly visit. We buried the hatchet six months ago and we haven't resurrected it since.'

Maire Madden answered the door and immediately threw her arms around Fiona, who responded with an awkward embrace. 'I heard what happened outside Tigh Jimmy yesterday. Some people in this parish don't know the meaning of the word respect.'

Fiona pulled back from the embrace. The reconciliation was ongoing and didn't need to be rushed. 'It was the drink,' she said.

'The drink be damned.' Maire stood aside to allow Fiona and Tracy to enter. 'You'll stay for tea. I've just baked a fresh batch of scones, and I'll put the kettle on.'

Fiona entered the living room. During her father's stay, it had been set up as his bedroom, permitting him to watch television if he woke at night. It had been returned to its former purpose and there was no sign of Conor Madden's residence left in it.

'She appears to be in good form.' Tracy sat on the sofa.

'She's relieved, like all of us.' Fiona sat beside him. 'She gets to move on at last. She's finally been widowed.'

'What about you?'

Tracy was taking lessons from Aisling. She liked him as a colleague, but she didn't want to go further than that. It might take more getting-to-know-you time before they exchanged deep feelings. 'I moved on years ago. In my eyes, the man we put in the ground yesterday died twenty-three years ago when he walked out on us.'

'I can't relate. I've always had my parents and I've always loved them.'

She could see Tracy tearing up.

He finally got control of his voice. 'You never said what happened between you and your mother.'

And I never will, she thought.

The silence in the room was broken by Fiona's mother, who arrived carrying a tray with the full array of cups, saucers, teapot and milk and sugar. She laid the table and poured the tea before returning to the kitchen for a plate of scones, cream, and strawberry jam.

'You're spoiling us, Mrs M,' Tracy said.

Maire put milk in her tea. 'You're a good lad. I saw you at the funeral yesterday.'

'We just dropped by to see if you were okay,' Fiona said. 'We've found a body in a bog down by Béal an Daingin. It's probably been there for a long time.'

'The people down there are weird,' Maire said. 'The islands were cut off for a long time before they built the bridges. There was a lot of inbreeding. I don't like going down there. You'll be careful.'

'I'm always careful and Tracy will be on hand if I get myself into trouble.'

'He's a handsome boy,' Maire said. 'It's a pity you're the other way inclined.'

Fiona smiled. It was a nice way of avoiding words like lesbian and gay. 'I thought you liked Aisling.'

'I think she's a great girl. But I always wanted grandchildren.'

Fiona put down her teacup abruptly and looked at her mother. 'Were you happy with the way the funeral went?'

'Yes.' She rose, went to a small bureau in the corner of the room and returned with an envelope. 'Conor had some sort of insurance in America. I can't make head nor tail of it.' She handed the envelope to Fiona. 'Can you check it for me? The funeral cost three-thousand euro and I borrowed more than half at the Credit Union.'

Fiona took the envelope. She looked at Tracy, who was finishing his scone. 'We need to get back to town.'

Maire jumped up, went back to the kitchen and returned with a paper bag into which she tipped the plate of scones. She handed the bag to Tracy. 'For later.'

Fiona stood and embraced her mother. 'I'll get back to you on the insurance business. Take care of yourself.'

In the car on the way back to Galway, she wondered how long the detente would last. She got the distinct feeling that her mother knew that her grandson was running around the country somewhere. At least they both knew that there was a son and grandson somewhere. A lot of strange emotions had surfaced during her father's illness. Fiona had been feeling her son's presence recently. It had roused conflicting emotions. She was his mother, and she felt protective of him. Every now and then, she put his name into the computer to see if he'd got himself into trouble. So far, she was happy to report that he hadn't. On the other hand, it was uncomfortable to know that there was someone out there who probably hated her enough to kill her.

CHAPTER SEVEN

Fiona parked the Kawasaki in its usual spot and made her way to the CID squad room. She had spent an hour in the dojo, showered and was at her desk at the appointed hour. DI Horgan had lately got the time bug, which meant that he had taken to poking his head into the squad room for a rapid head count at nine in the morning and five in the afternoon. Some of the group were annoyed, but Fiona knew this phase would pass. It was likely that Horgan was responding to an email he had received from Garda HQ regarding time keeping. The door opened and Fiona didn't bother to look around to check whether it was Horgan. The door closed, and, as no one had entered, she felt vindicated by her indifference.

Tracy entered and sat at his desk. 'Has he been?'

'Two minutes ago, he's upstairs, adding a demerit to your file.'

'I work loads of hours of overtime and there's never any budget and if I'm five minutes late, I get a bollocking.'

'Do me a favour and print off some of those photographs you took yesterday. And how come there's no takeaway coffee today?'

'I thought it was your turn. And apropos of the photos, I

had a reply to my request for information.' He took out his phone and opened it. 'Some guy says it was from the German Kriegsmarine and dates from nineteen-forty to nineteen forty-five. He said if it's genuine he'd offer fifty euros for it.'

'And what pray is the Kriegsmarine?'

'I looked it up. The Kriegsmarine was the name of the German Navy during the second world war.'

Fiona was quickly working out the math. If the corpse belonged to a seaman who was lost at sea during the war and washed up on the coast, he would have been in the bog for seventy-five years or more. But that didn't answer the question of how he got into the bog.

She was still pondering this problem when her phone rang.

'Detective sergeant Madden?' The voice was female, young and officious.

'Speaking.'

'It's Professor Daly from the Regional Hospital. You may remember we've already cooperated.'

'Of course I do, professor.' Fiona also remembered that the professor had screwed up but got away with it.

'We received the corpse that was disinterred from the bog in Connemara last evening. We've never dealt with a corpse in this condition and I am wondering what you want from us. A conventional post mortem appears to be out of the question.'

'We need the maximum amount of information from the corpse that we can get. Ideally, we'd like to know its name and last address, but I think that's unlikely. So we'd settle for the cause of death and an estimation of how long the corpse has been buried in the bog. We're currently checking on missing persons from the area.'

'I'm afraid you don't need a pathologist but an expert in forensic medicine. I've been asking around and the man for the job appears to be Timo Litmanen, who is the Professor of Forensic Medicine at Helsinki University. I've just been speaking to him on Skype and I've shown him the photos of the corpse. He's fascinated by the corpse's condition and if you're agreeable, he'd love to carry out a forensic examination and if so, he'll be here tomorrow.'

Fiona was thinking of Horgan's response to this news. 'What's this going to cost us?'

'Professor Litmanen has agreed to work pro bono and pay his own airfare. We would appreciate it if you could pay for his accommodation.'

'I'll look in to it.' Fiona decided not to bother Horgan with the details if possible. 'But we're agreeable.'

'Good, I'll let you know the arrangements.'

'What was that about?' Tracy asked.

She told him. 'Do you have room for a guest in your apartment?'

'Are you kidding? I don't even have room for myself in my apartment.' He tossed the photos taken at Béal an Daingin on her desk.

She picked out a clear one of the corpse and two showing the metal object and the cleaned-up button. 'Put those on the whiteboard.'

Tracy did as he was told, drew a large question mark at the top and wrote Kriegsmarine beside the button.

Fiona was about to examine her emails when Horgan entered the squad room. He made a bee-line for Tracy's desk and pulled himself up to his full height before facing him.

'Where were you at nine o'clock?'

'In the toilet, call of nature.' Tracy's reply was nonchalant.

'You mean you were here before nine and then went to the toilet?' He looked at Fiona for confirmation and she nodded.

Horgan's shoulders slumped. He turned and was about to leave when his eyes fell on the whiteboard and the recently-attached photos. He strolled over to it and pointed at the photos. 'Who is responsible for this?' He turned and stared at Fiona.

'Me, boss,' Tracy said before Fiona could answer.

'Who told you that the corpse in the bog was a legitimate investigation? I thought I told you we're not involved. Why do I have to keep reminding you two that we're the police and the police investigate crimes? Where's the crime?'

'We're investigating it in terms of identifying the corpse with a view to advising the family of the death,' Fiona said. She looked at the end of the room where Brophy was beavering away. 'Detective Garda Brophy, please join us.'

Brophy left his desk with some reluctance and stood beside Fiona.

'How are things progressing on the missing persons search in south Connemara?' she asked.

'I'm up to twenty-four and I've only gone back to 1995,' Brophy said. 'Those are the missing persons who have stayed missing.'

'That's a lot of unhappy families, boss,' Fiona said. 'Our corpse might have been a missing person and might be a cold case file down in the basement.'

'You're behind the times, Madden,' Horgan said. 'All the old files were shipped out of here years ago to a warehouse in Ballybrit.' He stared at the whiteboard. 'What's this Kriegsmarine shit?'

Fiona shuffled on her feet. 'A button found under the corpse has been identified as the kind of button used by the German Navy in the second world war.'

Horgan looked a bit green around the gills. 'Tell me the truth, Madden. Are we going to be getting involved with the German Navy?'

'Probably not, boss. Those buttons were probably all over the place.'

Horgan rubbed his stomach. 'I just got the strangest feeling down below. I think I need the toilet.'

'Need to know, boss,' Fiona said.

'There is no crime so there is no investigation, got it?' Horgan said as he made for the door.

'Absolutely, boss,' Fiona said.

'I assume we're not supposed to mention the involvement of Professor Litmanen,' Tracy said as soon as Horgan left the room.

Fiona went back to her desk. 'On pain of death.'

'Who is Professor Litmanen?' Brophy asked.

Tracy tapped the side of his nose. 'Need to know.'

CHAPTER EIGHT

The second body was brought up at mid-afternoon. O'Donnell had set up a mobile phone on a tripod so that Fiona and Tracy could watch the action from the comfort of the squad room. Brophy was invited along for the experience. The second body resembled the first. Set on the same white table, it was a brown blob with what looked like a face on one end. The arms and legs were curled into the body, which was in the foetal position.

'And look what we found underneath him.' O'Donnell held out a similar piece of metal to that found under the first corpse. 'And we've got some more of those buttons.'

'Bag the lot and send them to the lab,' Fiona said. 'And tell them to put a rush on it.'

'I have a bit of bad news for you,' O'Donnell said. 'A TG4 camera crew tried to gain access to the bog. One of the locals must have tipped them off. They wanted to know what we were up to, but I told them it was none of their business. We set up some crime scene tape and the local station will put a man on duty tonight. Maybe you guys could arrange to get this body to Galway this evening. And your boss might like to give the media a statement.'

Fiona nodded at Brophy, who took out his mobile and went to the end of the room.

'We've done a few passes with the Ground Penetrating Radar, but there doesn't appear to be any more bodies. We'll probably try to finish up this evening. We don't really want to waste time looking for something that isn't there.'

'I presume that you've taken photos of the second body,' Fiona said. 'If so, send them to us.'

'Will do.' O'Donnell waved. 'I'll be in touch.'

Fiona waved back. 'You still have that tingling feeling?'

'Stronger than ever.' The line went dead.

'The two bodies might mean that it was a murder suicide.' Tracy slid his chair over to his desk. 'What if one of the bodies is a male and the other a female? It could have been a suicide pact.'

'That would suit DI Horgan. Anything for a quiet life. Except this time I think he'll be sorely disappointed. Let's wait and see what Professor Litmanen comes up with.'

'Have you found him digs yet?'

'I'm working on it.'

Brophy appeared at her desk. 'The ambulance is on the way and the corpse will be in the Regional this evening.'

'Good man. Concentrate your search on the nineteen-forties and fifties.'

'Yes, sarge.' Brophy went back to his desk.

Fiona had never worked a cold case and a seventy-year-old case wasn't just cold, it was frozen. It would all depend on how the corpses died. She was still feeling a tingle, but she was also beginning to think like Horgan. A case that old would be hardly worth the effort. The hierarchy would decide that there were better ways of spending her and Tracy's time.

'The photos have come through,' Tracy said. 'Shall I print them off?'

'Do it and let me see them.'

Her phone rang. 'DS Madden,' she said.

'Professor Daly's office at the Regional Hospital. The Professor asked me to contact you. Litmanen will arrive in Dublin tomorrow morning at 8 a.m. and should be on the 9:15 Citylink to Galway, arriving at 12:15. Professor Daly has told him that he'll be met at the station. She asked me to remind you to organise accommodation.'

'It's in hand,' Fiona lied. 'And thank Professor Daly for her assistance.' She slid her chair over to Tracy. 'Litmanen is arriving in Galway at lunchtime tomorrow.' She kept her voice low. The walls in Mill Street station had ears and she wanted to keep Horgan in the dark as much as possible.

'Maybe you shouldn't have gone off the books.'

'Horgan would never have gone for it.'

'And if he finds out?'

'We'll cross that bridge when we come to it.'

Tracy stood up. 'I've printed the photos.' He left the office, returned with a sheaf of paper and sat down beside Fiona. They looked at the photos together.

'Same as the first one,' Fiona said. 'It may be my imagination but the face looks more recognisable but I still have no idea whether it's male or female.'

'Ditto.' He selected one of the photos. 'I'll put this one on the board.'

'It's as good as any.' Fiona looked at the office clock. 'Drink.'

Tracy smiled and nodded, then stuck the photo on the whiteboard.

'A Finnish Professor of Forensic Medicine,' Aisling said. 'I don't see why not.'

Fiona let out an audible sigh. She, Aisling, and Tracy were seated at the bar in the rear of Taaffes. She turned to Tracy.

'That's what it's like to have a partner.' Secretly, she'd been afraid that Aisling might not be so accommodating.

'I've never met an expert in forensic medicine,' Aisling said. 'Come to think of it, I haven't met a lot of Finns. So it should be an interesting few days all round. Show me the photos of the bodies.'

Tracy took out his phone and brought up the photos. He looked at Fiona before handing the phone to Aisling. 'We're not really supposed to do things like this.'

Fiona ignored him. It was part of her job in mentoring Tracy to ensure that he developed a flexible approach to police work. The people who write the rule books have generally never solved a crime.

Aisling took the phone and examined the photos. 'How long do you think they were in the bog?'

Fiona told her about the button.

'So it has to be after 1940,' Aisling said.

'I was in Finland once,' Tracy said. 'My parents took us to see the Northern Lights. It wasn't all it's cracked up to be. But you better be warned, the Finns drink like fish.'

'Speaking of which.' Fiona raised her hand to beckon the barman and called for another round.

Aisling handed the phone back to Tracy. 'This is the last round. I'm not really that accommodating. I get the impression that you guys are looking for a case.'

Fiona finished her pint and handed the glass to the barman as she took a fresh one with her free hand. 'At the moment, we're assisting the DPP in building a case against Charlie Grealish for James Mangan's murder. Our heart isn't in it and it's the case that nobody wants. We don't want it, the Super doesn't want it, the DPP doesn't want it and the Jesuits are running scared of it.'

'I wouldn't like to be the barrister that has to prosecute.' Aisling took her orange juice from the barman.

Fiona smiled. 'Most of the barristers I know would prosecute their grandmother as long as the money was right.'

'Okay, no more work talk,' Aisling said.

Fiona took a slug of Guinness. 'Then there'll be a lot of silence around here because us coppers can talk about nothing else.'

CHAPTER NINE

Maire Madden had a habit of saying "a watched kettle never boils" whenever they were waiting interminably for something to happen. Fiona knew that all kettles would eventually boil, but she also knew that time dragged when you waited for an expected event like the arrival of an expert in forensic medicine. Brophy was the only one of the three detectives who had work to do. Fiona spent most of the morning clearing the emails that had built up over the past few days. They had the obligatory visit from Horgan, but it had gone off pleasantly enough. He ignored the whiteboard and any mention of the bodies disinterred from the bog. In fact, it was a non-policework visit and more of a head-buried-in-the-sand visit. As long as he ignored what she and Tracy were up to, there was no case and all in Horgan's garden was rosy. If he had been more perceptive, he would have picked up on the nervous vibe in the squad room, but perception wasn't part of his extensive skill set. Horgan's main objective was to exit the Garda Síochána with his pension intact and anything that furthered that aim was to be welcomed. Fiona and Tracy left the office at 11:45, walked via Shop Street and Eyre Square and arrived at the Main Bus Station in Fairgreen Road just after the hour. The express from Dublin pulled into its slot at the rear of the station five minutes early, at five minutes past the hour. The two detectives stood at the entrance and watched the passengers descending from the coach.

'There he is.' Tracy indicated a short rotund dark-haired man who collected a rucksack from the driver, who was emptying the luggage hold.

'How the hell do you know?'

'I looked up the University of Helsinki and read his bio and checked out his photo.'

Fiona could have kicked herself. Tracy had out-thought her.

They stood back as the passengers filed into the concourse.

Professor Litmanen made straight for them. He had transferred his rucksack to his back. He held out his hand. 'Detective sergeant Madden, I presume.' His English was slightly accented, but not noticeably so.

Fiona had conjured up something like a Scandinavian god. She couldn't have been further from the mark. No one had told her that not all Finns were blond hunks. Litmanen's pleasant round face was half covered by a heavy moustache and beard. He had piercing blue eyes that peeked through spectacles and had a darker complexion than she had anticipated.

'Professor Litmanen.' Fiona took his hand. 'This is Detective Garda Tracy.'

'Call me Timo, please.'

'Can I take your rucksack, Timo?' Tracy said.

'No, thank you, your first name?'

'Sean.'

'I've been travelling since four o'clock this morning and now I'd like to eat. You have somewhere nice for lunch. Then I want to meet the bodies.'

Fiona normally didn't lunch in nice places, but she guessed that Litmanen would have assumed that an official visit by a noted European expert would have been expensed to HQ. He didn't know the visit was unofficial and that Fiona would be footing the bills. She tapped Tracy on the arm. 'Give Kirwin's Lane a call and see if they have room for three.'

Tracy raised his eyebrows but took out his phone.

Fiona headed for the exit accompanied by Litmanen while Tracy handled the phone call. 'The restaurant is a short walk away. Are you okay to walk?'

'I am fifty-one years old and despite my weight, I am in perfect physical condition. Please let us continue.'

KIRWIN'S LANE had room for three and Fiona was pleased that Tracy took the lead in the conversation at the table. Litmanen had never been to Ireland and had no desire to talk about work. The discussion centred on Finland and Ireland and Fiona marvelled at the way Tracy handled it. Her respect for her partner grew from day to day. She wouldn't be happy when it was time for him to move up. Litmanen managed to drink a pint of Guinness, a half bottle of wine and a double Jameson. Fiona and Tracy stuck to water. When the bill came, Fiona paid with a credit card and tried not to look at the amount.

It was a short walk from the bottom of Shop Street to the Regional Hospital where Daly had been kind enough to make the arrangements and they were led directly to the pathology suite where the bodies were already set up. Litmanen dropped his rucksack in the corner and accepted the scrubs that were presented by Daly's assistant. Fiona and Tracy accepted scrubs and washed up alongside Litmanen.

Fiona had attended dozens of post-mortems, most of which were aimed at finding out the cause of death. Litmanen was an academic and, as such, had a wider interest than her and Tracy. He was a bogman specialist.

'Let us begin,' Litmanen walked around the table, examining the body from every direction. 'This body has been remarkably preserved. Bogs are monuments to death; they're created by generations of dead, buried plants. They're also havens for anything buried beneath bogs and that includes human bodies.' He continued to circle the corpse. 'Some bodies may be kept in astonishingly good condition for thousands and thousands of years. Considering the level of decomposition here, I think that this body is quite recent, no more than one hundred years, and possibly a lot less.'

'We found some buttons in the grave that date from the 1940s,' Fiona said.

'That would fit. If I had more time, I would have visited the bog and tested whether the water running through it was acid or alkaline. The pH of the water can be important in preserving the body.' He very gently moved the arms and legs to lengthen the body. 'Decalcification of the bones is advanced but not yet completed. It would have taken another decade or two for the bones to disappear completely. The conditions in your bog were such that the moss was attracting the available nitrogen, which is also required by bacteria. That has slowed down the decomposition, but now that the body has been removed from the bog, we can expect the decomposition to accelerate. This is the body of a man, probably middle-aged. I would guess that he was a small man. Maybe no more than one metre sixty. Depending on the conditions, the bones of many bog bodies have softened, some to the extent of turning to jelly. That is not the case with your corpse.'

Fiona's mobile rang. She looked at the caller ID. It was Horgan and she killed the call.

Almost immediately, Tracy's mobile started to ring. He looked at Fiona before killing the call. 'We're toast,' he said.

Litmanen picked up a scalpel and slit the corpse's chest and Tracy recoiled as a slug of brown liquid exited the body and a fetid smell filled the autopsy room.

Litmanen bent to examine the open cavity. 'Some of the organs are still intact.'

'My boss has just tried to phone us,' Fiona said. 'Will you be able to establish the cause of death?'

'I already know the cause of death.' Litmanen remained leaning over the corpse.

'Would you mind telling us?' Fiona said.

Litmanen looked at her over his glasses. 'This man was shot in the head. The entrance hole is clearly visible.' He turned the body and pointed at a small entry wound in the back of the skull. 'I'm sure I'll find the bullet when I open the skull, which I will do almost immediately.'

'You mean he was murdered?' she asked.

Litmanen picked up the electric saw. 'I mean, he has a hole in his skull consistent with a gunshot wound. In Finland, it is up to the police to decide whether a crime has been committed or not.'

'Horgan is going to love this,' Tracy said.

'Is there anything more you can tell us about the body?' Fiona asked.

'I will now make a detailed analysis of this corpse,' Litmanen said. 'Then I will look at the other body. You can remain or leave as you wish.' He looked at his watch. 'I should be ready in two hours. You have arranged my accommodation.'

'I have a cottage outside Galway,' Fiona said. 'I thought you might prefer to be in the country rather than a stuffy hotel in Galway.'

'Excellent.' Litmanen took his scalpel and bent over the body. 'In two hours.'

CHAPTER TEN

Fiona passed the message to Aisling that they would be leaving later than usual and suggested that they meet in Taaffes, where there would hopefully be a traditional Irish music session underway. On the way back to the station, she and Tracy discussed breaking the bad news to Horgan. They decided to leave it for another day.

'If the two of them were shot,' Tracy said as they entered the station. 'I might have got it right about the murder suicide theory.'

'You might indeed.' But she very much doubted it. The two dead men served together in the navy. They were comrades and in war; men stuck together. She couldn't see it as a murder/suicide, but she's been wrong before.

'But you don't think so.'

'No, I don't. Murder suicides are more often personal. The shooter feels grief over the death of the murdered person and then kills himself in the same fashion. Also, murder suicides rarely take place on bogs. They more usually happen in or around a home. The hole that Litmanen showed us was in the back of the skull. It looked more like an execution than a murder. If the second body has a similar wound, we're looking at a double murder.'

They took their places at their desks. 'Will we have to investigate?' Tracy asked.

'We're the police. That's what we do.'

'The case is over seventy years old. The murderer is most likely dead and so are any witnesses. There'll be no DNA evidence worth a damn. There might not be any evidence at all.'

'You forgot to mention that there'll be no CCTV.'

'I don't think that there's a CCTV camera in the whole of Connemara.'

She thought that a slight exaggeration but didn't want to continue that conversation. 'Litmanen was confident that he'd retrieve the bullets. That'll be a start. We owe it to the families to do our best to bring the murderer to justice.'

Tracy took a deep breath. 'Despite the cost to ourselves. You're not so happy to see Charlie Grealish pay the price for murdering James Mangan.'

'No, I'm not happy and neither are you. Charlie had the makings of a decent human being. Mangan was a scumbag and a criminal. Charlie was a victim. I understand the motive behind the murder, but acting on it was against the law.' She understood better that Tracy knew. To hell with the law. She would have killed her rapist in a heartbeat if she'd had the chance. 'Perhaps not against a moral law, but certainly against the law of the land. Let's wait and see if Litmanen is as good as his word.'

Fiona was pondering the question as to who might have dumped two German sailor's bodies in a bog hole seventy years ago and what was the motive. It was a general perception in Ireland that murder began with the case of Shan Mohangi, who botched the abortion of his girlfriend, chopped her up and attempted to burn her in the fireplace. But murders were happening all the time except in many cases they went undetected not because of the ingenuity of the murderers but through the incompetence of the police. In the 1940s, Ireland was a poor rural country suffering the depravations of war along with the rest of Europe. It would have been easy for two murders to slip through the net. She was in the middle of this reflection when her phone rang.

She picked up the phone. 'DS Madden.'

'Fiona.'

She recognised O'Donnell's Northern lilt. 'Rory, what have you got?'

'You're all business.'

'That's why they pay me.'

'We did a bit of work on that piece of metal. I just sent you and Tracy the result. That tingle I felt on the bog is turning into a full blown excitement.'

Fiona entered her email, found O'Donnell's mail and opened it. She didn't speak. The techs had managed to bring up a faint representation of what had been on the metal. The title of the top was *Kriegsmarine* and beneath it was a name, Gunter Eich and a six digit number.

'We've looked it up,' O'Donnell said. 'It's a second world war German Navy dog tag. The two holes at the top had a string passed through them and it hung around the neck. We'll have the second one for you tomorrow. What the hell have you just walked into? Whatever it is, we're envying you.'

'I have good news for you. We might have a bullet for you by this evening.'

'You're kidding!'

She told him about Litmanen.

'And all this is off the books?' O'Donnell said. 'I'd heard that you were a character.'

'I'll be back to you.' She ended the call and turned to Tracy. 'Check your email. O'Donnell sent something interesting.'

Tracy hit a series of keys and stared at his screen. 'I don't believe it,' Tracy said. 'We have a name. So the body on the table this afternoon is this Eich guy. Remember, I had this theory that the bodies washed up from a German vessel that was sunk.'

Fiona sighed. 'I remember that theory.'

'But you don't believe it.'

'No, I don't.' Fiona thought that they were soon going to have to bring Horgan on board and that might seriously affect progress on the investigation into the bodies untimely deaths. But Horgan was their boss and there was no way that they could exclude him. The final decision would be his and it would be based on what would least impact on him and his non-existent career.

'So, what do you think?' Tracy asked.

'I'll let you know when I have a theory that I can add to the half dozen you've already come up with. But I'll need to have a lot more information.'

The squad room had emptied and Horgan was probably on his way home. They still had an hour to kill and there was nothing more they could do. Brophy had left a file on Fiona's desk of people who had gone missing in South Connemara in the 1940s. It was redundant, but she thought she'd take a look at it. She warmed to Brophy, who was a honest-to-God copper. He was a good researcher and methodical in his presentation. He had the makings of a good detective, but he was shy and didn't appear to be one of the boys. If Tracy ever moved up, she wouldn't mind taking him in hand. The front pages of Brophy's report had a list of names and the dates their disappearance had been reported to the police. She was astonished that the file contained five pages of names and the total came to more than three hundred. She skipped along the names. They were all locals who had left their homes and never returned. Her father had cleared off, and she assumed that most of the names on the list had done the same. She couldn't remember whether her mother had made a missing persons report. She doubted it but decided that when she had time, she'd look it up. Most of the disappeared would have ended up in towns across the UK and the US. Like her father, they'd left their past and their families behind. She stopped in the middle of the third page. The name wasn't local. It was German. Professor Heinrich Baum had disappeared from Letter Mullen in December 1944. He'd probably returned to Germany but it had been a peculiar time to disappear. The war was ending, and Germany was in turmoil. Life in Ireland at the time wasn't rosy, but it was a lot better than in a devastated country. About the same time, a German sailor had been shot and deposited in a bog not too far from Letter Mullen. It was a co-incidence and Fiona didn't believe or like co-incidences. She made a note that Brophy should look into the disappearance of Heinrich Baum.

CHAPTER ELEVEN

Litmanen was having a coffee with Daly's assistant when Fiona and Tracy arrived in the autopsy suite. The Finn had divested himself of his scrubs and his rucksack was sitting by the door.

'All done?' Fiona asked.

Litmanen turned to face her, fished around in his pocket and produced a plastic evidence bag with two bullets in it. 'The experience was not as exciting as I thought. I think that had Professor Daly known that the corpses were relatively recent, she would not have bothered to call me. Both men were executed. They were shot in the back of the head. The condition of the skin didn't allow me to conclude if they were tied. There are some scraps of clothing which I have collected and placed in an evidence bag. William,' he nodded in the direction of Daly's assistant. 'Has put the bag away safely. I have taken X-rays of the jaw area. Both men have had extensive dental work and you may be able to identify them from records in Germany, if they exist.'

Fiona took the bag from his hand. It had been sealed and signed by both Litmanen and Daly's assistant. The chain of evidence had been maintained. The bullets were in good condition but smaller that standard 9mm. She was not sufficiently well-versed in weaponry to hazard a guess at the calibre or what weapon might have fired them. That would be O'Donnell's job. 'Anything else you can tell us about the men?'

'They were probably in their thirties and both were reasonably fit. They were also both short in stature. Their internal organs were not totally decomposed, but what remained was not suitable for testing. I'm sorry, but that's about it.' He sighed. 'To come all this way from Helsinki for something that was not really that challenging.'

'It depends on how you look at it, Professor,' Daly's assistant said. 'We've never had a case like this in Galway. I think you did a terrific job.' He raised his teacup to the Professor who responded in kind.

'We have a name for one of the dead men,' Fiona said. 'Gunter Eich.'

'A good German name,' Litmanen said. 'Now I must thank William for his help and the excellent cup of tea. I have arranged to leave in the morning and I shall send a full report when I get home. Now, how shall we spend the remaining hours of my visit?'

'There's a pub close by where there's possibly some traditional Irish music.'

'And dancing?' Litmanen asked. 'I have seen Riverdance on TV. Do all the girls in this country have the long flowing hair?'

Fiona turned to leave. Litmanen had obviously never heard of extensions. 'I'm afraid not.'

Tracy picked up the rucksack.

THE MUSIC from Taaffes could be heard up the street. They found four seats at the bar and Fiona order a round. Aisling and Litmanen hit it off the moment they were introduced. They immediately became immersed in a conversation about working in academia and the merits of their relative universities. Meanwhile, Fiona and Tracy took a class in passive listening. Fiona eventually tuned out the highbrow conversation and watched with amazement as Litmanen lowered two pints of Guinness and two double Jamesons in the first hour. She was reflecting on the investigation. Horgan had already declared that there was no case, but somehow she would have to overcome his reluctance. She remembered the excitement in O'Donnell's voice. That was how people would respond to the details they had uncovered. There was enough of a mystery to pique the public interest. O'Donnell had shooed TG4 away, but Tracy could always drop a word in his girlfriend Cliona's ear. Possibly during pillow talk. She leaned towards Tracy. 'How are things between you and Cliona?'

'Mind your own business.' He nodded at the two academics. 'Those two must have been injected with gramophone needles. They only stop talking to draw breath.'

'Or in Litmanen's case to drink.'

'He can certainly lower it.'

'We may need to tip Cliona a wink on the two dead Germans.'

'That thought had also crossed my mind. She working on a film being shot in Mayo. I'm on the phone with her every night.'

'It's still going strong then?'

Tracy took a sip of his drink.

'How's your dad?'

'Shocked. The word cancer tends to do that to people. He's busy researching and he seems to have calmed down a bit. They're doing some genetic testing at the moment and looking at possible solutions.'

Fiona looked in disbelief as Litmanen had his hand in the air again to summon a barman. 'Timo, do people drink a lot in Finland?' she asked.

Litmanen laughed and leaned towards her. 'Two Finns go

into a bar and order two pints of beer. They drink silently until they finish and then order two more. After the third beer, one turns to the other and says *Skol* and the other says, did we come here to talk or did we come to drink?' He slapped his knees and laughed while the barman deposited another pint and a double whiskey chaser in front of him.

Tracy and Aisling joined in the laughter, and Fiona smiled. She liked Litmanen, and she was glad that she hadn't mentioned his visit to Horgan. There was now no chance that the two bodies would be unceremoniously bagged and buried. And there was also the affair of the missing Professor Baum. She ordered additional drinks for herself and Tracy. Aisling was the nominated driver and still had an orange juice sitting on the bar. If it was going to be one of those nights, then so be it.

CHAPTER TWELVE

Fiona rubbed the sleep from her eyes and looked at the clock. 'No way,' she rolled over. There was a steam hammer working in her head and from experience she knew six in the morning was way too early to get rid of it.

'Your guest,' Aisling shouted in Fiona's ear. 'Professor Litmanen is about to be driven into town by yours truly and the least you can do is to thank him and wish him bon voyage.'

'Not at six a.m.' Fiona forced her eyes open and saw Aisling directly above her face.

'His bus for Dublin Airport leaves at seven and there's only one flight to Helsinki today.'

Fiona pushed herself out of bed, pulled on her robe, and staggered after Aisling. How many drinks had they had before heading home and did they really continue the party in the local pub? Litmanen must be devastated. She entered the living room and found the Finn standing at the door, rucksack in hand. He appeared totally ready to attack the day.

He stuck his hand out to her. 'Thank you, Fiona, for a truly memorable visit. Aisling has invited me to return and stay with you, and I will be happy to accept.'

Fiona took his hand. 'Thanks and bon voyage.'

'We have to leave,' Aisling said from the door.

The handshake turned into a hug and Litmanen was out the door.

Fiona staggered back and flung herself on the bed. In seconds she was asleep.

SHE WOKE two hours later to the realisation that she had no transport; the Kawasaki had been left at Mill Street. She immediately searched for her jacket and ensured that the plastic bag containing the bullets was still in the pocket. Relief flooded through her when she found it. She dumped her robe and headed for the shower, convinced that Litmanen or possibly all Finns had a wooden leg. She'd never seen anyone lower that amount of liquor and still remain standing.

SHE ARRIVED at the station at half-past nine, aware that Horgan was already inscribing a minus behind her name in his little black book. She was three cups of coffee to the good and the steam hammers were still there but working at a lower decibel level. She had suffered the bouncing bus and Horgan's demerit gladly.

'Hard night.' Tracy had slithered away early in the proceedings. 'I'm glad today that I didn't get caught up in the session.'

'It continued at the local pub. The last thing I remember was Litmanen on a darts team in a competition. He had a whale of a time.' She handed Tracy the bullets. 'I don't recognise the calibre but there'll be some tech in Dublin who'll be an expert.'

Tracy looked into the bag. 'These two little pieces of metal took the lives of two men.'

'Get them off to O'Donnell as soon as possible. Give Brophy a call for me.'

'Why not call him yourself?'

'I don't want to shout.'

Tracy went to the rear of the room and returned with Brophy.

Fiona nodded at the file on her desk. 'I went through the file you prepared on missing persons in south Connemara. One name stood out: Professor Heinrich Baum. Find out everything you can about him. If there's nothing in the files, find out if there's a local historian in Letter Mullen and discover what Baum was doing there.'

'On it.' Brophy scuttled back to his desk.

Tracy watched him go. 'You've certainly got that guy on a string.'

She smiled. 'The same as you then.'

Tracy walked up to the whiteboard and wrote Gunter Eich under the photo of the first corpse.

Fiona tossed a ten euro note on Tracy's desk. 'Be a good lad and get us three takeaway coffees.'

Tracy picked up the note. 'Still seeing pink elephants crawling up the walls?' He turned towards the door and almost walked into Horgan.

'Where are you off to, Detective Tracy?'

'The toilet, boss, call of nature.'

'Well, you better hold on to it until I'm finished in here.' He went to Fiona's desk. 'Nice of you to join us today, Madden.'

'Sorry I was a bit late, sir. Trouble with my partner's car. You know us women, we're useless with mechanical things. We had to wait around for a man to sort the problem out for us.'

Tracy started sniggering and Horgan looked confused.

'Stay a half an hour extra this evening.'

Fiona stared him in the eye. 'I stayed two hours extra last evening. Will that do?'

'You always have an answer. Don't you, Madden?' He

looked at the whiteboard. 'I thought I told you to get rid of that stuff.'

'I don't think so, sir.' Fiona looked at Tracy.

Horgan followed her gaze. 'Don't bother backing her up. I want it off the whiteboard. There is no case.'

'There have been some developments, sir,' Fiona said. 'You may notice that we have the name of one of the corpses. The pathology department at the Regional Hospital did a post mortem on the bodies, and it appears that they were both shot in the back of the head. We identified the first corpse because his dog tags were under him. His dog tags are...'

'I know what dog tags are,' Horgan interrupted. 'We've all seen a war film.'

Fiona gave him her sweet smile. 'Both bodies are male and they appear to be German naval personnel. Their dog tags date from the 1940s. I think the idea of bagging them up and sticking them in the ground again might be out the window. As well as the fact that they both appear to have been murdered. Also, there was a German professor living in Letter Mullen who disappeared about the same time. Lots of questions to be answered and lots of coincidences.'

Horgan paced the top of the room before stopping at Fiona's desk. He had a perplexed look on his face and she concluded he was having a problem assimilating all this news. The good news was that he wasn't asking difficult questions like, who did the post-mortem? And how did they know the men had been shot in the back of the head?

She decided to pile on the information. 'Detective sergeant O'Donnell is cleaning up the second dog tag so we should know the identity of the second man before the day is out.'

'The situation has suddenly become more complicated,' Horgan said. 'And I'm sure that your hand is in there somewhere. Is your hand in there somewhere, Madden?'

'Perish the thought, boss. I am simply following procedure,

from the moment the bodies were discovered until this minute, you are completely covered.'

'And what do we do now?'

It was a quintessential Horgan question. 'We are dealing with two German nationals who have been found murdered. Either you, the Super or the Commissioner will have to inform the German Embassy.'

Horgan had continued pacing. 'Will that mean that we'll have a load of German coppers here looking over our shoulders?'

'I suppose that will be between the Park and the German Ambassador. I think we should ensure that we keep control of the case.'

'You're right on that one, Madden. It's our case and we're keeping it.'

Fiona suppressed a smile. Horgan had been taken from a no-case position to defending Galway CID's right to pursue the investigation. 'I'm sure the Super and the Park will agree with your decision.'

'Keep me informed,' Horgan started for the door and passed Tracy. 'I thought you needed the toilet.' He kept walking and muttering to himself.

Tracy was holding in the laughter. 'It's gone off me, boss.' He guffawed when Horgan left the room. 'That was priceless. I noticed you didn't tell him about the slugs.'

'I think he'd reached the limit of his ability to absorb information. The slug might have caused a severe case of information overload and we would have required an ambulance and paramedics.'

'You'll be the death of that man. I don't know why you do it. You're not a rebellious person by nature.'

'How little you know about me and we'll try to keep it that way. Perhaps it's just me being me.'

'I think it has more to do with you being in control of your environment. You should have learned by now that it's impossible. Nobody is really in control of their environment. Things happen and you have to respond to them. The disdain you display for Horgan and O'Reilly comes from the fact that you think you're a better copper than them. It's pure vanity.'

'No wonder you and Aisling get along so well. If you're finished psychologically assessing me, maybe you'll finish up the Grealish papers for the DPP.'

Fiona spent the rest of the morning with a pen and paper, trying to make sense of what they already knew. Tracy might be right that the murderer was already dead. There were no modern tools like DNA and CCTV to help them, but she was attracted by the puzzle. How had two members of the German Navy got themselves shot in a tiny corner of the Irish Republic as the second world war wound down? And what happened to Professor Baum and what had he been a professor of? And what was he doing in south Connemara? As she jotted the questions down, it was clear that solving the puzzle of the murders would require finding answers. Only the dead men might know what they were doing in Ireland, and only the murderer might know why they had to die. It was either investigate this case or concentrate on putting Charlie Grealish away. She knew what she'd prefer.

They had lunch at McDonagh's fish shop. Tracy was quieter than usual. She put it down to his father's scare with prostate cancer and the possibility that it had been passed on through a random gene. Tracy was a young man and the thought of mortality should have been a million miles from his mind. The young think they're never going to die. They talked about some of the questions Fiona had raised in her review, but Tracy remained remote. They needed to develop some momentum in the investigation and she needed to get Tracy's mind off his impending death by keeping him busy.

O'Donnell called at around three o'clock. His email arrived at about the same time. The inscription on the second dog tag was faint but legible. The second murder victim was

Dieter Muller. Fiona sent an email thanking O'Donnell and asking whether he had received the bullets. They hadn't yet arrived, but he would rush the examination. She liked working with the techs. They generally had more pride in their job. She asked Tracy to put Muller's name up on the whiteboard. They were making progress, but this was the easy stuff. They'd identified the victims, established that they had been murdered, and they had the slugs that had killed them. So far so good, but there was a long way to go and she didn't yet see a line of enquiry. There was a process to follow. Every murder investigation looked for motive, opportunity and method. They had the method but the motive and opportunity were complete unknowns. They were wandering around in the dark, picking up bits of information that might turn out to be absolutely useless.

She was packing up for the day and thinking about a warm bath and a couple of cold glasses of wine when Brophy came to her desk.

'The file on the disappearance of Heinrich Baum has disappeared. That is, if there ever was a file. I've done an Internet search and have come up with nothing. That's not surprising, but if Baum had been preeminent in his field, he might have been written up in Wikipedia. I've been on to a local historian, a guy called Noel Leavy. He'd never heard of the guy, but was instantly interested. There are still a few locals who were around at that time, and he'd be glad to accompany us if we decide to interview one of them. That's pretty much it.' He handed her a piece of paper with Leavy's number on it. 'I told him you'd call.'

Fiona picked up the phone and dialled.

'Noel Leavy.' The voice was strong.

'DS Madden, Detective Garda Brophy said we'd call.'

'Yes, I'm intrigued by the German professor. I've been researching this area for the past twenty years and I've never heard tell of him. There's an old guy in the care home in

Carraroe who lived in Letter Mullen from the 1930s onwards. He might be able to help. Do you have Irish?'

'I'm from Glenmore.'

'You're that DS Madden?'

'I am. Can we meet this man tomorrow?'

'I'll make the arrangements,' Leavy said. 'Eleven o'clock in Carraroe. I'll meet you in the care home reception.'

'Looking forward to it.'

CHAPTER THIRTEEN

Dark rain clouds were massing overhead when Fiona left Mill Street. She raced the clouds home and lost arriving drenched to the skin at the cottage in Furbo. She dumped her leathers just inside the front door and the rest of her clothes made a trail from the door to the bathroom. She ran a bath and submerged herself in the hot water as soon as it was ready. When she ran out of air, she surfaced and found that Aisling was preparing to join her with two glasses of wine in hand. She took her glass and, after touching Aisling's, sipped the cold liquid.

'That bad a day?' Aisling said.

'I can't handle the drink the way I used to.'

'It's a question of age.'

'Or I might be out of practice.'

They both laughed.

'Litmanen must be suffering the pains of hell,' Fiona said.

'He was as fresh as a daisy when I left him at the coach station.'

'That guy's my hero.' Fiona had finished her glass. 'Did you bring the bottle?'

Aisling leaned over the side of the bath, retrieved a bottle, and refilled both their glasses.

'I was a bit groggy this morning,' Fiona said. 'Do I remember something about Litmanen and his wife being invited to stay with us for a holiday?'

'I invited them, but I had an ulterior motive. Timo showed me photos of his holiday home in a place called Hanko at the end of a peninsula that juts into the Baltic. And we're invited to stay there any time we want.'

'Great, as long as Timo isn't there pouring grog down his and our throats.'

'Let's check the flights and go. You've just buried your father and now would be the ideal time to go to a house in a fantastic location far away from home.'

'Let's get it straight. We just buried a total stranger. Anyway, I can't leave right now. We have a murder investigation.'

'You always have an investigation. Give it to someone else.'

'I'm worried about Tracy.' Fiona held out her glass for a refill.

'I'm worried about you.' Aisling emptied the bottle between the two glasses.

Fiona let her mouth sink under the water.

'Alright, why are you worried about Tracy?'

'His father's been diagnosed as having prostate cancer. Tracy thinks it's hereditary. I think he may have suddenly realised that he's mortal.'

'And he's angry.'

'More like withdrawn.'

'He'll be angry, but won't want to show you. First, he'll be angry with his father for having a disease that might be hereditary. Then he'll be angry with himself that he now knows he might get something that will kill him.'

'He should be grateful now he knows what to do when the time comes.'

Aisling stood up. 'The water's gone cold.' She stepped out of the bath and wrapped herself in a towel. 'I can talk to Sean and reassure him. He's probably not going to die next week, but nobody can guarantee that. But I wish you would recognise that you need to grieve for your dead parent. You're carrying enough emotional baggage. Don't add more.'

Fiona downed her wine, placed the glass on the floor and submerged herself in the tepid water. She was worried about Tracy, but she had a son out there somewhere and anything could be happening to him. As she had done with her father, she had locked him away in a box in her mind and thrown away the key convinced that she didn't care. Why the hell hadn't both of them stayed away? But they didn't. Now she was playing the worried mother. Was she carrying a gene that would give him something horrible? Was it more likely that his father's genes were screwed up? Perhaps there was a rapist gene. Years ago, people just died. Nowadays, technology is able to discern the small building blocks of the human body and decide what illnesses are in the individual's future and where they came from. Maybe her son would die a horrible death because of a gene that she gave him. The temperature of the water had gone from tepid to cold. She shivered, stood up, and climbed out of the bath. The mirror above the handbasin was fogged and she rubbed it with her hand. She looked at her reflection. She wasn't sure who stared back at her. Was this really Fiona Madden, or was that someone else?

'Fish and salad?' Aisling shouted.

'Coming.' The mirror was steaming up again and her reflection was hidden behind the fog. She thought it was appropriate.

CHAPTER FOURTEEN

Tracy manoeuvred around a parked ambulance and turned into the carpark of the Carraroe Care Home. It was a modern, single story building located in the centre of the village.

A man came to greet them as soon as they entered the reception area.

'Detective sergeant Madden?' The speaker was a short squat man whose face was almost obliterated by a fuzzy black beard. He had two bright hazel eyes and a red nose. 'Noel Leavy.' He held out his hand.

Fiona took his hand and shook. 'This is Detective Garda Tracy.'

Tracy and Leavy shook hands.

'Willie Gerry is waiting for us in the conservatory.' Leavy pushed a button on the wall and the door to the interior opened. He led the way along a corridor with bedrooms on either side before turning right and heading towards the rear of the building where there was a glass enclosed day room. He pulled two chairs along and indicated a third to Tracy. Their objective appeared to be an old man whose bald head was covered in liver spots. He sat upright in an easy chair in the corner. Leavy set up the two chairs facing the old man and Tracy placed the third beside them.

'Cé caoi bfuil tu, Willie?' *How are you?* Leavy said as he settled himself in his chair.

'Ah tá me alright.' Willie Gerry hawked and spat into a handkerchief.

Fiona said, 'Does Willie speak English?'

'Of course, I do,' Willie said. 'You'll be Fiona Madden. I've heard about you and I seen you on the television a couple of times. You look better in the flesh. Where are you from?'

'Glenmore.'

'And how do they call you there?'

'Fiona Maire beag.'

'I know you now,' Willie said.

Tracy had his notebook out.

'I don't know so many people around here,' Fiona said. 'I left when I was sixteen and only returned to Galway a few years ago.'

'They tell me I'm ninety-one and I suppose that I believe them.' Willie Gerry looked from Leavy to Fiona and then Tracy. 'You're a fine looking couple.'

'They're not a couple, Willie,' Leavy said. 'They're detectives from Galway.'

Willie Gerry sucked on the end of an unlit pipe and looked at Leavy. 'I remember a dance in Tigh Darby. T'was well before your time.' He turned to look at Fiona. 'They tell me Tigh Darby is gone. Is that true?'

'It is,' Leavy said. 'The detectives have come all the way from Galway to ask you a few questions. About a German man that was living in Letter Mullen.'

Fiona pushed her chair forward. 'Were you in Letter Mullen in the 1940s?'

'I've been there all my life. I never went to America or England like the rest of them. My father and mother needed help with the cows and the land.'

'Do you remember a German professor called Heinrich Baum ever being there?'

Willie Gerry scratched his chin. 'Indeed, I do. He had wonderful Irish, but it was the Donegal dialect. I don't remember his name, only he was a German.' He smiled, exposing a set of bare gums. 'Sure, I don't remember the names of many of my neighbours. They said that he wanted to learn Connemara Irish. He had the words but not the accent. He used to sit in the pub drinking pints and listening to all the old stories. He wasn't slow to put a drink on the table, either. If you entertained him, you got your glass of whiskey.'

'Where did he live, a hotel?' Fiona asked.

Willie Gerry laughed. 'There wasn't a hotel within fifty miles. He was a big, strong man. He had a little beard and was always well dressed. He wanted to learn Irish, so he stayed with different families.'

'Do you know the names of the families?'

He shook his head. 'No, I don't remember.'

'What became of him?' Fiona asked.

Willie Gerry looked around the room. 'I don't know. He went as quickly as he'd come. I heard tell that he left his clothes behind. I never heard what became of them clothes.'

'You're sure you can't remember any of the families that he stayed with?'

'No.' Willie Gerry looked at Leavy and smiled. 'Is it tea time yet?'

A careworker was hovering close by. 'It'll be tea time soon.'

Leavy leaned towards Fiona. 'I think you've got about as much as you're going to get.'

Fiona stood. 'Thanks Willie, it was nice to meet you.'

'Do you have to go? I don't get many visitors.'

'Yes, Willie,' Leavy said. 'They have to go. They're very busy.'

Leavy led them back to the reception area. 'Do you have

time for a coffee? There's a cafe on this side of the church that makes a nice cup.'

'I suppose we could spare ten minutes.'

LEAVY DEPOSITED three coffees on the table and sat in a chair facing the two detectives. 'I've been researching the Letter Mullen region for the past twenty years and I've never heard of this Professor Baum. How did you guys come across him?'

'He was reported as a missing person and the file is still open,' Fiona said. 'When crime takes a break, we turn to the cold cases to convince our superiors that we're worth our salaries.'

'Any specific reason for picking this German fellow?'

'List of names and a dart.'

'I suppose he was the only German on the list. That was quite a coincidence.'

'We go where we're told. Are you from the Letter Mullen area?'

'Lord no, I've lived in Galway city all my life.'

'Then why your interest?'

'It's one of the last real Gaelic areas in the country. I'm hoping to turn my research into a book.'

'Sounds like a plan,' Fiona said. 'What do you do as a day job?'

'I was a civil servant, but I took early retirement. I do a bit of consultancy.'

'Then we're probably keeping you from your work.'

'I took the morning off. It's a pity Willie wasn't much help. Looks like the man you're looking for is a ghost.'

'You're probably right,' Fiona said. 'There are plenty of other missing persons on our list.' She stood. 'We've taken up enough of your time.'

'You haven't finished your coffee.'

Fiona looked at the untouched cup. 'The next time is on me.'

'What was all that about?' Tracy said when they were in the car.

'I haven't worked it out yet. I got the impression that Mr Leavy is interested in knowing why we're looking into Professor Baum and what exactly we know.'

'I thought he was being helpful.'

Fiona took her place in the passenger seat. 'You're too trusting. I think he tossed us a bone to see what we'd do with it. He already knew what Willie Gerry would say. You know what they learned at Troy: beware Greeks baring gifts. I bet when we look into Noel Leavy, we're going to find that he's as white as the driven snow. We have two murdered men, and I'll be willing to bet that Baum is underground somewhere. They're connected and so might Leavy be. How they're connected is just another mystery that we have to solve.'

CHAPTER FIFTEEN

They arrived back in Mill Street in the early afternoon after picking up their lunch of a sandwich and takeaway coffee at a small cafe in Furbo. Fiona checked with Brophy and there was nothing new to report.

Tracy pulled his chair over and sat beside Fiona. He opened his roast beef sandwich and took a bite. 'A seventy-five-year-old murder case. Are we out of our minds?'

Fiona laid her lettuce and tomato sandwich on the desk. 'We can't win them all. But I'm beginning to think that we're on to something. For instance, I don't think that the file on Baum's disappearance is missing by chance. Police files don't just disappear. People remove them and they are generally instructed to do so by someone higher up the food chain. That thought opens some interesting possibilities.' She motioned for Brophy to join them.

'How did the meeting with Leavy go?' Brophy sat down beside them.

Fiona told him about the conversation with Willie Gerry.

'Dead end then,' Brophy said.

'How did you come across Leavy?'

'Internet search. I was looking for someone who might have known about Baum. I found nothing, so I wondered whether there was any local knowledge. The South Connemara Heritage Society came up and showed Leavy as a contact.'

'There's an actual group?' Fiona took a bite of her sandwich.

Brophy laughed. 'It's a group of one. The address of the Society is Leavy's house and he appears to be the only member. There's a heritage officer with the County Council, but I drew a blank with him.'

'I want you to find out what you can about Leavy,' Fiona said. 'I don't expect much, but I didn't get a good feeling from him. I think he wasn't there to give information but to get it.'

Brophy stood. 'I'll get on it.'

'You're not going to let it go.' Tracy lobbed the sandwich container into the waste bin.

'Are you kidding? It's a puzzle that's been waiting for seventy-five years to be solved.' She showed him the notepad she had been working on. 'I've come up with ten questions I need answers on already, and we've only scratched the surface.' Tracy read through the list of questions. They began with: what were two German sailors doing in Béal an Daingin? And continued on to why did someone want to shoot them in the back of the head and dump them in a bog hole?

'When I have the answers to those questions and whatever else I can come up with, I'll let it go.' She tossed the residue of her lunch into the waste bin. They had established that Baum was in Letter Mullen and that he stayed with local families. He also disappeared, leaving his baggage behind him. That might be a fact, but it might also be local folklore. Baum would have been a personality in the area. There would have been stories about him. Most of them would have been fiction, but some may have been fact. Willie Gerry had been a teenager at the time. He would have listened to the adults talking, but she didn't think he retained much.

'Only if Horgan lets you.' Tracy slid across to his own desk.

The Garda Síochána is a hierarchical organisation that doesn't appreciate mavericks. From the top down, the main ethos is to have your arse covered. She knew she didn't fit in, but she loved the job. Aisling had told her more than once that her choice was either to play the game or move out. Playing the game was anathema to her, but she didn't want to leave. As a frustrated puzzler she would not want to give up on the case of the murdered seamen but she knew she might have to develop a strategy to frustrate the hierarchy's desire to sweep it under the carpet.

She switched on her computer and the usual flood of emails filled the screen. In the middle was one from O'Donnell. It said: Skype? followed by O'Donnell's Skype name.

'O'Donnell wants us on Skype,' she called over to Tracy.

External programmes were not permitted on official Garda computers. The Irish Health Service Executive had recently been hacked by the Russian mob and money demanded, but not paid. The cost of fixing the hack had been crippling, and the alarm bell had been rung through the entire Irish Public Service.

Tracy pulled his personal laptop out of his satchel and put it on his desk. 'Email back that we'll be on in five minutes.'

Fiona smiled and sent the email.

Five minutes later, O'Donnell's smiling face appeared on Tracy's laptop. 'Hi guys, how are things in Galway?'

'Getting more interesting by the moment,' Fiona said. 'What have you got for us?'

'We've rushed the tests on the bullets. They're 7.65mm which we don't see around here very often. Our local expert has no idea what gun they came from, but his contact in the Met got very excited. He's apparently the oracle on World

War Two weapons and he's positive that they were fired from a Mauser HSc. I'm sending through the information that he sent us.'

Fiona's computer pinged, indicating the arrival of an email. 'Thanks, I don't know what that's going to do for us.'

'You'll see when you read the information. In the Second World War, most of the German Army was issued with the P1908 Luger. The Luftwaffe had the Sauer 38H and the Mauser HSc but the Kriegsmarine only used the Mauser HSc.'

Fiona immediately got the point. 'The men were most likely shot with their own weapon.'

'I think that's a safe conclusion. There wouldn't have been many Mauser HScs about the place in the mid-nineteen forties. Now you find the gun and we'll tie it to the bullets.'

'That gun is probably long gone,' Tracy said.

'Maybe not,' O'Donnell said. 'Our GPR didn't pick up anything, but just in case we missed something, we're going to send someone along with a metal detector. You might be in luck.'

'You're really invested in this case,' Fiona said.

'It's not your everyday case.'

'Thanks. Let us know how your guy gets on.'

'My boss will flip when we submit the costs. Maybe you and I will soon be looking for new jobs.'

'Either that or we'll be heroes.'

'Sayonara.'

'Same to you.'

Fiona slid back to her desk while Tracy read through the information on the Mauser HSc.

'Nice looking gun.' He swivelled his monitor towards her.

He was right, it was a neat gun. 'Looks like the kind of gun a woman would choose.'

'I wonder if it's buried in the bog.'

'If it is, it'll be bugger all use to us by now.'

Fiona thought that it would have taken some brass to have killed the two naval personnel with their own gun. They were trained soldiers. They must have trusted whoever they gave their gun to. Another tiny piece of the puzzle had fallen into place.

CHAPTER SIXTEEN

'Upstairs, now.' Horgan was in his no-nonsense mood. Fiona returned the handset to its cradle and nodded at Tracy. 'Our presence is required.'

Once inside the office, Fiona could see that Horgan was in distress. His face was red and blotchy. 'What's up, boss?' She took a seat in front of his desk and Tracy sat beside her.

'I moved the German sailor issue up to O'Reilly and he passed it on to the Park for instructions. They were trying to develop a strategy when the Commissioner received a phone call from the German Ambassador who was contacted by one of the dailies about a report that the bodies of two German World-War-Two sailors had been located in a bog in Connemara.' He looked sharply at Fiona. 'Be honest, Madden, was that you leaking?'

Fiona put her right hand on her heart. 'On my mother's life, no. If I was to make an educated guess, I'd say the guy who was working on the bog has been talking. After that, it could be the ambulance crew that brought the bodies to the hospital, the assistant to the pathologist, a member of the tech team. God forbid, but it might be a colleague who was examining the whiteboard in the CID squad room. But it wasn't us.' Fiona felt like looking at Tracy but she kept her gaze steadfastly on Horgan. It was one of those occasions when a leak would be beneficial.

Horgan leaned forward for emphasis. 'The bottom line is that someone from the German Embassy will be coming here tomorrow morning for a briefing. Tell me that I'm aware of everything you've been up to.'

Fiona kept a straight face. 'There is one further piece of information that's come to light. Another German, a Professor Heinrich Baum, disappeared from Letter Mullen about the same time that the sailors were murdered. According to the computer, his disappearance was reported to the Guards at the time. But the file on the disappearance can't be found. Also, we recovered the slugs from the two bodies and it looks like they were fired from the type of sidearm the two men would have carried. There's no sign of that gun.'

Horgan had buried his head in his hands. 'I told you what to do with those bodies, but you knew better, You never listen to me. Now we have the Commissioner and the German Ambassador and soon it'll be in the newspapers. They already have the bones of the story. Why couldn't you just have left well enough alone?'

'Because we're the police and there are specific procedures to be followed when we find bodies that might have been subjected to violent death. Those men were murdered and they deserve justice. We couldn't just stick them back in the ground. What about their families? They should know what happened to their loved ones.'

Horgan rubbed his forehead with his left hand. 'Let's get this straight. Two German sailors were murdered and dumped in a bog. We have no idea what they were doing in Connemara and we've only just started the investigation. What in heaven's name does the missing professor have to do with the murders?'

'We don't know.' Fiona decided to leave Litmanen and her disquiet in relation to Leavy out. 'The whole case might just fizzle out, but I reckon the Germans will want the bodies back.'

'Are we finished with them?'

'They're in the freezer at Galway Regional. I'm told that once they're out, they'll decompose at a rate of knots.'

'Okay.' Horgan had tipped his chair back. 'I want the two of you at this meeting with,' he searched his desk and found a note he'd made, 'Siegfried Von Ludwig, First Secretary of the German Embassy. And for God's sake, keep it simple, Madden. What we don't want is a whole load of German coppers running around Connemara.'

'Tracy and I have got the picture, boss. What time will Siegfried be here?'

'Eleven. O'Reilly has a previous engagement and can't attend. If I call in sick, you'll handle the meeting.'

'Is that likely to happen?'

'I have a bit of a twinge in the stomach. I just hope it doesn't get worse overnight. Now piss off.'

'I NEED A DRINK,' Tracy said as they made their way downstairs.

'Make that several drinks and I'll keep you company.'

Fiona sat at her desk. The situation was escalating. She'd known that the Germans would eventually be involved, but she'd hoped that it would be further down the line. Possibly when the investigation had ground to a halt. She never heard of anyone in the Garda investigating a seventy-five-year-old murder. Whenever she thought of the time elapsed, she wondered if it was sensible to waste time on a crime where the murderer and any witnesses might be underground themselves. The excitement she felt about the investigation was still there, but the obstacles they faced appeared insurmountable. However, it was in her nature to continue to the end whatever that might turn out to be.

Brophy came and dropped a sheet of paper on her desk. 'The life and times of Noel Leavy,' he said.

She picked up the sheet, which contained four paragraphs. 'I don't suppose he'll be writing his autobiography, then.'

'Unlikely. He's exactly what it says on the tin. Ex-civil servant, dabbler in local politics, took the pension and spends his time playing around with his heritage hobby.'

'And the South Connemara Heritage Society?'

'Membership of one, Noel Leavy.'

Over the years, Fiona had learned to trust her intuition. She couldn't get over the feeling that there was something phony about Leavy, but perhaps she'd been mistaken. She read quickly over the page. As Brophy had indicated, Leavy was squeaky clean. He'd never even had a speeding ticket. You're beginning to lose it, girl, she thought to herself. She wasn't pleased at the thought. Her intuition had been her edge as a police officer.

FIONA RATTLED her empty pint glass on the bar to attract the barman's attention. When he responded, she made a circular motion with her right hand to indicate another round was required. She and Tracy had retired to Taaffes as soon as the office clock showed five. It had been a peculiar day which had started with a level of optimism but had ended on a note of frustration. It was probable that Willie Gerry was the only one living who remembered the German professor. The person who 'lost' the police file would be impossible to find and the German government would soon be aware that two members of their navy had been murdered in an obscure location on the edge of the Atlantic. The only possible note of positivity had come via O'Donnell with the identifying of the type of gun used in the killings. Fiona assumed that the gun itself would be long gone.

'Slainte.' She raised her glass and Tracy tipped his glass to hers. 'I'm afraid it's going to be this far and no further.' She noticed that Tracy had been more open than usual to the suggestion of more than one drink. 'Any sign of Cliona on the horizon?'

'The shoot is scheduled for two weeks. There are some fairly well-known local actors taking part.'

'Are you afraid someone's going to run off with her?'

Tracy laughed. It was the first time since they'd entered the bar.

'What's so funny?'

'I was thinking back to when I was about sixteen. I invited my girlfriend to join me and my parents on a holiday. She arrived several days after us and when I met her at the airport, I saw her being chatted up by another boy. I was as jealous as hell, but by the end of the holiday we'd split up.'

'I can just imagine the scene,' Fiona said, and they both laughed.

'I've matured since then, so if someone runs off with Cliona, I know there's very little I can do about it. But I am looking forward to seeing her.'

'What's the story from Wexford?'

'Nothing new. I gave a blood sample in Galway yesterday and we'll just have to wait and see.'

Aisling arrived behind Fiona's back. 'That's the second time I've caught you two canoodling. Once more and I'll be getting worried.'

Fiona's face reddened. 'It's been a strange day, so no dramatics, please. I've left the Kawasaki at the station, so you're on the orange juice.'

'Thanks,' Aisling said. 'I have strange days, too. I've been working with a client who was sectioned at the age of fourteen and has been in an institution for the past fifty-one years without ever receiving treatment for her so-called mental problem. Seeing someone who has had their life taken from them isn't exactly uplifting.'

Fiona got off her stool and hugged her partner. 'Sorry, we're consumed with our own problems. I'm cooking tonight.'

'I was reliving an embarrassing teenage moment.' Tracy pulled over a stool for Aisling while Fiona ordered the juice.

'Okay,' Aisling said as soon as she was seated. 'I want to hear about the dead Germans. What's the latest?'

Fiona and Tracy looked at each other and smiled.

CHAPTER SEVENTEEN

She supposed that it was inevitable that the discovery of the bodies would find its way into the news. The initial break came from the local Irish speaking TV station, TG4. O'Donnell had probably tried his best, but the camera crew had footage of the Technical Bureau vans and a departing ambulance. There was no comment from the local Garda. There was speculation that the bodies had been in the bog for a considerable number of years. The early morning newspapers had followed up on the story, which didn't make the front pages. The news cycle had shortened to the stage that the discovery would be forgotten in a couple of days.

Horgan had reported in ill with a bad dose of diarrhoea and O'Reilly was away for his prior engagement. Fiona was in charge of the Criminal Investigation Division for the day. For once, she looked the part. The leathers had been left at home and she had put on her best clothes: flat black shoes, a pair of skinny black trousers, a white blouse and a dark blue linen jacket.

'Looking good,' Tracy said as soon as she walked into the squad room. 'I hope Siegfried approves.'

She did a twirl for him. 'Horgan's an asshole. Every time

there's a tricky situation he ducks out and if the shit hits the fan, which it invariably does, he's the first one to point the finger of blame.'

'How are we going to play it?'

'Upfront. You and I have nothing to lose. We've been doing our job. Then we try to find out what Siegfried knows.'

'He's a diplomat. He'll try to get most out of us and give us the minimum in return.'

Brophy joined them. 'Anything I can do, sarge?'

Fiona couldn't see where to go next. The lines of enquiry were drying up. Horgan and O'Reilly would be delighted if they knew that she and Tracy were stumped. 'Check whether the conference room has been booked. Work up a set of photos from the bog and the post mortem. Also the photos of the dog tags. Put them in one of those plastic sleeves. And tell the gang downstairs that we're expecting an important guest and have coffee and biscuits on the table. DI Horgan is paying.'

Brophy nodded and went back to his desk.

'What do we do?'

'Maybe we should go to the Augustinian Church and say a few prayers.'

THE CALL from the reception came at ten minutes to eleven. Their guest had arrived and had already been shown to the conference room. Fiona and Tracy rushed upstairs and found Siegfried Von Ludwig standing just inside the conference room door.

Fiona extended her hand. 'Detective sergeant Madden and Detective Garda Tracy.' Von Ludwig was in his thirties, over six feet, fair-haired, broad-shouldered and narrow hipped. He wore a well-cut dark blue pin-striped suit, a white cotton shirt with a blue silk power tie. He looked every inch the up-and-coming diplomat. The new laid-back Tracy could take dress lessons from him.

Von Ludwig bent forward as he took her hand. 'First Secretary Siegfried Von Ludwig.' He almost clicked his highly polished leather shoes together, but didn't. As soon as he let Fiona's hand go, he extended his own to Tracy and they shook.

'You've just driven from Dublin,' Fiona said. 'Please take a seat and can we offer you some coffee?'

'A cup of coffee would be most welcome.' There was no hint of his nationality in his accent, which was a mix of British and American. He sat and the two detectives moved around the table so that they sat facing him. 'My ambassador would have liked to attend but he has an important meeting in Dublin. Will Detective Inspector Horgan be joining us?'

'I'm afraid DI Horgan got ill last night.' Fiona nodded at Tracy and then at the coffee.

Tracy's sigh was audible. He poured three cups of coffee and offered milk and sugar, both of which were refused by the diplomat.

Von Ludwig sipped his coffee. 'Excellent.'

He really is a diplomat, Fiona thought. Either that or someone in the kitchen had learned to make coffee overnight.

She laid the sleeve containing the photographs on the table. 'DI Horgan has informed us that you wish to make enquiries about the two bodies that have been recovered from the bog at Béal á Daingin.'

Von Ludwig put down his coffee cup. 'Until the Ambassador received a call from the press yesterday, we had no information on the matter of bodies being found.'

'Detective Garda Tracy and I have been tasked with investigating the discovery.' She opened the plastic sleeve, took out two photos taken at the bog, and passed them across the table.

Von Ludwig examined the photos. 'They are hardly recognisable as human beings.'

'Bogs have that effect on bodies. We found a small piece of metal under each of the bodies and we also found some buttons. The lab at the Garda Technical Bureau cleaned up the pieces of metal, which turned out to be German Navy dog tags.' She passed photos to the diplomat.

'Gunter Eich and Dieter Muller.' Von Ludwig's voice was soft.

'An autopsy at the Galway Regional Hospital established that both men had bullet holes in the back of their heads.'

Von Ludwig sat up straight. 'You mean these men were murdered?'

'That's our conclusion.'

'But why?'

'We have no idea. The bodies have been in the bog since the mid 1940s. As you can imagine, investigating a crime that happened over seventy years ago presents challenges.'

Von Ludwig put the photos on the table. 'These men were both members of the German Navy. What were they doing in the west of Ireland?'

'We thought you could help us there.'

'We will endeavour to find out what we can about these men. They will, of course, have to be repatriated. When will the bodies be available?' Von Ludwig was going through the file of photos that had been prepared by Brophy.

'You may have the bodies whenever you wish,' Fiona said.

'I will contact Berlin for instructions.'

She hadn't known what to expect from Von Ludwig, but she was pleased that he hadn't come across as heavy-handed. She was at one with Horgan on the question of the German police not being part of the investigation. 'We'd be grateful for any information you could supply. A crime was committed in our jurisdiction and we are obliged to investigate that crime. You may take all these photos for your report to your superiors. We haven't yet received the autopsy report and we'll forward it to the embassy when it's available.'

Von Ludwig collected up the photos and put them in his briefcase. 'I don't know whether we can assist you. That is for Berlin to decide. I would now like to view the bodies. The

Embassy will arrange to transport them to Dublin and for eventual shipping to Germany for proper burial.'

Fiona took a business card from her pocket and pushed it across the table. 'If we can be of assistance just call. I'll contact the pathologist at the Regional Hospital, you can go straightaway.'

He looked at Fiona. 'Thank you. You are your colleague have been very proficient in difficult circumstances.' He handed Fiona his business card. 'You may contact me at any time.'

'And you'll get back to us with any information concerning what Eich and Muller were doing in Connemara. Unless you have any other questions, Detective Garda Tracy will show you out.'

Von Ludwig stood and picked up his briefcase. He shook Fiona's hand. 'Thank you, I must endeavour to visit Galway again.'

Tracy was holding the conference room door open. The two men left Fiona alone in the room.

It was going nowhere. But there's a point in every investigation when the situation looks bleak. She didn't think that Von Ludwig would come up with anything. And if he did, someone at the Foreign Ministry in Germany would probably want to bury it. Politics and crime didn't mix.

'He fancies you,' Tracy said as soon as he sat behind his desk.

'Then I hope you put him straight.'

'He asked me if you were married. Might not be a bad life married to a handsome German diplomat travelling the world.'

'Except I'm gay.'

'That might not matter to him. At that level, they're all bisexual and running around having affairs with each other's wives and husbands.'

'You know this how?'

'I read John Le Carré.'

Fiona was silent.

'Penny for them.'

'We're losing momentum.'

Tracy picked up a piece of paper from his desk. 'I was looking over the list of questions that you developed. The majority of them are unknowns and behind them are lots of unknown unknowns. Questions that we haven't even thought of yet. Normally, the unknowns would shine a little light on the unknown unknowns, but since there are questions we can't possibly answer like what were two German sailors doing in Connemara, we're stymied.'

'A little knowledge is a dangerous thing,' Fiona said. 'Get back to preparing the Charlie Grealish evidence while I ponder some of the unknown unknowns.'

CHAPTER EIGHTEEN

Horgan had made a miraculous recovery and returned to the station for the afternoon, which relieved Fiona of her responsibilities as chief of the CID. Since she didn't have any pressing work, she decided that she had caught the same bug as Horgan and called in sick. It was a fine day. There was a nip in the air but the sky was clear so she went back to the cottage in Furbo and changed into her leathers. Aside from the visit to the bog at Béal an Daingin, it had been twenty years since she had visited the part of south Connemara known as the Islands. It was time to reacquaint herself with the area. She gassed up the Kawasaki at the local garage and headed south west past Carraroe and in the direction of Letter Mullen. She crossed the island of Letter Mór and stopped at Tigh Lee at the causeway between the two largest islands. It was a wild area that jutted directly into the Atlantic Ocean. She ordered a BLT and a pint of Guinness, sat at an outside table and stared at the sea as she ate. Two young sailors had lost their lives somewhere around here. Their reason for being in Connemara might remain a mystery, but the answer to why they died and who killed them was somewhere in this area. But the investigation so far had produced only one piece of evidence, the slugs from the dead men's heads.

She watched as two old men exited the bar and sat at a corner table, cradling their pints of Guinness. She sat back and listened as they conversed in Irish ,the topic was her. They speculated on who she might be and then moved on to what they might have done to her sexually when they were younger. She knew they had no idea she was a native speaker, and she smiled inwardly. It was natural that in an area such as this, any stranger would be of interest to the local population. She looked at the two men and guessed that they were in their late seventies, which would have made them children when Baum was about. Maybe there were others, aside from Willie Gerry, who were alive when the German had lived in the area.

'Cén aois atá sibh?' she asked their age.

Their jaws dropped. 'Cé as tu?' *Where are you from?* One of them said when he eventually recovered the power of speech.

'Glenmore, is mise Fiona Maire Beag.' In Connemara, few of the locals use a surname but prefer the old system of patronymics, or in the case of Fiona matronymics. The name includes the first name of the person, then the first name of the father or mother, and sometimes the first name of the grandfather or grandmother.

They hung their heads in embarrassment as they realised she had understood every word of their conversation.

The speaker continued in Irish. 'I know you. You're a Guard. I'm seventy-seven and Noel here is one year younger.' Both men shuffled and looked ill at ease. The islands of South Connemara were like islands the world over. The inhabitants were suspicious of outsiders even if the outsiders came from thirty kilometres away and spoke perfect Irish.

'Is there anyone around that was ten-years-old in 1944?' Fiona asked.

She could see the men calculating in their heads. Such a person would be eighty-eight years-old.

'Brídt Josie would be that age,' one of them said.

'Where can I find her?'

'She has a thatched cottage in Trá Bán. You can't miss it.' The men picked up their drinks and moved into the pub.

Fiona rode over to the small hamlet of Trá Bán, which is the Irish for White Strand. The beach in front of Fiona more than lived up to its name. There were several houses behind the beach, but only one was thatched. She pulled up outside the cottage. She knocked on the door but received no reply. She was halfway to her bike when she heard the door open behind her and an elderly woman stood in the doorway.

The woman looked her up and down. 'What do you want?'

'Bríd Josie?'

'Sea.' I am.

Fiona walked to the door. 'Mise Fiona Maire Beag as an Gleann Mór.' There was no invitation to enter. Bríd looked every bit her age. Her grey hair was pulled back from a face that was heavily lined. She was small, rotund, and wrapped in a shawl. She could have stepped out of a picture postcard.

'You father died recently,' the old woman said in Irish. 'I heard it on the radio. You're the Guard.'

'I'm looking for someone who can tell me about a German professor who lived around here in the 1940s.'

'Come in.' She stood aside to allow Fiona to enter. Inside, it was dark inside and the only illumination was a single bulb that hung from the ceiling. 'Will you take tea?'

'No thanks,' Fiona sat on a kitchen chair and Bríd Josie sat in an easy chair that was pulled up to a smouldering turf fire that gave off no apparent heat. 'Do you remember the German professor?'

Bríd leaned and warmed her hands at the fire. 'I was only a slip of a girl in the 1940s. I had no more sense than a jenny.

But I remember he lived around here for a couple of months. Then he moved on.'

'Do you remember who he stayed with?'

'He stayed with us for a month or more, but he stayed with others. I can't remember who exactly. I often heard my parents say that he paid good money. And money was scarce at the time. I don't remember much about him. He liked to take long walks and he liked talking with my father. I think I might have a photo of him somewhere.' She stood with difficulty, crossed to a wooden trunk, opened it, and removed a tattered photo album. She returned to her chair and flipped through some pages. A smile creased her face.

Fiona went and stood over her. Bríd was examining an old sepia photo of a group standing in front of the cottage. She put her finger on a distinguished gentleman with a goatee beard and wearing a suit. The other people in the photo were dressed in old clothes and were locals. 'That's him with my mother and father on either side of him.'

'Can I borrow that photo?'

'You'll bring it back.' The photo was held in the album by the four corners. The old lady used her nail to free it and handed it to Fiona. 'You'll not forget.'

Fiona put the photo carefully in her pocket. 'Do you think you might be able to remember the other families he stayed with?'

Bríd tried unsuccessfully to stir the fire to life with a poker. 'My memory comes and goes. I think some of our neighbours took him in.'

Fiona could see that Bríd was tiring. 'I'd be grateful if you'd try to remember. It's important. Would you mind if I come back and ask you some more questions?'

'Bring me a cake from Galway when you come. They have a fine cake shop there close to Eyre Square.'

Fiona nodded. 'I won't forget.'

CHAPTER NINETEEN

Fiona switched on her computer and watched the screen fill with recently arrived emails. She read the subject lines and clicked on one from the Garda Office of Corporate Communications that had been forwarded by Horgan. They wanted to have further details on the bodies that had been discovered in the bog. She looked across and smiled at Tracy.

'What have I done now?'

'It's what you're going to do. I just forwarded you a message from HQ. They want additional information on the bodies in the bog.'

'Cliona rang me last night and told me it featured on the local news. I don't usually watch TG4. What will I say?'

'The minimum, two German navy personnel, Gunter Eich and Dieter Muller, in the bog since the 1940s, working in cooperation with the German Embassy, bodies will be repatriated soon, Garda investigating the deaths.'

'You could have done that yourself.'

'But English is my second language. I don't have the facility with words that you have.'

Tracy read the email and started to type.

Fiona was about to answer her emails when she stopped

and sat back in her chair. A quote from somewhere suddenly came to her: the difficult we do immediately, the impossible takes a little longer. She had no idea where it had come from or who said it, but it had relevance to their case. Investigating a seventy-year-old murder case was most detective's definition of impossible. She was only a few days in and the frustration was already building. The questions were clear, but the answers were too far in the past. She heard the door to the squad room open and the footsteps on the floor were recognisable. 'Boss,' she said without looking up. 'Fully recovered, I hope.'

Horgan came around her desk and faced her. He looked the picture of health. 'Mind your mouth, Madden. It'll be the death of you. The word from the Park is that we're to tread water in the German bodies' case. It's a complete waste of police time. The bodies will be driven to Dublin this evening and they'll be transferred to Germany tonight. They'll be interred in a military graveyard in the next few days. Case over and we all go home.'

Fiona locked eyes with her boss. 'Those men were murdered. Isn't anybody interested?'

Horgan laughed. 'Fancy yourself as a Don Quixote, eh Madden? Up for a tilt at windmills yourself. Pity we can only charge the civilians with wasting police time.'

'Aren't we supposed to investigate a bit before we throw the towel in? Maybe the boys in the Park should start watching late night TV. In the past few months, investigative journalists have made us a laughingstock for screwing up the Kerry babies investigation and the botched investigation into the death of Father Niall Molloy. I hope this one doesn't come back to haunt us. I wonder who'll play you in the movie. Probably Brendan Gleeson.'

Horgan put both hands on her desk and leaned forward until her computer monitor stopped him. 'I heard about you before you were landed on us. You're a shit-stirrer, plain and simply. A shit-stirrer who doesn't follow orders. The DPP are complaining that you and Tracy are swinging the lead on the preparation of the Grealish evidence.'

'That's not true,' Tracy said. 'It's the DPP that is holding the process up. The case is a can of worms, as you well know. The powers that be want that can kicked down the road for as long as possible and there's no way we're going to take the blame.'

Horgan's mouth twisted in a grimace. 'The white knight rides to the aid of the damsel in distress. Take it from me Tracy, Madden is no damsel in distress. In fact, she not even...'

'Don't say it,' Tracy shouted. 'Because if you do, you'll be carried out of here.'

Horgan looked around, everyone in the squad room was staring at him. 'Tread water on the German case,' he said as he stalked out of the room.

'Horgan nearly overstepped the mark,' Tracy said when the door closed behind him.

Fiona smiled. 'He was only going to say what other people think.'

'Who put the bug up his arse?'

'I don't know.' She didn't have a great deal of respect for Horgan, but she wasn't lying about this case hounding them. The Garda were taking a pummelling on TV programmes investigating old cases. She would have thought that Horgan would be happy that they were willing to spend time on a case that might only frustrate them. She'd never been a conspiracy theory junkie, but she was getting the feeling that there was something more to this case than met the eye. It smelled like something political. Perhaps the two seamen were spies sent to Ireland to foment trouble. They might have been arrested by Irish Army Intelligence and shot. Ireland was neutral during the war, but there was plenty of evidence that there were German spies in the country. On the other hand, Baum might have murdered his countrymen before disappearing. The possibilities were endless, and so would the investigation be.

Maybe Horgan had got the message right. 'Let's get the Grealish evidence business out of the way. If we remove the stick, the DPP won't be able to beat us.'

FIONA AND TRACY lunched at The Quays at the bottom of Shop Street. They found a seat in the rear and they each ordered a salad and water. Fiona told Tracy about her trip to the Letter Mullen and made him laugh when she told him about the old men and what they would have done to her if they'd been younger. Their food arrived and they chatted while they ate. Fiona went to the toilet and when she returned, she sat close to Tracy. The bar was full and consequently noisy.

Fiona leaned into Tracy. 'Across from us, there's a middle-aged, clean-shaven man wearing a donkey jacket and a flat cap who was outside Mill Street when we left. I'm not sure, but I think he followed us here and every now and then I catch him looking at us. Does that sound crazy?'

'Galway's a small city. It's easy to run into the same people several times.'

'So it is crazy.'

'Nothing about you is crazy. If you say he followed us, then he followed us.' Tracy stood up and went to the toilet.

Fiona sat and tried to look like a girl would when the only man she wanted to talk to left the room.

Tracy returned and sat facing her.

'Take out your phone and bring up the camera,' Fiona said. 'Then pass it to me.'

Tracy did as requested.

Fiona picked up the phone and took a photo of Tracy, making sure to get the man she thought was following them into the picture. As soon as she lifted the phone, the man stood and exited. Fiona looked at the photo. She had just caught him before he stood and disappeared. 'I don't think I'm crazy,' she said. 'He appears to be camera shy.' She could feel a pang of anxiety grab her stomach. She'd been convinced that there had been something off with Leavy. Now someone had tailed her and Tracy to the Quays. People didn't tail the police, it was usually the other way around. She asked for the bill and paid. 'Let's get back to the station.'

CHAPTER TWENTY

The afternoon dragged. For once, Fiona decided to heed Horgan's instruction and she reviewed the correspondence from the DPP regarding preparation for the trial of Charlie Grealish. Reading between the lines, she could see that there was little appetite for the prosecution. The evidence they had produced was compelling, but there was a constant demand for more. Grealish had repudiated his confession, which had been made at his request and without any pressure on their part. She knew that it was one of those cases that would hang in the air until the spin could be developed. The consequences for the various actors dictated a slow grinding process. That didn't suit Fiona. After reading the correspondence, she put it aside and asked for Tracy's mobile. She found the photo she'd taken in The Quays and brought the man in the corner of the photo into focus. Who the hell are you? And why were you so interested in Tracy and me? She knew most of the local characters and she was sure that her man wasn't among them. He had a hard set to his face, but she couldn't understand a local criminal tailing two police officers. She called Brophy and asked him to blow up the section of the photo showing the man and print it off for her.

Perhaps there was an innocent explanation. Grealish's mother had hired a top-class legal team to defend her son. Maybe they were looking for some reason to call the investigation into question. Perhaps they hoped to catch Tracy and her in a sexual moment in order to impugn them. Or maybe she was just being her paranoid self, questioning everything and everybody. Brophy returned with the photo and she told him to attach it to the board and write underneath: *Who are you?*

She had no stomach for reading through the Mangan murder book again and her stomach wouldn't allow her to sit quietly and digest the crap that passed for administration. She could have sat on the toilet and ruminated, but instead she decided to go for a walk. As soon as she left the station, she looked for the man who had tailed them earlier. There was no sign of him, but she had no doubt that in The Quays he'd realised that they were on to him. She crossed O'Brien's Bridge, stopping to view the Corrib as it rushed towards the sea. She turned sharply, nobody behind her slid into a doorway or took cover behind a van. She told herself to relax, there was no reason why someone should be following her. She continued down Bridge Street until she came to the roundabout, then cut into Cross Street. Her heart, which had been pounding back in the station, was beating more regularly. The two dead Germans had somehow conspired to spook her. She had no idea why, but she felt that she and Tracy had stumbled into an investigation that someone wanted to keep hidden. She turned back and caught a glimpse of a man changing direction and disappearing up Bridge Street. She quickened her pace and saw that the man wore a donkey jacket and a flat cap. He was fifty metres ahead of her. She walked faster and closed the distance. She was ten metres behind him when he turned and she got a look at the side of his face. He was younger than the man in The Quays. Her heart rate slowed and she turned back the way she had come. You are being ridiculous, she told herself. This whole thing about being followed was bullshit. She recrossed the bridge and made her way back to the station.

'Out for a ramble?' Tracy said. 'Didn't meet your new friend by any chance?'

She sat at her desk. 'Oh ye of a little faith. At lunch, you said you didn't think I was crazy. Looks like you've changed your mind in the interim.'

'I don't think you're crazy, but I don't think someone followed us. There's no reason. Unless Aisling really believes that there's something going on between us and has hired a private detective.'

'She isn't that stupid or that well paid. Maybe I'm a bit anxious.'

'Time of the month?'

Fiona stared at Tracy and sighed.

'I'm sorry,' he said. 'It was out of my mouth before I had time to stop it.'

'Don't bother to apologise. You were just being a man. You know that one hundred and forty-four women have been murdered in Ireland since 1995. And most of them were killed by men who had professed to love them at some point. This is holy Ireland and it's open season on women. Misogyny hasn't gone away.'

Tracy looked at the office clock, a half an hour to the end of shift. 'I fancy knocking off early. What about a drink?'

'Not this evening. I want home and bed.'

CHAPTER TWENTY-ONE

Fiona woke early but she'd already had eight hours of continuous sleep. Just prior to waking, she was being pursued by a man in a donkey jacket and a flat cap. Aisling was still asleep when Fiona got out of bed. She made herself a coffee and dressed. Although the clouds surrounding the west looked ominous, she rode into Galway and went straight to the dojo. A class for juniors was just about to begin and she assisted the teacher for half an hour before moving to a quiet area and practicing some katas. She entered a deep meditative state and exited half an hour later, feeling energised.

There was a coffee and croissant sitting on her desk when she arrived.

'A peace offering,' Tracy said.

'Not necessary. I'm a woman, so I'm used to the snide remarks, the catcalls and the leers from the drunks at the bar. During a recent spate of attacks on women, a woman was asked whether she felt unsafe. She answered that as a woman she always felt unsafe. It's part of being female. But thanks all the same. I know that you're one of the good ones.'

'What's on the agenda for today?' Tracy asked.

Fiona took a bite of her croissant. 'You heard the boss. Let's make the DPP happy.'

'Screw the DPP. They have some balls for putting the blame on us.'

'What end of the stick do we always get?'

'The shit end.'

Fiona finished her coffee and had just switched on her computer when the phone rang. She listened and then turned to Tracy. 'There's some guy in reception who wants to talk to me.'

'About what?'

'Our dead Germans.'

When Fiona entered the reception area there was only one citizen present. She guessed that he was in his late twenties or early thirties. He was pale faced but handsome with high cheekbones, fair-hair, and the most perfect blue eyes peered out from behind designer spectacles. At his feet there was a large briefcase. She walked straight to him. 'I'm Detective sergeant Madden. I understand you want to talk to me about the bodies of the two German seamen we found.'

He stood and offered his hand. 'My name is Berthold Hindrichson and I'm the grandson of Kapitän Gunter Eich. I got your name from Herr Von Ludwig at the German Embassy in Dublin. You are the person investigating my grandfather's death?'

'Please sit.' Fiona indicated a bench.

Hindrichson picked up his bulging briefcase and sat.

Fiona sat beside him. 'Firstly, my condolences on the death of your grandfather. We have already released his body and I understand arrangement are being made to repatriate him and his colleague to Germany for burial. How did you learn of his death?'

'I have put his name on a search and whenever it appears, I get a notification. I will, of course, be returning to Germany for the burial. My mother never met her father, but we hear many stories from my grandmother. My grandfather was very famous in the Kriegsmarine. He was young to have been promoted to kapitän, and he won the Iron Cross for his bravery.'

'I'm sure that you're very proud of him.'

'I am an investigative journalist for a small newpaper in Mainz and I have spent many years researching my grandfather.' He held up his briefcase. 'This is the result of my research. Herr Von Ludwig has told me that you will be examining the death of my grandfather. I would like to help you.'

'Thank you for the offer. But I'm afraid the investigation will be low key given that the events happened seventy-five years ago.'

Hindrichson frowned. 'I understood from Herr Ludwig that my grandfather had been murdered.'

'It appears to be the case, but we have no idea why and who might have been involved.'

Hindrichson pushed his spectacles higher on his nose. 'Perhaps it has something to do with the gold.'

CHAPTER TWENTY-TWO

Fiona asked the duty sergeant to show Hindrichson into an interview room and to find a cup of coffee for him while she went to fetch Tracy. In the CID room, she flopped into her chair.

Tracy scooted over to her. 'That bad?'

She kept her voice low as she told him the content of her conversation with Hindrichson.

'Gold!' Tracy had his excited face on.

'Let's not get carried away. Hindrichson is in an interview room and I needed an opportunity to assimilate the news. Let's go and see what he's got to tell us.'

The duty sergeant managed to drum up a decent coffee for Hindrichson. In the interview room a mass of paper covered the table and the briefcase lay on the floor. Fiona introduced Tracy and Hindrichson.

Fiona and Tracy sat facing the young German. 'Before we start, I want to tell you where we are with the investigation,' Fiona said. 'Then you can tell us about your research.'

She went over the salient parts of the investigation, the discovery and disinterment of the two bodies, the autopsy, the discovery that the two men had been shot in the head. They had no idea what Eich and Muller were doing in Ireland. 'That's it,' she said when she was finished.

Hindrichson sifted through some of his papers. 'I can fill in some of the blanks, but for others we may have to draw some conclusions. Before I begin, what do you know about Germany during the final days of the Second World War?'

Fiona looked at Tracy, who raised his eyebrows. 'You can take it that you'll have to start with the basics.'

'First things first, Gunter Eich, my grandfather, spent his entire career in the German Navy and, more particularly, the Kriegsmarine.' He searched for a document on the table, found what he was looking for and offered four stapled pages to Fiona who took it. 'This is my grandfather's file.' He looked at Fiona who looked puzzled. 'You don't understand German.'

'No,' Fiona and Tracy said in unison.

'That file spans Gunter's twenty years in the Kriegsmarine. He rose from Fähnrich zur See to Kapitän, I'm sorry from midshipman to captain. He was a devoted Nazi and a highly decorated naval officer. Have you ever heard of the Abwehr?'

Fiona shook her head. 'Assume that we know nothing about the institutions in Germany.'

'The Abwehr was the military intelligence organisation for the German Army from 1920 until the end of the war in 1945. Like all such organisations, it contained officers of every hue. Some supported Hitler and the Reich, while others were part of plots against Hitler. Many secret documents are now in the public domain, and I have been diligently searching these documents.' He put several documents on the table, all of which had the emblem of an eagle at the top. 'As the war was coming to an end, military intelligence launched a plan to continue the Third Reich with a Fourth Reich, which would be located in Argentina. Many ardent Nazis had escaped Germany and made their way to South America on the so called *Rat Lines* via Portugal. They had already formed an organisation called

ODESSA and they would need money to establish the new Reich.'

Fiona could see many comparisons between Hindrichson and Aisling. They both fell easily into lecture mode.

'They came up with lots of schemes to move money from Germany to South America. I'm sorry, I don't mean German money because Reichsmarks were worthless. I'm talking about dollars and gold. My grandfather was brought into one of these plots. He and his fellow officer Muller were part of a group trained to operate a small submarine of the SEEHUND class.' He put a schematic of a submarine on the table. 'My grandfather and Dieter Muller underwent significant training to familiarise themselves with this type of submarine. Only the most motivated officers were chosen for these missions. The submarine was designed to carry two torpedoes but for this mission, the weapons had been removed and the tubes modified to carry gold and currency in one and additional fuel in the other. My grandfather and Muller left Wilhemshaven on 1st September 1944 heading for a disguised Kriegsmarine naval base in the Canary Islands en route to Argentina. Their route took them around Scotland and the west of Ireland.'

'So that's how they came to be in Galway,' Fiona said.

'It would appear so,' Hindrichson said. 'They might have had engine trouble or they may have run out of fuel. Before they left, they were given the names of contacts along their route who they could depend on.'

'Do you know if there was a contact in the west of Ireland?' Fiona asked.

Hindrichson looked puzzled. 'No, but until yesterday I thought they were probably lost in the mid-Atlantic, since they never arrived in the Canaries. The bodies being found in Ireland changes everything.'

'Can you find out for us if they had a contact called Henrich Baum?'

'It would probably be in one of the files I already have on my computer. Who was he?'

'A German professor who in 1944 was living in the area where your father and Muller were buried. He was consequently reported as missing to the police. Nothing was ever heard of him again.'

'How much gold are we talking about?' Tracy asked.

Hindrichson shuffled some of his papers. 'The documents I've seen mention a payload of at least one hundred and fifty kilogrammes. It might be a lot more.'

'And what would that be worth today?' Fiona said.

'About nine million American dollars,' Hindrichson said.

'And in 1945?'

'Around three hundred thousand dollars.'

Tracy was busy Googling. 'That would have been a fortune in 1944.'

Hindrichson gathered his papers together. 'These are copies I prepared for you. I'm sorry but they are in German but they corroborate the story I told you. I'm scheduled to meet the German Ambassador and Herr Von Ludwig tomorrow. Then I return to Germany for my grandfather's funeral.' He handed the bundle of papers to Fiona. 'I have a photograph of my grandfather. Would you like to see it?'

Fiona nodded.

Hindrichson removed a photo from his satchel and handed it to her. 'It was taken at Wilhelmshaven several days before he left on his final mission. He's the one in the middle.'

There were three men in the photo. Hindrichson's grandfather was at least six inches shorter than the other two men. Only Eich was shown full face. He was smiling and he had several days of beard on his narrow face. He wore his captain's cap at a jaunty angle and around his neck was an Iron Cross hung from a leather strap. His eyes were lined and hooded. Despite the smile, he had a haunted look. 'He looks haggard,' she said. 'More tired than haggard.' She handed back the photo.

Hindrichson took it and stared at it before handing it to her. 'You may keep this copy. Anyone would be exhausted by five years of war. He went on a record number of missions. That was why he received the Iron Cross. Will you find who killed my grandfather?'

Fiona passed the papers to Tracy. 'It happened a long time ago. The murderer is most likely dead.'

Hindrichson picked up his briefcase. 'You will keep me informed.' He handed Fiona a business card.

She put the card in her pocket and handed him her card. 'Of course we will. Are you staying in Galway tonight?'

'Yes, I will catch the train to Dublin, tomorrow. My meeting at the Embassy is in the afternoon. I have already reserved a hotel. I have spent many years trying to find out what happened to my grandfather. Maybe at last there is a chance we might solve the mystery.' He extended his hand to Fiona. 'Thank you for finding my grandfather. My mother also thanks you.'

She shook his hand. 'I'll arrange for a police car to take you to the hotel.'

'That is not necessary.' He and Tracy shook.

'It's the least we can do.'

CHAPTER TWENTY-THREE

Fiona and Tracy retraced their steps to the interview room and sat facing one another. She handed Tracy the business card. 'Google him. Go on the newspaper in Mainz site and check him out.'

Tracy took out his phone and followed Fiona's instructions. He handed her the phone. 'Berthold Hindrichson investigative journalist.'

Fiona looked at a picture of the man who had just recently been in the room. 'The story is so off the wall that he could have been a fantasist.'

'He appears genuine.' He took back the phone and started Googling. 'The Abwehr actually existed. There are hundreds of sites related to Nazi gold. There was a small submarine class called Seahund.'

Fiona picked up the bundle of papers from the table. 'We have to fact check every aspect of this story. Aisling will have a contact in the university who teaches German. We'll get an opinion on the validity of these papers. If we go to Horgan with a story about mini-subs and Nazi gold, he'll have us committed.'

'The existence of the gold changes everything,' Tracy said.

'If Baum was a spy, maybe he's the one who murdered the crew and made off with the gold. That's why he disappeared with only the clothes on his back.'

'I can't see him humping one hundred and fifty kilos of gold on his back. He would have needed transport. Moving a load of that size from a remote part of South Connemara would have attracted a lot of attention. But it's something we should consider. There are a lot of people who would be very happy if Baum turned out to be the villain of the piece.'

'You mean it was the German what done it?'

'Hindrichson is going to research Baum. If he turns up somewhere in Germany post war, then I think he might have been our man and we can put this investigation to bed.' Fiona's intuition told her that this wouldn't be the case.

'In the meantime?'

'In the meantime, we fact check Hindrichson's story. And we keep all this gold and money stuff to ourselves.'

'YOU'RE JOKING.' Aisling hadn't eaten a bite of her lunch, so engrossed had she been in Fiona and Tracy's story. 'Murdered German seamen, a missing professor and now Nazi gold. I wonder what's next.'

They were sitting at one of the outside tables in Munroe's Tavern in Upper Dominick Street. It was perhaps a little crisp for outside dining, but Fiona didn't want to be overheard.

'Fiona didn't tell you that she thinks we were being tailed yesterday.'

Aisling looked sharply at her partner. 'Really?'

'Definitely,' Fiona said. 'Although Tracy thinks that my anxiety had something to do with the time of the month.'

Aisling switched her look to Tracy, whose face was ruby red. 'Maybe he was right.'

'I think we're being watched right now,' Fiona said. 'I don't know why. It's not the same guy as yesterday, but there's a guy across the road that I've seen three times since we left Mill Street.'

'Galway's a small place,' Aisling said, turning to her neglected sandwich.

'That's what I told her,' Tracy said.

'We'll see.' Fiona took the Hindrichson papers from her bag. 'This is where we make you pay for your lunch. These are the papers Hindrichson gave us in support of his story. Tracy Googled him and he's the real thing. But these papers are in German and we need someone to review them for us. We don't need them translated, but it would be reassuring if someone could give us the gist of what's in them.'

'I have a colleague who might help.' Aisling pushed her plate away.

'There's one condition,' Fiona said. 'They can't talk to anyone about this. We haven't told Horgan about the gold and possible money. If it gets into the newspapers, the investigation will go down the toilet.'

'I won't be able to guarantee silence,' Aisling said.

'Horgan will have your guts for garters if this leaks out,' Tracy said.

Fiona already knew that. 'What about saying you're writing a book about Nazi gold?'

'My colleague probably wouldn't believe me.'

'But he probably won't be able to put two and two together. There's no mention of the bodies in the newspaper today.'

Tracy signalled to the server to bring the bill. 'That's because they haven't put two and two together. When they do, it's going to be bigger than the naked man on the platform with a knife in his chest at Dun Aengus. Think of it, two, maybe three murders, a fortune in Nazi Gold and US currency, ODESSA, mini subs, spies. What a cocktail. The press are going to love it.'

Fiona stared at Tracy. 'You're not being helpful. We need

to corroborate Hindrichson's story, and Aisling's colleague is the only one who can do that for us. We have to take a chance.' She handed the bundle of papers to Aisling, who took them with some reluctance and shoved them into her bag.

'I hope none of us are going to regret this arrangement. I'll organise it this afternoon. How soon do you want an opinion?'

'Yesterday,' Fiona said.

Tracy paid the bill and they left.

At the door, Aisling turned to the two detectives. 'I know that you guys are too smart not to have thought of this, but there's someone out there who appears to have made off with a fortune seventy-five years ago. That same person has murdered at least two people. He's not going to be very happy when he finds out that two detectives in the Garda Síochána have stumbled across his misdeed.'

'You're right,' Fiona said. 'We have already thought of that.' She could see by the look on Tracy's face that he hadn't.

Aisling looked at her watch. 'I've a lecture at two o'clock.' She kissed Fiona and rushed off.

Fiona and Tracy strolled along Dominick Street in the direction of the station.

'We might be poking a hornet's nest,' Tracy said. 'That could be dangerous.'

'It is what it is.'

CHAPTER TWENTY-FOUR

Fiona stood before the whiteboard and stared at the face of the man she photographed in The Quays. Hindrichson's story was wild, maybe even a fantasy involving his grandfather. But if even a scintilla of it were true, someone had managed to cover up murder and a heist of monumental proportion for seventy-five years. She thought that such a man, or men, had to be respected and feared. The man in the photograph was in his forties and therefore had no role in murdering the two men in the bog. Maybe she was overthinking the situation. But Aisling was not a trained detective or even a police officer, but she had concluded that whoever had pulled off the crime would not be pleased with their investigation. If he, or they, knew how little chance she and Tracy had of a successful conclusion, they wouldn't be worried. But if they were, she and Tracy would have to watch out. She returned to her desk and tried to concentrate on dealing with her paperwork. There was an email from Aisling saying that her colleague would take a look at the Hindrichson papers and would revert back in a couple of days. She brought up her browser and searched for *dead seamen and Connemara*. A page of results appeared, only two of which were Irish. The rest were in German. She cursed herself for her inability in languages. She clicked on one of the German results and saw that it was a small piece that had appeared in the prestigious Frankfurter Allgemeine. There was an obvious interest in the German media. She went back to her emails and spent the rest of the afternoon fighting boredom.

Fiona and Tracy were preparing to call it a day when Horgan entered the squad room. He moved around the various desks discussing cases with the other detectives, but it was clear to all that his major interest was in buttonholing Fiona and Tracy. There was no way that she could tell him about Hindrichson's story. She was feeling guilty about it. When you joined the police, you accepted that you have become a member of a hierarchical organisation. Information flows upwards through the chain of command. She knew that what they had learned, if true, was of enormous importance. It changed everything. The two murdered seamen's deaths could be passed off if there was no apparent motive. The gold and the money changed all that.

'Anything new?' Horgan asked when he finally reached Fiona's desk.

Her first reaction was to wonder whether he had heard about the gold and money. But only she and Tracy knew. Hindrichson wasn't meeting the embassy staff until the following day. 'We're moving ahead on the evidence for the DPP, as you requested. There's not much more we can add. I think that Tracy will draft a clever letter for your or O'Reilly's signature that will put the ball firmly back in their court.'

'Good work.' Horgan circled her desk. 'And the German seamen?'

She felt another blip of fear that he knew something. 'They'll be back in Germany tomorrow and I assume they'll be buried with military honours.'

'And there's been no comeback from the Embassy?'

'Not so far.'

'Good.' He was preparing to leave the room when his gaze fell on the whiteboard and the photograph of the man in The Quays. 'Is someone here trying to be a comedian?'

'No, sir.'

'Who wrote, *Who is this man?* Beside that photograph, and why?'

'That was me, boss,' Fiona said. 'He was taking an unusual interest in Tracy and myself when we lunched at The Quays yesterday.' She left out the bit about him tailing them from Mill Street. 'Do you know him?'

Horgan laughed. 'Everybody who put in their twenty years knows former DI Sam Darker. He caused more trouble that most of the criminals we put away and he never served a day. I met him once or twice and thanked God I never had anything to do with the man. Maybe he fancied you, Madden. His bad luck.'

She gave him a withering look. 'Could be, boss. Have a nice evening.'

Horgan suddenly remembered he'd been on his way and started for the door. 'Sam Darker,' he muttered as he left. 'On my patch.'

She gave the middle finger to his departing back.

'Drink?' Tracy asked.

'Not just yet.' She dialled the number from memory.

'Dominic Geraghty.' The voice was deep and hoarse, like sand running over gravel.

'It's Fiona.'

'How's Galway? I've been following your exploits in the papers and on YouTube.'

'You can't believe all you read or see. You have to take the context into consideration. But Galway is great. I always wanted to move west.'

'Strange, I thought you said you'd never go back there.'

'You weren't really listening then.' She looked around.

Only she and Tracy were left in the room. 'Mind if I put this call on speaker phone, Dominic?'

'As long as we're not going to discuss our respective love lives.'

She pressed the speaker button. 'You have nothing to worry about.' She turned to Tracy. 'DCI Dominic Geraghty was my old boss. He's retired these days and spends his days walking his dogs.'

'This is not one of those calls where we're going to reminisce about cases we worked together on. I didn't think you were the type.'

'I'm not. I need to ask you a question.'

'Fire away.'

'Did you ever run across a fellow officer called Sam Darker?'

There was silence on the line for a minute. 'Why do you ask?'

'Someone followed my partner and I from the station to the pub where we had lunch. He sat across from us and I caught him looking at us a couple of times. I took his photograph and stuck it up on the whiteboard with the question, who is this man. My boss, DI Horgan, recognised the photo as a former DI called Sam Darker. He didn't know him well and given the case we're working on at the minute, I didn't want to press the point.'

There was silence on the line.

'You still there, Dominic?'

'I ran across Darker now and then. He generally worked the other side of the aisle. He spent some time in the Special Branch, worked ministerial protection, took part in some special ops stuff that nobody wanted to talk about. Most of the work he did was on the edge. I didn't like the guy. I stayed away from him, and I advise you to do the same. He's been retired for about six years and I heard that he hires himself out these days.'

'As a private investigator?' she asked.

'I think he takes on the jobs that a private investigator wouldn't touch with a barge pole. I was enjoying this conversation until his name was mentioned. What kind of case are you working on?'

'A need-to-know one.'

'You were the best pupil I ever had. I wouldn't like to see you getting mixed up with someone like Darker.'

'And you were the best teacher and mentor that I could have wished for. Forewarned is forearmed. I'll make sure that we stay on the right side of the guy.'

'Yeah, and I'm supposed to believe that. It's not your style, Fi.'

'How's retirement treating you?'

'Jane is still teaching, so I've taken over as house husband. I can even iron to my wife's exacting standards. You get to Dublin much?'

'Not as much as I'd like to.'

'Next time you're here, give us a bell and I'll introduce you to my new hobby, cooking.'

'You're joking. I'll put it in my diary. Thanks Dom, take care of yourself and give my love to Jane.'

'I hope you got the message, Fi.'

'Loud and clear. Have a nice evening.' She put down the phone.

'Fi,' Tracy said. 'Can I use that?'

'No, you can't. And if you try, you'll regret it. And not a word about the contents of that phone call to Aisling.'

'You think this Darker guy is dangerous?'

'Dominic Geraghty was one of the hardest men I've met. If he stayed away from Darker, the guy is to be avoided.'

'Is it Charlie Grealish or Eich and Muller?'

'I don't know, but I have a feeling we're going to find out.'

CHAPTER TWENTY-FIVE

Fiona woke at five to three. In her nightmare, someone was trying to take her boy away. Her son had been taken from her at birth, but in her dream he was maybe four or five. When he was gone, she felt the deepest loneliness that she could imagine. She touched her face. It was wet. She was surprised that she displayed mothering instincts after all. Sleep wasn't going to come, so she got up, went to the kitchen and made herself a cup of coffee. Her son had turned up unexpectedly and the reunion didn't go well. She was partly to blame but according to Aisling her son exhibited symptoms related to extreme abandonment issues culminating in a desire to kill his birth mother. He'd stolen her prized Vincent Black Shadow and ran. That had been more than eighteen months ago. Why hadn't her son contacted her in the meantime? She had scoured the advertisements for the Vincent Black Shadow, but there was nothing. Perhaps he had sold it privately. She was a detective and she couldn't find a trace of her son. She sat at the kitchen table and held her head in her hands. She'd always thought that she was who people said she was, a hard-hearted bitch who had packed a lot of living into not many years. Recently, she had made peace with her mother and failed to do the same with her father. She would be the first to admit that she had never wanted to meet the child she had given birth to, but now she longed to meet him again. She had done him wrong at birth and again when he tried to become part of her life. Maybe they could make a go of it but she was afraid that there was a lot of his father in him. And he was a serial rapist. Her view of herself was crumbling, and she wasn't comfortable with what was emerging in its place. She sipped her coffee and thought of returning to bed. The kitchen clock showed three-thirty, three and a half long hours before Aisling would wake at seven on the dot. Plenty of time to mull over all the mistakes she'd made. Perhaps the anxiety she was feeling had nothing to do with the murdered men in Béal an Daingin. Only time would tell. She remembered a part of her nightmare had contained a shadow that threatened her and her little boy. She thought about the man sitting across from her at The Quays. Was he really so dangerous? She respected Geraghty's opinion. But how did he fit in? Charlie Grealish or the German sailors? It had to be one of them since they were the only two cases she and Tracy were working on.

She was considering TV and a rom-com when the telephone rang. She didn't like calls in the middle of the night they were seldom good news.

'DS Madden?'

'Yes.'

'Sergeant McDonagh, I'm on the desk at Salthill. A young man was assaulted earlier this evening. He was mugged and his briefcase was stolen. He was transferred to the Regional and triaged there. Two of our lads were with him. He had your card in his pocket, so I thought I'd give you a call. It's a German name, Hindrichson.'

'How is he?'

'He has a nasty cut on his head and he was concussed. They're keeping him in overnight and possibly longer. I checked with the doctor and they told me they're planning some scans and he'd been settled for the night. He's not in any danger, he's being observed.'

'Thanks.' Fiona killed the call. Someone wanted to know what was in Hindrichson's satchel. She'd gone to the front door of the station with him. There must have been someone watching who followed him. When they got the opportunity, they mugged him and lifted his satchel. Now they were aware that she and Tracy knew about the gold and the money. She and Tracy might have been safe before, but that knowledge might be their undoing. Poor Hindrichson, he had no idea what he had walked into.

CHAPTER TWENTY-SIX

Hindrichson was lying on a trolly in a corridor directly outside the Accident and Emergency Department. His head was bandaged and the side of his face was bruised. The corridor was packed with patients on trollies and sitting in chairs. Fiona assumed that such sights were rare in an ultra-modern hospital in Mainz, but they were all too usual in Galway. Hindrichson's eyes fluttered before opening when Fiona put her hands on the trolly. 'How are you feeling?' she asked.

Hindrichson's eyes widened. 'I have a big headache and the side of my face hurts.'

'Do you remember what happened?'

'Not clearly. I had dinner in a restaurant, then I listened to Irish music in a pub. I was on my way back to my hotel and then I woke up here. They told me that two policemen had found me in the street and that I had been mugged. My satchel was missing, but thankfully my passport and money were not taken.'

'You don't remember anyone following you?'

'No.'

'Were you drinking in the pub?'

'Just one pint of Guinness. Everyone talks about it, but I didn't like it.'

'It's an acquired taste. I just spoke to the doctor and you have a nasty blow on the head. They're taking you for a brain scan this morning and they might hold on to you for a couple of days. The Beds Manager is trying to find you a bed, but I wouldn't hold out much hope. I'll get my boss to give them a call.'

'This kind of thing happens a lot in Galway?'

He hadn't managed to put two and two together yet. 'No, it's a rare occurrence. Galway is a pretty safe place.'

'Whoever mugged me wanted my satchel.'

'More likely they wanted to see what was inside it.'

A porter arrived behind Fiona. 'I have to take the patient for a scan.'

'I'll call back later and see how you're progressing.'

THEY SAT TOGETHER in one of the interview rooms. Fiona had brought the coffees and she sat facing Tracy and Brophy. She briefed Brophy on her conversation with her former boss and then told them about Hindrichson. And her visit to the hospital.

'Poor bastard,' Tracy said. 'You obviously think the worst.'

'I think someone is interested in our investigation. I think he was picked up at the station, followed, and when it was convenient, mugged. And the only item stolen was his satchel. We have a bent copper on the case who I assume is trying to put the frighteners on myself and Tracy. We need to find out everything we can about this man.'

'Tricky,' Brophy said. 'He was obviously no run-of-the-mill copper, ministerial protection, Special Branch, operations possibly involving terrorists. Those kinds of people generally keep their heads down.'

'I suppose there's no chance of getting his police file?'

Brophy frowned. 'About the same chance that a snowball would have in hell.'

'But you can try,' Fiona said.

'I can try, but I might leave a trace. If he still has friends in the Force, they might let him know that someone is checking up on him. And I doubt I'll get anywhere.'

'It's a risk we have to take,' Fiona said. 'We have to know why he's involved.'

Tracy tossed his coffee cup into a waste basket. 'I thought your old boss said to leave him alone.'

'That doesn't mean he's going to leave us alone. The more we know about this character, the better we'll be able to handle him.'

Tracy shifted uncomfortably in his chair. 'If your old boss was a hard man and he stayed away from Darker, what chance do we have handling him?'

The door opened and Horgan stuck his head in. 'Is this meeting private or can anyone join? Well, not quite anyone, but what about the head of CID?' He entered the room and sat in the free chair at the table. He looked directly at Fiona. 'Would anyone like to tell me what's going on here?'

Fiona finished her coffee before speaking. She wanted to keep Horgan involved, but she didn't want to mention Hindrichson too soon. 'You should have received the latest set of papers requested by the DPP in the Grealish case with the cover note for you to sign. They've been giving us the run-around for months, bombing us with requests for additional evidence. We're discussing whether there are any further gaps that we might have filled.'

'And you couldn't discuss this in the squad room?'

'In all honesty, boss,' Fiona said. 'There are times in that room that you can't hear yourself think with the sound of phone calls and computer keyboards. This room was empty and we decided to use it.'

'You must think I was born yesterday, Madden. You're up

to something and it involves those seamen. The bodies are gone to Germany. We don't do cold cases here. There's a special group that deals with those investigations.'

'No boss, there's a special group that deals with the way we handled investigations in the past and it's very likely that someday they will look into how we screwed up the German seamen investigation.'

'What lines of enquiry are you following?' Horgan asked.

'We're a bit stumped at the moment, but there are one or two questions that need answering.'

'Well, you better find the answers soon because I'm about to pull the plug on this investigation of yours. It's a waste of police time.' He rose and went to the door. 'And no more secret meetings.' He opened the door and turned back. 'Madden, I sometimes think that you're a monkey holding a live grenade and I don't want to be around when it goes off.' He closed the door behind him.

'Why didn't you tell him about Hindrichson, the gold and the money?' Tracy said.

Fiona lobbed her cup at the waste basket. It missed. 'Because it will freak him out.'

'Then how are you going to stop him from pulling the plug?' Brophy asked.

'I'm not.'

FIONA WAS TRYING to put a viable scenario together. She started with the hypothesis that Baum was a German spy. He could have been a linguistics professor before the war, and his knowledge of Donegal Irish indicates an interest in Ireland. Maybe he was initially posted to Donegal, which is close to the border with Northern Ireland, which was part of the United Kingdom. He was probably spying on happenings in Lough Foyle and Derry. Then he could have been moved to Connemara, again under the guise of learning Irish, and was in

Letter Mullen as a contact for the transports heading for the Canaries. That was where he ran into Eich and Muller. What happened then? That was the sixty-four thousand dollar question.

'You're on to something,' Tracy said. 'You go all glassy when you're coming up with a theory. Spill it.'

She told him.

'There's a certain logic to it,' Tracy said when she finished.

'It's a hypothesis based on the facts.'

'And you can go further.'

'I have no basis in fact for what followed, but it could be something like this. Eich and Muller either needed fuel of something went wrong with their submarine. They probably radioed their contact, Baum, who steered them into the Islands and that's how they ended up in Connemara.'

'Then Baum found out they were carrying gold and currency, killed them and disappeared with the money,' Tracy concluded.

'Who's making the leaps now? Baum being the villain throws up a whole series of questions. How did he keep the submarine secret? What happened to it? In 1944, there was no transport from Letter Mullen. He would have had to transport the gold and currency by wagon. Where did Baum disappear to?'

'That one is easy. Back to Germany?'

'We'll need to check that out when Hindrichson is operational.'

'One step forward and two steps back,' Tracy said.

'Like every other investigation,' Fiona said.

'Like to enlighten me on how you plan to keep Horgan's feet to the fire?'

Fiona smiled. 'Who did the money belong to in the first place?'

'The Germans.'

CHAPTER TWENTY-SEVEN

How do you investigate a seventy-five-year-old murder? The simple answer was with great difficulty. Fiona had been pondering the question along with a more important question for her. How would Horgan react to her subverting his desire to bring the investigation to an end? She was sure that her plan to involve the German Embassy in pursuing a continuation of the investigation to seek justice for their countrymen, and also to retrieve the money that had been stolen, would eventually become known to the Garda hierarchy. That was probably inevitable, although she would try to avoid it like the plague. It might spell the end of her glittering career. And might that be a bad thing? Like her colleague, Sean Tracy, she wasn't entirely sure that her future lay in the Garda Síochána. Involving the Germans was a high-risk scenario, and she normally considered herself as risk averse. So why was she willing to play that card? Aisling had often upbraided her when she claimed she hated her job by saying she'd do it for nothing. That was an exaggeration, but it wasn't a million miles from the truth. She wasn't sure where it came from, but Aisling thought it came from her need for recognition. Tracy would say she suffered from the sin of pride. She knew she was a good detective, better than most of the colleagues she worked with. All she knew was that she enjoyed solving the puzzle that murder generally created and bringing the guilty to book. Maybe it had something to do with her errant father. As a teenager, it galled her that he had gotten away with dumping her mother and her. He had done something she considered at the time to be reprehensible and he hadn't had to pay the price. Over the past several months, seeing him disintegrate before her eyes made her believe that, in a perverse way, he had paid. In the end, everyone paid a price for the decisions they made. She took out the card that Von Ludwig had given her and called the number on it.

'Siegfried Von Ludwig,' the voice was officious.

'It's Detective sergeant Madden.'

'Good afternoon, detective sergeant, we have sent the bodies of Eich and Muller to Berlin. Muller has no family and Eich only has the Hindrichsons. They will be buried in a military cemetery tomorrow. I thought that concluded our business.'

'Have you spoken with Hindrichson?'

'He should meet with us this afternoon.'

'I'm afraid he's going to miss the meeting. He was mugged in Galway last night and is currently in hospital.'

'Good God, is he alright?'

'A bad bang to the head, some concussion, but the prognosis is for a full recovery. Has he told you of his research into his grandfather?'

'Yes, he did.'

Fiona felt that she was trying to get blood from a stone. 'What did you think?'

'It is historically correct and I think very plausible. He was bringing papers to substantiate his claims.'

'Do you still think that our business is concluded? What about the question of who murdered Eich and Muller?'

'We have the impression that there is a certain reluctance on the part of the authorities to pursue that issue.'

'I can assure you that there is no reluctance on my part to continue the investigation. But I might require some assistance. Do you understand?'

'My Ambassador had already expressed some dissatisfaction that the case is not being pursued as he might have wished.'

'Then I can count on you to keep pressure on from your end.'

'You're an interesting young woman. I think I am going to pay a visit to Galway soon to become better acquainted.'

'I'll introduce you to my partner. She's a professor at Galway University.'

'I would love to meet her. I hope we are not embarking on a journey that will injure our careers.'

'The crime was committed seventy-five years ago. Our chances of success are not great.'

'Then we better enjoy the experience. Good day, sergeant.'

'Thanks, Siegfried.'

'How did it go?' Tracy asked.

'He's on board.'

'Not the Titanic, I hope.'

CHAPTER TWENTY-EIGHT

Fiona was happy with her day's work. For the second day in a row, she had declined an invitation from Tracy to have a drink before heading home. She picked up the Kawasaki from the parking and headed out along the coast road. There was a speed limitation and plenty of cameras to enforce it, so she kept to the limit and enjoyed the mental benefits of the ride in terms of the countryside and the ocean. She stopped off in Barna and bought some fresh hake and two bottles of Sauvignon Blanc. She was looking forward to a nice glass of white wine and a fish dinner as she pulled into the space in front of the cottage that she and Aisling shared in Furbo. The cottage had belonged to her grandfather, and he had bequeathed it to her when he died. She loved the cottage and lovingly renovated it. She'd just turned off her bike when Aisling pulled in behind her.

Fiona put her helmet on the seat and peeled off her leathers. She opened the front door, kissed Aisling as she passed, and followed her into the living room. 'I picked up some fish and white wine for dinner.' She held up her shopping bag.

Aisling was standing in the centre of the living room.

'What's that smell?'

Fiona got it too. 'Perhaps it's the fish. The shop told me that it was straight out of the sea.' She knew it wasn't the fish. The cottage had been closed up all day, and the smell of cheap aftershave still hung in the air. They'd had a visitor or visitors, but Aisling shouldn't know.

Aisling continued to sniff. 'I don't think it's the fish. But I can't put my finger on it.'

'I turned down a drink with Tracy, but I'm gagging for a glass of wine. I picked up two bottles of Entre Deux Mares.' She started for the kitchen. 'Take your work clothes off and I'll have two glasses ready on the deck.'

Whoever had visited her home had wanted her to know he'd been there. It was the classic *we-know-where-you-live* situation. Sam Darker would have pulled the same ploy during his days in the Special Branch. Now he was giving her a message. She got it, but she didn't know yet what it meant. She had no doubt she was about to learn. Dom had said that Darker was dangerous. When she joined the police, she accepted that her job might put her life in danger. But Aisling was a civilian. There used to be an unwritten code that civilians were not part of the game between the police and the criminals. But that code had been broken so many times that it no longer had meaning. Darker hadn't been outside Mill Street by chance and he hadn't been in The Quays because he heard that the lunch was good value. He was on her and Tracy. And someone had stuck him on them. She had no idea who that might be. She opened the coldest of the two bottles, poured two glasses and put the full and half-empty bottles into the fridge. She opened the glass doors to the rear and set the two glasses on a rattan table. The sun was disappearing into Galway Bay. She sat in a chair and watched it descend. The deck was one of her additions and she wished that her grandfather might have seen what a difference it had made to the cottage.

Aisling had changed into a shirt and harem pants. 'I'm still trying to work out what that smell is.'

'It'll be gone tomorrow.' Fiona handed her partner her glass and they clinked.

Aisling sat on a rattan chair similar to Fiona's. 'It's weird.' She looked thoughtful as she sipped her wine.

Fiona watched the light fade on the hills of Clare across the bay. 'It's the country. We once had a rat die in the house in Glenmore. My mother and I tore the place apart until we found it. Believe me, you never want to have a rat die in your house.'

'My colleague finished with what you call the Hindrichson Papers.' Aisling leaned back and looked at the setting sun. 'She found them very interesting.'

'But are they original?'

'She thought so. She's the head of the German Department and her grandfather was in the Wehrmacht, the German Army. He told her lots of stories about the war. She told me to tell you that it all rings true, the Fourth Reich, Argentina, ODESSA, the whole story. She gave me back the papers.'

'Did she ask any questions?'

'She didn't, which surprised me.' She came upright quickly, almost spilling her drink. 'I've got it. My ex used an aftershave called Old Spice. That was the smell.'

Fiona burst out laughing. 'You should see the doctor and get him to check your olfactory system. The smell was something completely different.'

Aisling got up and went into through the patio doors, which Fiona had left open on purpose. She returned some moments later. 'The smell has dissipated. I could have sworn it was aftershave.'

'Who's making dinner tonight?' Fiona stood and picked up the two wine glasses. 'If you cook, I'll refill the glasses and find us something interesting to watch on TV.'

'Deal.'

CHAPTER TWENTY-NINE

Fiona slept fitfully. The lack of decent sleep was getting to her. She would have liked to have an opportunity to check out the cottage, but she didn't want to alert Aisling. There was a possibility that the message would be somewhere where she could find it. She hated the psychological bullshit. Why didn't Darker or whoever had creeped her cottage come out and tell her what they wanted? At least she and Aisling had been spared the phone calls with the heavy breathing on the other line. While on the job in Dublin, she'd had limited contact with the Special Branch. At first, she had been over-awed by these supposed super-cops until she realised that in the main they were sociopaths enmeshed in a macho culture that wasn't far removed from the criminals they were chasing. They were also a rampant group of misogynists. She was afraid that the visit to her cottage would only be the beginning. Their speciality was messing with people's heads. They had been given psychological training and they loved using it. She decided that she wouldn't play their game. She would ignore all the psycho shit and wait for Darker to explain exactly what he had in mind. Then she would tell him to go fuck himself.

. . .

SHE WAS in the squad room when Tracy strolled in at nine o'clock exactly. She slid her chair over beside him as soon as he was seated. 'Remember your theory about the source of my anxiety.'

'I already apologised for that.'

'Someone visited my cottage yesterday while Aisling and I were at work. They purposely left the smell of cheap aftershave hanging in the air.'

'They wanted you to know.'

'It was a message. They're telling me that they know where I live. I've been thinking about our little encounter with Darker the other day. He's a highly trained operative. If he wanted to tail us and not be seen, he could easily have done so. He wanted us to know that he was following us and he allowed me to take his photo because he wanted us to know who he is and what he represents to us. But it's only the start. Whoever Darker is working for wants me to be shit scared before they're going to tell me what they want.'

'Can we get at them?'

'Get at who? I only know that someone creeped my house. I think it was this guy Darker, but I have no evidence and I bet he didn't leave a trace behind.'

'Get the techs to give the place a once over. They'll find something.'

Fiona shook her head. 'No way. They'll freak Aisling out and that's the last thing I want to do.'

Brophy approached them and handed Fiona a sheaf of paper. 'I can't access Darker's Garda file. But I've concentrated on what's available on the Internet.' He pointed to the first three sheets. 'These are photos of Darker in the background during his ministerial protection phase.'

Fiona looked at the first photo which showed Darker off to the side while some minister or other was being interviewed for television. The second photo showed him opening the rear door of a large Mercedes to allow a VIP to exit. The third showed him walking behind some important looking woman.

Tracy was taking the photos from Fiona's hand as she finished. 'That's our former Minister of Justice,' he said. 'And those are prominent politicians.'

'I have no interest in politics,' Fiona said. 'They're all the same, feathering their own nests.'

Brophy handed over another page. 'His company, Darker Inc, has an upmarket address just off Fitzwilliam Square in Dublin. I looked it up in the Companies Registration Office and the list of what they can do is as long as your arm.'

Fiona took a second look at the photos. Darker mixed with the great and the good. They would have a use for someone with his skills. 'So he's not just a retired police officer who has become a private detective?'

'From the filings I've seen,' Brophy said. 'I don't think investigation is the company's primary offering. I think Darker responds to his client's needs, whatever they might be.'

'Like throwing a scare into a serving police officer.' Fiona looked at Tracy. 'This doesn't look good.'

'Any chance we can find a client list?' Tracy asked.

'No chance,' Brophy said. 'I didn't realise that we had characters like this hanging around. His annual accounts show that the company turned over close to a million euros last year. So he's not cheap and the clients are not poor.'

Fiona handed Brophy back the photos. 'File these away and keep digging.'

Brophy took the papers and went back to his desk.

Fiona and Tracy sat together. 'At some point,' Tracy said. 'This guy is going to find out that you've been looking into his background. That might not be good for you. I assume your friend Dom is solid.'

'Dom's no fool. He's out of the game and he'll stay that way.'

'Where do we go next?'

'You remember that stomach bug I had several days ago? Well, I'm not over it and I've spent more time in the loo than the office this morning. I think I need to sign off sick.'

'What are you going to do?'

'I'm going to nose around the cottage while Aisling is at work. I don't think I'm going to find anything, but you never know your luck.'

CHAPTER THIRTY

Fiona gunned the Kawasaki around the corner at the Galway Golf Club and onto the Coast Road. There was a hint of rain in the air, but she was leathered up and wasn't worried about getting wet. The large black Audi behind had picked her up as soon as she left Mill Street and was not hiding the fact that it was tailing her. She didn't react by carrying out crazy manoeuvres aimed at losing the tail. She wanted them to know that throwing a scare into her would require more than stalking her. She was aware that the situation could escalate quickly, but she didn't have many cards and Darker was the dealer. It was a well-known fact in games of chance that the house always won.

She parked in front of the cottage. There was no sign of the Audi, but she knew it wasn't far away. She took off her gear, dumped it on the bike, and entered her home. There was something about any home invasion that gets under your skin. She knew nothing had been taken, but she still felt violated. It wasn't because her home was her castle, it was more that it was part of her. Once someone uninvited had entered and had spent time there examining her possessions, it was impossible to feel the same. She had handled enough burglaries to understand the mental impact on the victims. There were the feelings of mistrust, isolation, and fear. Many victims suffered depression, anxiety, and panic attacks, as well as PTSD-like symptoms. But worse of all are the feelings of vulnerability. The person or persons who invaded her home wanted to engender all those feelings in her and if she were totally honest, they hadn't completely failed. Her main worry was not herself, now that she understood the game, she would be prepared when the next incident occurred. And she was certain there would be another incident and it would be an escalation. Her main worry was Aisling. Having a copper for a partner wasn't the easiest job in the world. The hours were long and for Fiona, there was her commitment to the job. Aisling was made of stern stuff, but no civilian, no matter how psychologically strong, can fail to be affected by either stalking or the invasion of one's private place. If Darker wanted to screw with her, that was fair game, but if he started to screw with Aisling, all bets would be off.

She made herself a cup of coffee and started in the living room. She did a quick tour, making sure that everything was pretty much where it should be. She moved on to the bedroom and went through the wardrobe and sideboard. She wondered if Darker and his crew might have a fetish for women's undergarments, but their pants were all neatly stacked. She went back to the kitchen and sat at the table, nursing her coffee. It was a good clean job carried out by professionals. She finished her coffee and washed the cup.

As soon as she heard Brophy's briefing on Darker Inc, she realised that Charlie Grealish could be ruled out. The Grealishes had money, but not the kind of money that Darker was used to charging. Darker had been brought on board by someone to monitor the situation on the murdered German sailors. Someone was worried by the investigation and that someone had money. Fiona couldn't believe that the man who murdered Eich and Muller could still be around. That would count double for Baum, who was already in his forties when he was in Ireland. If the murderer was dead, why should anyone worry about an investigation?

The rain that was promising earlier had come and gone while she was in the cottage. She dried the bike's seat and sat wondering what to do. She remembered she had promised Bríd Josie to bring a cake from Galway. She wasn't going back to the office, so a cake from Spiddal would have to suffice.

THE AUDI PICKED her up as she turned onto the main road. Maybe her little side trip would give them something to think about. She picked up a fancy cake at the supermarket and drove out to Letter Mullen and the small cottage behind the beach at Trá Bán. She enjoyed the ride. She didn't think too much about the car behind, but concentrated on who might be hiding in the woodwork.

The sun was shining when Fiona stopped outside Bríd's residence. The Audi breezed by as she parked. The tinted windows concealing the driver. She had to knock on the door twice before Bríd opened it. She saw that the old woman didn't recognise her, so she held up the box containing the cake. 'You asked me to bring you a cake from Galway the next time I visited. It's Fiona Maire Beag.'

'Tar isteach.' *Come in.* She took the cake in her hand.

Fiona entered the small living room. 'Will I put the kettle on?' She smiled when she remembered it was the kind of thing that she would have said when she visited her grandparents.

'That would be lovely.'

Fiona spied an electric kettle on the sideboard, filled it with water and set it in motion.

Bríd went to the kitchen table and removed the cake from the box. 'It's many a long day since I had a cake as fine as this.' She walked to a dresser, took down two side plates and put them on the table.

Meanwhile, Fiona had made the tea and put the pot on the table. When the table was set and the cake cut, they sat facing each other.

'Have you lived all your life here?' Fiona asked.

'I was born in this house and I suppose I'll die here. Everybody else I knew is already gone. But we had good land and I only got rid of the cows five years ago.'

'What about your relations?'

'Most of them are in America. They have their lives there and the young ones don't bother to visit. I suppose they're waiting for me to die so they can sell the bit of land I have left.'

'You have lots of years in you yet.' Fiona ate some cake and drank her tea.

Bríd smiled. 'The doctor says my heart isn't good. They won't have long to wait.'

The old woman reminded Fiona so much of her own grandmother. 'Do you have a neighbour to look after you?'

Bríd drank a slug of tea. 'I have, they're very good, but like myself they're getting on. There are no young ones about.'

'Did you think any more about the German professor?'

'Did we talk about him?'

'We did the last day I was here. You remembered him. He was learning Irish, and you told me he stayed with several families. You loaned me a photograph of him.'

'I remember he was a big strong man, and he spoke Irish like someone from Donegal.'

'That's right.'

'I think he stayed with the Gannons and the Griffins and he might have stayed with the Farmers. He spent his day talking with people and taking notes. He looked out to sea a lot. I suppose he was homesick.'

'Are any of the families he stayed with still around?'

'The Gannons moved away to Galway after the war. Sold their land and left, lock, stock and barrel. They did well, I heard. The Griffins left for America in the fifties. The Farmer sons went to London and when the old people died, they came back for the funeral and sold the house and land. They're all gone.'

Fiona's phone rang. It was Tracy. 'What's the problem?'

'Some dude turned up from HQ and you're the reason he's here. I told Horgan you were home sick and he's threatening to send a car out to Furbo to pick you up.'

'Tell him I'm at the doctor's and that I'll be in as soon as he sees me.' She killed the call, gave Bríd a hug, and rushed out of the cottage. She jumped on her bike and roared away. As she crossed the bridge between Tiernee and Letter Mullen, she saw the Audi sheltering down a narrow laneway. She didn't give him a second thought as she sped towards Galway with her stalker in tow.

CHAPTER THIRTY-ONE

Fiona parked her bike, climbed out of her leathers, and made her way to the squad room. She was about to sit down when Tracy shook his head.

'Upstairs immediately.'

She dumped her gear and ran her fingers through her hair. 'Who is the dude from HQ?'

'DI Peter O'Neill, ever heard of him?'

Fiona raised her eyes. 'Oh yes indeed, they call him *The Fixer*. He can generally be found up a certain part of the Commissioner's anatomy. Let's go.'

'I'm not invited.'

'Lucky you.' She left the room and went upstairs to Horgan's office, where she found her boss and *The Fixer* conversing over coffee.

'How did you get on at the doctor?' Horgan asked.

'I'll live, but thanks for asking.'

She locked eyes with O'Neill.

Horgan put down his cup. 'This is DI O'Neill. Have you met before?'

'I don't think so,' Fiona said. She heard enough about him.

The Commissioner kept him around to cover his arse and as a sycophant to boost his ego. He was the equivalent of Lear's Fool but anyone who took O'Neill for a fool was making a big mistake. O'Neill resembled a large stick insect dressed in a blue business suit. His face had a deathly pallor and his head was too big for his matchstick frame. His eyes were dead and Fiona was suspicious of people with dead eyes.

O'Neill made no move to rise to shake hands. They both held the stare like two animals that were about to indulge in a fight to the death.

'DI O'Neill was anxious to meet you.' There was a nervous catch in Horgan's voice.

Fiona relaxed her stance. 'Well now he has, perhaps he'll tell me why.'

'Sit down, Madden,' Horgan said. 'This is a friendly conversation.'

'Thank you, sir, but I think I'll remain standing.'

O'Neill rubbed the side of his nose with a bony finger. 'The Commissioner had a meeting with the German Ambassador this morning. He asked for a briefing on the status of the murder investigation into the deaths of the two German sailors. The Commissioner wasn't aware that any such investigation existed.'

Fiona looked at Horgan, who in turn looked at O'Neill.

'I told DS Madden on several occasions that she was not to begin a murder investigation,' Horgan said.

'Have you been leading a murder investigation, DS Madden?' O'Brien asked.

Fiona wasn't going to forget Horgan's attempt to throw her under the bus. 'My partner and I were called away from my father's funeral to view a body that was found in a bog not far from Béal an Daingin. That body and another were disinterred by the Technical Bureau and sent to Galway Regional Hospital where an autopsy was performed and it was concluded that both men died were shot in the head. It is usual for the police in such circumstances to investigate. We have been doing so but at a leisurely pace.'

'The case is cold, Madden,' O'Neill said. His small red tongue flicked out across his thin lips. 'The Commissioner wants an end to it.'

'I'm personally associated with this investigation,' Fiona said. 'If it's going to fold, I'll need a written order from the Commissioner.'

The two men looked at each other. 'Out of the question,' O'Neill said.

Horgan's face had lost its customary colour and he looked like he was about to be sick.

'I'm afraid that's what it's going to take,' Fiona said. 'If the Commissioner wants it done, he's going to have to put his name on it.'

O'Neill leaned forward. 'You career is in the balance here.'

'And so is my integrity and that of the Garda Síochána. I hope that neither you nor the Commissioner will have to face a TV investigation. I wonder why everyone is so keen to sweep the death of two men under the carpet.'

Horgan opened his arms as though preparing an embrace and he forced a smile. 'Let's not hurl threats around. How long do you think you need on the investigation?'

'Give me a month,' Fiona said.

O'Neill laughed. 'You've got a week.'

Fiona gripped the edge of Horgan's desk. 'Solve a seventy-five-year-old murder in a week. You can't be serious.'

O'Neill sat back. 'In one week, we will call the German Ambassador and tell him that the murder investigation failed to establish who murdered the men and we have been obliged to drop it. And then you'll be mine.' He pointed his finger at the door.

Fiona stood her ground. 'If it ever comes to that, I'll be out of my own accord. I wouldn't give you the pleasure.'

'A week, Madden.' Horgan stood, opened the door and nodded at Fiona. 'You're wasting time.'

'Fucking Judas,' Fiona muttered audibly as she left the room.

CHAPTER THIRTY-TWO

When Fiona entered the squad room, she nodded at Tracy and Brophy and they followed her to the whiteboard. She told them what had transpired in Horgan's office. 'I'm about to be skewered, but I'll do my best to keep you two out of it.'

'You don't appear too bothered,' Brophy said.

Tracy was frowning. 'Don't be fooled by the tough exterior. She's bothered. And when she's down and out is when she's at her most dangerous.'

She looked up at the whiteboard. 'We've come a long way since the bodies were pulled out of the bog. We have the bullets and the type of weapon that fired them. We know that the men were transporting gold and currency and we can assume that's the reason they were killed. They landed in a poverty-stricken area of Southern Connemara. There's an old woman in Trá Bán who remembers Baum.' She took the photo Bríd had given her from her desk and put on the board. 'The well-dressed man with the goatee is Baum. What would you do if you just became the owner of one hundred and fifty kilos of gold bars and God only knows how much currency?' She looked from Tracy to Brophy.

'Bury it,' Tracy said.

'Maybe you could do that in Wexford,' Fiona said. 'But that wouldn't work in South Connemara. I remember I went out fishing with my grandfather one time and we didn't manage to get a single lobster. I was only a child, and I suggested we pull some of the traps that didn't belong to us. My grandfather laughed. He said that there were at least four pairs of eyes staring at us at that moment. Every move was being observed. The situation in the Islands is worse. Most of the people there are related either by blood or marriage. Someone would know.'

Brophy looked at Fiona. 'What do you think?'

'Baum is in the frame.' Tracy said.

Fiona nodded. 'I don't think he is. Eich, Muller and Baum were all fanatical Nazis. And, as such, they were most likely committed to the rebirth of the Fourth Reich in South America. They'd never steal the gold and they would never kill each other. Their mission was to get the gold and currency to the base in the Canaries, and they would have been dedicated to that. Baum is underground somewhere close to where Eich and Muller were found, and I bet he has a slug in his head that'll match the ones we have.'

'Are you going to tell us what you think happened to the gold?' Brophy said.

'When someone wins the lottery, all their neighbours know about it. They buy a new big house and a big car. Hiding wealth isn't easy. Finding the killer is going to be about following the money trail. I have no doubt the gold is long gone.' She sighed.

'The murderer has had seventy-five years to hide it away,' Tracy said.

'I can't imagine that in 1945, someone walked into a bank and said *I happened to find a hundred and fifty kilos of gold last week, can you change it into cash?* Even at that time, questions would have been asked. The killer was sitting on a fortune that he couldn't use for fear of being asked where he got it. It's the modern-day dilemma of the drug dealer. And what do they do?'

'They launder it,' Brophy said, smiling.

'Tomorrow we start following the money.'

CHAPTER THIRTY-THREE

Aisling put a twenty euro note on the bar and handed Fiona and Tracy their drinks. 'Drink up. If you get fired we don't have a mortgage and we can live on my paltry lecturer's salary.'

Fiona picked up her pint of Guinness. 'Slainte.'

Tracy raised his glass. 'All we have to do is to find the murderer and the money in the next week. That's not too much to ask, is it?'

They burst out laughing.

'It's great that you two can laugh about it,' Aisling said. 'This could genuinely be the end of your careers.'

Fiona sipped her drink. 'Tracy is safe but I might have to wait until he gets a big job in the Park until I get rehabilitated. The knives have been out for me since that bloody video on YouTube.'

'This O'Neill character appears to be rather unsavoury,' Aisling said. 'Does he really have the power to fire you?'

'At the stroke of a pen,' Fiona said. 'Of course, there would need to be some reason, but I've given them enough ammunition.'

'And the possibility of clearing the case of the murdered Germans?' Aisling asked.

Fiona and Tracy looked at each other. 'Possible but not probable,' Fiona said. 'We'd need a significant break and O'Neill isn't the only creepy individual about.' The words were out of her mouth before she could stop them. She looked at the glass in her hand as though it were responsible.

'Who else is there?' Aisling said.

She doesn't miss a trick, Fiona thought. 'There's a former Garda officer who is currently a private detective in Dublin who might be interested in the case.'

'And he's creepy because?' Aisling said.

'I told you he followed Tracy and me to lunch one day.'

'Fi thinks he followed us to lunch one day,' Tracy said.

Aisling almost dropped her juice. 'Fi?'

'That's what the old boss in Dublin calls her. She said I could use it.'

Fiona punched him in the upper arm. 'I did not say that you could use it.'

Tracy rubbed the spot she had struck. 'That hurt. I bet your hands are registered as lethal weapons in California. I could arrest you for GBH.'

Fiona began smiling but the smile faded. 'I think we might be in over our heads this time.'

'Then let it go,' Aisling said. 'There'll be other cases.'

Fiona could see the logic. The men had been dead for seventy-five years and could be considered as casualties of war. And she didn't give a fiddler's curse about the recovery of the gold and cash. Maybe if she hadn't seen the huddled corpses that had been taken out of the bog. But she didn't think so. Major crimes had been committed. She wouldn't be doing her job if she walked away, and she had already told herself that if the day came when she didn't live up to the oath she'd taken, she would quit the Force. She leaned forward and kissed Aisling on the cheek. 'I love you,' she whispered in her ear.

Aisling smiled. 'There's no way you're going to give up the case.'

'I can follow it for the next week, officially, but unofficially I'll never let it go. Every old copper has a cardboard box in the attic with the files of the ones that got away. I'd prefer to quit with an empty cardboard box, but it will be what it will be. As for this case, it bothers me that so many people are anxious that we drop it. That's a conundrum I want to solve.'

Tracy finished his drink. 'I'm away. Cliona is back for the evening and I have something special planned.'

'I'll bet you have,' Fiona said.

'You've a dirty mind.' Tracy kissed Aisling and headed for the door.

'No kiss for Fi?' Aisling called after him.

He turned and blew a kiss.

'I hope to God you don't get that boy fired,' Aisling said when Tracy was out of earshot.

'Take me home.'

They worked their way along the length of the bar and were almost at the front door when Fiona looked to her left into the small snug.

Darker sat in the corner.

They locked eyes and for a moment Fiona was tempted to confront him. Then she felt the tug on her jacket and saw that Aisling was following her gaze.

Darker tipped his cap to her and broke off eye contact.

'One of the creepy ones?' Aisling asked.

'The creepiest.'

CHAPTER THIRTY-FOUR

The envelope was sellotaped to the screen of Fiona's computer when she arrived in the squad room. She put on a pair of latex gloves before removing it. It was plain white with no writing and although she would send it for fingerprint analysis, she knew they would find nothing. The flap hadn't been sealed and she tipped out the folded single sheet of A4 paper onto her desk.

Tracy arrived and stood beside her. 'A love letter?'

'I doubt it, probably a poison pen.' She opened the sheet and laid it out on the desk. The letters had been cut from a newspaper and the message was clear: *DROP THE INVESTIGATION.*

'A bit melodramatic,' Tracy said. 'They might have added or else.'

'Perhaps. It's like something from a bad movie but I think the threat behind it is real enough.'

'Come on, you don't send something like that to a Garda. Whoever did this is watching too much Netflix.'

'I'll send it off to the lab, but I wouldn't expect to get anything useful. They didn't even bother to put my name on it. Darker was sitting in the front snug in Taaffes last evening. We had a staring contest when Aisling and I left. I suppose this was his work. I'm not taking the hint, so he might have to escalate and that bothers me.'

Brophy joined them and looked at the paper on Fiona's desk. 'Are you going to take the advice?'

Fiona folded the paper and returned it to the envelope. 'What do you think?'

She took the envelope, went to the reception and entered the back office where the Duty Sergeant was examining a file. She showed him the envelope. 'This was sellotaped to my computer when I arrived this morning. It's a note threatening me. How did that happen?'

He continued examining the file. 'Search me.'

'Wrong answer. You control entry and exit to and from this station. A person entered the CID squad room and delivered this envelope. So that person gained access not only to the station but to the CID squad room. You should realise that I'm doing you a favour by coming to you first. If we clear this up here, there'll be no need to go to the Chief Super. Sooner or later, the finger of responsibility is going to be pointing at you.'

The Duty Sergeant looked up at her. 'Didn't happen on my shift.'

'So you know when the note was delivered?' She controlled the tone of her voice. She only got angry when it suited her purpose. She had spent years learning how to keep her emotions in check.

He put the file aside. 'This place is like Grand Central Station sometimes. I do the best I can with the staff I have, but when we're busy, there's a possibility that someone could have snuck in. Show me it.'

'I'm sending it to the lab. There's a remote possibility that there are fingerprints. But I am making a report and you'll need to have a better answer than 'search me'.'

She returned to the squad room, put the envelope in an evidence bag and sent it to the lab for testing, then she flopped into her seat. It was all part of the process of attempting to break her down. It started with the show of interest, then the 'we know where you live', next was the stalking and finally the threat. So far, it was pretty low level stuff but there was an implied threat and it was getting to her.

She motioned for Tracy and Brophy to join her at the whiteboard.

'I've got the names of three families that left Letter Mullen lock, stock and barrel during the nineteen forties or early fifties.' She went to the whiteboard and wrote *Gannon, Griffin,* and *Farmer* on the board. 'Three families who left that area for ever and took everything, which wouldn't have amounted to much, with them. We need to trace them and see what became of them.' She looked at Brophy. 'How long will it take?'

'How long is a piece of string?' Brophy replied. 'These are pretty common names. First, I have to get the records from Letter Mullen and then I have to expand the search. The nineteen forties and fifties were at the height of the emigration boom. Lots of people went to England, the US, Canada and Australia. We might even have to take a look at East and South Africa.'

'How long?' Fiona asked.

'I don't know,' Brophy said.

'Then get busy.'

Brophy went back to his desk.

'You know he'll give you his best,' Tracy said.

Fiona went to her desk and slumped into her chair. 'I wish they'd given us more time. I hate working against the clock. That's when the mistakes get made.'

'What will we do?'

'We go back to the beginning and see if the paperwork throws up any new leads.'

'Grunt work,' Tracy said.

'This afternoon, we go for a trip.'

. . .

By mid-morning Fiona had finished her review of where they were. There were positives like the slugs and the raft of information that Hindrichson had supplied. But they were no nearer to identifying a prime suspect than when they stood in the bog and examined Eich's bare arm sticking out of the ground. She stood up and went to the toilet. She spent a few minutes staring at herself in the mirror. There were lines where there had been smooth skin. Life events were piling up on her. There was the return and subsequent death of her father, a rapprochement with her mother and her ongoing relationship with Aisling, who had assisted her through her problems but who had received little or nothing in return. A partnership wouldn't last long where one of the partners was using up more than their fair share of the available psychic energy. Still staring at herself, she resolved to give Aisling more attention. There was no point in returning to the squad room. She needed to refreshen her brain. She left the station and walked into Dominick Street to the Arabica Café, where she bought a Soy Wax Candle of Connemara Heather for Aisling. Outside, she took a seat with a view of the Corrib River and ordered a coffee and homemade carrot cake.

The coffee and cake had just arrived when the man who had been following her sat down across from her.

Fiona smiled. 'Mr Darker, I was wondering when we were going to meet face to face. Can I get you a coffee?'

'No thanks.'

Darker was dressed in an expensive leather jacket over an equally expensive pullover. He had a single day's stubble on his lightly tanned face. He had regular features and was not unattractive, but he had a hard face that probably didn't smile often. His black hair was tinged with red. He had a habit of laying his left hand slightly forward, exposing the gold Rolex on his wrist.

'Then you won't mind if I enjoy my coffee and cake.' She used her teaspoon to hive off a piece of cake and put it in her mouth. Her heart was beating faster and she used a breathing exercise to slow it.

'Not at all.' He removed three sheets of paper from his pocket and placed them on the table.

Fiona ignored them and concentrated on her coffee, which was excellent.

Darker leaned back in his chair. 'Aren't you interested to know what's in the papers I just put on the table?'

'Not really.'

'You're a cool one. Old Dom Geraghty's prize pupil and he trained you well. Dom says you were the best he'd come across and that's praise indeed.'

'I contacted him about you and he said you were dangerous. Are you dangerous, Sam?'

Darker smiled. 'I knew you were going to be a God-awful nuisance.'

'Can I ask you a question?'

'That depends on the question.'

She leaned forward. 'Why did you go over to the other side?'

Darker laughed. 'Haven't you worked it out yet? There is no other side. There's only people. I got tired of earning buttons protecting people who earned millions through corruption and graft. I had skills that were being undervalued by my employer, so I went private. Question time is over.' He nodded at the papers on the table. 'That's the life and times of Fiona Madden. You are a very interesting lady. Are you sure you don't want to read about yourself?'

'Quite sure.'

'Your bosses might like to see what we dug up.'

Fiona shrugged. 'Then give them the pages.'

'We're going to take your career away.'

Fiona broke off some more carrot cake and ate it. 'You can do that?'

'You have no idea who you're playing with.'

'This is beginning to sound like the dialogue of a bad nineteen fifties crime movie. I prefer the dialogue in *Chinatown* it's more to the point. I got your message. Why don't you fuck off and let me enjoy my coffee and cake in peace.'

Darker picked up the papers from the table. 'Dom told me not to get mixed up with you. Said you were relentless.'

'And that's when you started playing silly buggers with me. I don't suppose Dom told you that I don't scare easily?'

'Everyone told me that.'

'But you decided to go there anyway. One piece of advice: don't get too close to me and those I love.'

Darker shrugged. 'It's not personal. It's a job and someone's got to do it. Drop the investigation and we'll all go home.'

'Why demean yourself with this kind of work?'

'It's a living.'

She stared at the watch on his wrist before eating another piece of cake. 'And the money offered was too good.'

'And the money was too good.' His lips crinkled. 'See you around, doll.'

She watched him as he walked along the Corrib. She made herself a promise that if they took away her career, she was going to fuck them up personally.

CHAPTER THIRTY-FIVE

Fiona sat at her desk. She would have loved to know who Darker's client was, but there was no point in speculating. Not for the first time in her life, she was afraid that someone was going to take away something that she prized. Most days she was blasé about what she did for a living, but today she cared. Hearing that Dom rated her so highly gave her a warm feeling, but Dom was the exception that proved the rule; Fiona Madden was high maintenance. She was sure that Aisling could tell her why she'd gone through life looking for approbation from others. Possibly she hadn't got any when she was young. Joining the police was not compatible with her need for praise. Being good at the job was generally viewed as a threat. She remembered the proverb; those that the gods wish to destroy, first they call promising. Darker's cool demeanour bothered her, as did his confidence that he could finish her career. She had lied about not being interested in what was on the pages. There was a period of her life that she had kept secret. She had been clever enough to live under a different name when she had gone off the tracks. But people like Darker have ways of penetrating the cover that she had set up. If that was the case, then the presentation to DI O'Neill of a dossier would certainly scupper her. The walls were closing in on her and all because someone murdered two German sailors and stole gold and currency from them. The smart move was to drop the case and get both Darker and O'Neill off her back in one fell swoop. But if she did that, she wouldn't be able to look at herself in the mirror. She would give the investigation her best shot and see where the cards fell.

TRACY CLOSED a file and slid his chair across to Fiona's desk. 'You have the look of someone who's off somewhere else. I hope it's a beach beside a blue ocean under a blazing sun. And in your hand, you've got one of those colourful cocktails with an umbrella stuck in it.'

Fiona came out of her reverie. 'I wish. I had coffee with former DI Sam Darker. I'm not proud to admit that it shook me.' She told him the details of her conversation with Darker.

'You have got to be crazy,' Tracy said when she finished. 'Sitting down with someone who is trying to ruin you.'

'He's just doing what someone has paid him to do. This is what happens when you rattle someone's cage.'

'Whose cage have we rattled?'

'Think about it. Two bodies are discovered buried in a bog. Horgan had it right straight away. Stick them in another hole and forget all about them. That would have made everybody happy, especially the person who has been looking over his shoulder for seventy-five long years, afraid that his crime would be discovered. But we start behaving like police officers. We bring in the Technical Bureau and start collecting evidence. We identify the victims and inform the German Embassy. The find is reported in the German papers. A reporter arrives in town who has a personal stake in the story and has been researching it for years. Hey, this is getting serious for the murderer. He needs to find out what we know. I think that our friend Leavy was a trip wire.'

'What's a trip wire?'

'It's all in the name, a wire set up that you trip over and announce your presence. It's like ringing an alarm. Leavy gave us nothing but asked a lot of questions. He probably reported back that there was nothing to worry about, but someone was getting anxious about an investigation. Sam Darker was the go-to man in this situation. Former detective inspector with all the contacts, he'd find out what was happening. Darker finds that DS Madden is on the case and the bitch is relentless. That was the description Dom Geraghty gave him. Relentless is bad. The murderer needs to get the investigation to go away, so he develops a two-pronged attack. Get the Garda hierarchy to pressure us to drop the investigation and, at the same time, let Darker loose to intimidate me into acquiescing when the hammer falls. Then the reporter is mugged. Maybe that will get him out of town. How does that sound?'

'Fucking crazy. There's nothing tangible that connects all those coincidences together.'

'I thought you might say something like that. Right now, it's the only hypothesis that fits what we know. But there's still a lot that we don't know.'

'The famous unknown unknowns.'

Brophy came and handed Fiona a sheet of paper. 'The Farmer family emigrated to America. There's be no sign of them returning. I'm about to start on the Griffins.' He shuffled on his feet. 'I don't think I'm the man for this job, sarge. I'm okay at running down people who have been to school, who get married, have children, have a residence, a social security number and pay their taxes. I have no idea if the Farmers loaded a large crate containing gold bars onto the ship when they sailed to America. I don't think I'm doing a good job.'

'You're doing fine,' Fiona said. 'The more information we

have, the better chance we have of finding the culprit. Just keep on as you are.'

'What do we do?'

'We pray that either the Gannons or the Griffins were the last places that Baum stayed.'

CHAPTER THIRTY-SIX

When Fiona returned from lunch, Horgan was standing at the top of the squad room, examining the whiteboard. She slipped into her seat and switched on her computer. Horgan finished his examination, turned, and sat in Tracy's chair.

'You made quite an impression on CI O'Neill,' he said.

'Did I?'

Horgan looked at her and nodded. 'Not many front up against the Fixer. I suppose you know that he's about to move up to superintendent and will be in charge of HR at the Park.'

'I'm not in the circle that receives the rumours from the top. But I can well believe that he's riding the golden trail right to the top.'

Horgan frowned. 'What are you intimating?' he said.

She looked at Horgan with distain. He'd hit rock bottom in her estimation. He had the leadership qualities of a poisonous snake. 'Nothing, boss. It's just that some people's road to the top is paved with gold.'

Horgan's frown deepened. 'I can't figure you out, Madden. You had a chance to ingratiate yourself with the hierarchy and you throw it back in their faces.'

'I don't think I'd make it as one of the boys.'

A smile broke out on Horgan's face. 'Anyway, that's not why I came to see you. Detective Garda Brophy has had to go to Dublin. They found a place on a course that he applied for some months back. I already told him and he's off home to pack.'

'How long is the course?' Fiona asked.

'He'll be away for a week at least.'

'I thought that might be the case. Lucky man, finding a free place on a course at the last minute.'

Horgan smiled exposing a bottom row of stained teeth. 'Yes, it's a pity he won't be around to help you.'

Tracy entered the room, walked over, and stood at his desk.

Horgan stood. 'I'd best let you get on with your work.' He marched toward the exit.

Fiona waited until he was at the door. 'Thanks for your help, boss.'

'What's all that about?'

'Brophy is a lucky man,' Fiona said. 'He apparently applied for a course several months ago and somehow a place became vacant today. So he's off to Dublin for a week and the investigation just lost one third of its manpower. Resources are the lifeblood of any investigation. It takes people to dig up and watch hours of CCTV, witnesses have to be interviewed and alibis checked. It takes people to research backgrounds and review phone records and bank statements. Cutting off people means cutting off the blood supply and the investigation dies as a result. This is just another ham-fisted attempt to get us to throw in the towel. There must be a one percent chance of success, otherwise they wouldn't bother hobbling us. But we'll only give up when our seven days run out and I'll take the consequences.'

Tracy took his seat. 'With this kind of juice, it's got to be political.'

'Someone important is upset. Otherwise, they wouldn't be trying to crack a hazel nut with a sledgehammer. Whoever is behind screwing up the investigation should pick up a dictionary and look up the word *subtle*.'

Her mobile rang. She didn't recognise the number but she took the call. 'I'm putting you on speaker.' She laid the phone on her desk and Tracy came close.

'Sorry, sarge.' Brophy's voice was just above a whisper. 'I tried to resist, but Horgan said the order came from upstairs. I have no idea what course I'm going on. I don't remember applying for any course. I think that they just want to get me out of Galway and away from the investigation.'

'I know,' Fiona said. 'Don't worry. Enjoy whatever course they've thought up for you.'

'I've sent you an email with the research I did on the Griffins. They emigrated to London and lived in the East End in a place called Leytonstone. I don't think they would have pitched up there if they had money. Anyway, one of them returned and has fixed up the old house in Letter Mullen. If I were you, I'd concentrate on the Gannons. I was about to start researching them when I was pulled. The preliminary stuff is in the email.'

'Thanks. Enjoy.' She cut the call.

'Looks like we just entered the Last Chance Saloon,' Tracy said.

Fiona brought up her emails and printed the attachment to Brophy's short message. 'I hope there's plenty of drink there because I have a feeling we may need it.'

'What do we do without Brophy?'

'We continue to follow the money. According to Bríd, the old lady in Trá Bán, only those three families left the area in the period just after the war. The Farmers are out and so are the Griffins, so that leaves the Gannons. You're the guy with the degree. Can't you think like Brophy?' She always was a bad loser, but it was difficult to win when your own side is tying your hands behind your back.

Tracy opened his computer. 'Let's start by looking at the number of Gannons in Galway.'

Fiona smiled. 'Let's look at the 1911 Census.' She opened the National Archive website and brought up the Census. Then she looked for the name Gannon in the townland of Letter Mullen. Three possibilities came up. She printed off the census forms and handed them to Tracy. 'Ignore the parents and concentrate on the children.'

Tracy took the papers. 'Does everyone in Connemara have ten children?'

'Television only arrived in the west of Ireland in the 1960s. Draw your own conclusions.'

Tracy continued muttering under his breath as he started with the first name on the list.

Fiona wondered whether she had pushed too hard. Every hierarchical organisation had their unwritten rules, not the rules they put in the HR manual, the real rules by which the organisation operated. One of the main ones in the Garda Síochána was not to rock the boat. That was closely followed by don't embarrass the top brass. She was breaking both of those rules. Mavericks might be appreciated in a tech start-up, but they received short shrift in large organisations. The answer to Fiona's problem was easy; stop being a maverick. Screw them.

CHAPTER THIRTY-SEVEN

Tracy had a date and Aisling had a drinks event at the university. Fiona had been invited but she didn't feel like company. Eich and Muller had waited seventy-five years for justice and it was beginning to look like they would never get it. She had parked her bike at the cottage and walked the one and a half kilometres to the local pub. There was no one inside when she entered. This was one of the few remaining pubs in the area and it hadn't changed since Fiona had first entered it as a young girl. She ordered a pint of Guinness and retired to the corner of the bar. She sat in her grandfather's seat. He was a great man for a drink, a story and a song. He was also great at giving advice and one piece he had given Fiona was never to drink alone. For him, it was the road to rack and ruin. She had sent Aisling a message that she was in the local pub. She examined her phone and saw that the message had been read, but there was no answer. She finished her drink, took her empty glass to the bar, and ordered another.

The owner of the pub looked up from his newspaper before putting it away and pulling the pint. 'We don't see you in here much,' he said, watching the Guinness settle.

'I used to come in here with my grandfather when I was a little girl.'

'Your grandfather was a regular. He was one of the best, honest as the day was long and never did harm to man nor beast.'

'He was also a good grandfather.'

He handed her the drink and refused the money she offered. 'This one is on the house.'

'I don't think my grandfather would approve of me drinking alone. Can I at least buy you a drink?'

The pub owner laughed. 'Never touch the stuff. The motto for running a successful pub.' He picked up his paper. 'Of course, betting on the nags will ruin any man.'

'Large white wine.'

Fiona turned and smiled. Aisling was standing just inside the door to the bar.

They took their drinks and went back to where Fiona had been sitting.

Aisling lifted her glass and they clinked. 'Your message was innocuous but I got a funny feeling when I read it. It arrived as the Dean began his farewell speech for the visiting professor. It's always the same. The Dean should video the speech and they should just play it. You know the kind of rubbish, Professor X has had a very successful sojourn with us and we wish him all the best with the rest of his brilliant career. Now on to the drinks and canapes. I was wishing that I could eat my head and I didn't like the sound of you here drinking alone. What's up?'

Fiona explained about Brophy being pulled from the investigation. She was careful not to mention her talk with Darker.

'And of course, you being DS Fiona Madden, there was no way that you were going to pack in the investigation. They're increasing the pressure bit by bit.'

'I know. Remember we watched that programme about the killing of Father Niall Molloy?'

Aisling nodded.

'That was one totally screwed up investigation and the court case was a joke. That's why members of the public think that we're just a bunch of Keystone Cops. Two men were murdered in Letter Mullen and I think that there's another man we haven't found. I can't believe the level of pushback we're getting. A senior officer comes from Dublin and tells me to end the investigation or he'll end my career.'

'But he'll deny he ever said that.'

'Of course he will.'

'And you intend to go to the end?'

It was Fiona's turn to nod.

'Is there anything you haven't told me?' Aisling asked.

'No.' Fiona finished her drink and made to stand up. She and Aisling had agreed that they would never lie to each other. Fiona wasn't good at keeping her promises.

Aisling put her hand on Fiona's arm and pushed her back into her seat. 'Let's finish with this one. I think we both need an early night.'

'I'd prefer to get sloshed.'

'It won't help. You need to keep a clear head. Otherwise, you're handing it on a plate to this Fixer individual.'

CHAPTER THIRTY-EIGHT

The explosion sounded like it was in the bedroom and Fiona's first reaction was to look for Aisling. The room was flooded with a bright light, and she was relieved that the woman lying beside her was unhurt. She thought she heard a car revving and speeding away. They both sat bolt upright.

'What the hell was that?' Aisling rubbed sleep from her eyes.

Fiona jumped out of the bed and ran into the kitchen. She grabbed the fire extinguisher, sped through the living room, and opened the front door. Flames were rising from the Kawasaki, but the petrol tank was still intact. She knew she had a matter of minutes to put the fire out before the tank blew and sprayed burning petrol over the cottage. The smell of burning rubber and faux leather assailed her while fumes of burning petrol caught in her throat. White foam shot from the nozzle of the extinguisher and blanketed the motor bike. Fiona coughed but kept the pressure on the extinguisher and gradually the foam won out and the fire subsided. She felt the heat around her feet and was surprised when Aisling knocked her to the ground and threw a duvet over her.

'Your pyjamas were on fire,' Aisling said. 'Are you alright?'

She caught the sweet smell of burnt flesh. 'I think my calves might be singed.' She stood up and hugged her partner. 'Thanks.'

They looked at the smouldering wreck that was once her bike.

'You broke the rules,' Fiona was muttering to herself.

'What are you saying about rules?' Aisling asked.

'Nothing. I had a mechanic check that bike before I bought it.'

'How can that happen? We could have been killed.'

'Probably something in the ignition system.' She hoped Aisling hadn't noticed the shards of glass lying on the ground beside the bike. Someone had tossed a Molotov cocktail and run. It wouldn't have been Darker, but he was behind it. They could have been killed, and it was an escalation that couldn't go unanswered. She gave the bike a final blast of foam. 'What time is it?'

'Five past three.' Aisling held her. 'You loved that bike.'

'It's insured, but the insurance company won't like it.'

'It's probably a design fault.'

'Could be. Let's go back inside, make a nice cup of camomile tea and see if we can get back to sleep.' Fiona guessed that she wouldn't sleep easily until she had neutralised Darker. The man must have been out of his mind or the money must be really good. She had received several messages from the opposition, and it was time that she sent a message of her own. She put her arm around Aisling and led her back into the house. 'That's enough excitement for one night.'

'That's enough excitement for a lifetime.'

I wish, Fiona thought.

CHAPTER THIRTY-NINE

Fiona looked up as Tracy deposited a coffee on her desk.
'Why the face?' he said. 'Don't tell me you're still in a strop about losing Brophy.'

'Somebody torched my bike last night.' She picked up the coffee and removed the lid. After the camomile tea, she had gone back to bed with Aisling, but she hadn't slept a wink. Her mind was racing with plans of what she was going to do as a reprisal. She decided that she was going to deal with Darker, working on the theory that if confronted by more than one attacker always deal with the most dangerous one first. Her calves still hurt despite Aisling using an ointment on them that was intended to counteract the stinging pain.

'You're kidding.' Tracy sat at his desk.

'I never kid.' Fiona sipped her coffee.

'I know. It was just an expression. Are you going to report it?'

'I already have. The insurance will check up. I told the duty sergeant it was probably the work of some local idiots.'

'What happened?'

She told him in detail about the events of the night.

'That's heavy duty. If the fire had spread, you and Aisling would have been in danger.'

His brow furrowed. 'I don't like it when you go all cold. You're going to do something crazy.'

She gave him her false sweet smile. 'Why the hell would I do that?'

'Because you could have taken whatever they threw at you, but this time they went for you and Aisling. I have no idea what you're planning, but if I can help.'

'I want to get on with the investigation. What have you got on the Gannons?'

'I've just started. Brophy established that they moved closer to Galway city. Give me the morning and we'll see how far I get.'

Fiona nodded. She couldn't really spare a half a day, but research wasn't Tracy's thing and she would have to cut him some slack.

Tracy sat at his desk. 'You look like a balloon that's had all the air let out. It looks like they finally found a button that worked.'

'Aisling is my Achilles heel. She's a civilian and therefore out of play. Darker should have known better. If he's a real professional, he expects me to retaliate.'

'Which means he thinks that he can handle you.'

'I already thought of that.'

'Can he?'

'We're about to find out?'

HORGAN ENTERED the squad room at mid-morning and made a point of stopping at every desk and conversing with all the members of his team, but Fiona knew that he would make his way slowly to her.

He finally arrived at her desk. 'DS Madden, the duty

sergeant tells me you reported that your motor bike was torched last night.'

'Yes, boss, a group of local ruffians having a night out.'

'And they picked on you? That sounds unlikely. I suppose most of the people in Furbo know that you're a police officer.'

'I keep a low profile.'

'It happened in the middle of the night?'

'Around three in the morning.' Fiona had a thing about three o'clock in the morning. The phone had rung at three o'clock announcing her grandfather's death and her own father had died at six minutes past three.

'Must have given you a fright.'

'Not so much. We had the fire quickly under control. The fuel tank didn't blow, but it was almost empty. I noticed that the fuel gauge was on reserve when I arrived home last night.'

'What about the bike?'

'Finished. I'll be putting in a claim to the insurance.'

'Looks like you'll have to lower the profile further.'

'Don't worry, boss, I'll take care of it.'

'Anything happening on the German investigation?'

Fiona shook her head. 'I'll let you know if there's anything new.' She smiled. 'Thanks for your concern.'

'See that you do. The Commissioner himself seems to have an interest in your investigation.' Horgan made to leave.

All bets were now off between Fiona and Horgan. 'I suppose Chief Inspector O'Brien has returned to Dublin?'

Horgan frowned. 'He went back this morning. Why are you interested?'

'I thought that he might have friends in the city.'

'I sometimes wonder what goes on in your head, Madden. You seem to be interested in all sorts of things.' Horgan weaved his way through the desks and exited the room.

In her mind's eye, she saw O'Brien and Darker exchanging notes in some secluded restaurant. O'Brien would have passed the message that the investigation was continuing and Darker would decide that drastic action was required. The Americans had an expression about not being able to fight City Hall. Fiona knew what they were talking about.

Tracy slid his chair over to her desk. 'The research into the Gannons is throwing up some issues.'

'What issues?'

'They live in a large house near Moycullen and that's where they moved to when they left Connemara.'

'Again, what's the issue?'

Tracy turned his computer in Fiona's direction. 'This is a picture of Trabane House, the Gannon residence.'

Fiona whistled. 'Did you check how much that cost when they bought it?'

'There were no records of the purchase price paid at the time.'

'Maybe it was a dump and they spent the last seventy-odd years rebuilding it. We need to dig deeper.'

Tracy looked at his notebook. 'I've already established that they own the Gannon Group, which covers a whole range of businesses from construction to agriculture. The family has become mega rich over the past seventy years. The father, Peadar Gannon, died in the 1960s and the business was taken over by his son, Tim, who is now the chairman of the Group with the next generation running the various businesses.'

'I suppose that makes the Gannons the prime suspects in the murders of both Eich and Muller, but we'll have a hell of a job proving it. Does Galway University have a business school?'

Tracy took out his phone and typed with his thumbs. 'Bingo.'

Fiona took out her mobile and called Aisling.

CHAPTER FORTY

Oscars restaurant wasn't one of Fiona's normal haunts for obvious reasons principally financial, but Aisling assured her that if she wished to land the man that would help her, she would have to stump up for lunch there. Fiona arrived first and had a chance to examine the menu before the others arrived. It wasn't as expensive as she anticipated, and she liked the understated vibe of the place. There were only seven tables, and Aisling had booked a small booth in the left-hand corner.

Aisling's companion was in his thirties. His dress was California cool, with a white open-necked shirt, a light-blue cotton jacket and a pair of blue jeans. He had a full head of prematurely grey hair that was cut to perfection. His attractive face was lightly tanned and he strode into the restaurant like he owned the place.

Aisling steered him towards the booth and put him sitting beside Fiona. She introduced him as Professor Tom Patterson. Aisling had briefed Fiona on Patterson. He had graduated from Trinity College Dublin in business studies and had earned a master's degree and a doctorate from the University of California at Berkeley.

'So, you're Aisling's partner.' Patterson's accent was mid-Atlantic.

'Yes, detective sergeant Fiona Madden, but please call be Fiona.'

'Call me Tom.' They shook hands. 'How long have you guys been together?'

Fiona looked at Aisling. 'Just over three years.'

'Cool.' Patterson looked around. 'This is my favourite restaurant in Galway for lunch.' He looked at Aisling. 'I wonder how you knew.'

They picked up their menus and examined them.

'I recommend the cod.' Patterson put down the menu and turned to Fiona. 'Aisling tells me you're currently investigating an interesting case. Like to tell me about it?'

Fiona began with the finding of the bodies at Béal an Daingin and continued to their development of the first prime suspect. Her exposition was only interrupted by the arrival of the waiter to take their order, which was three pan-fried cod and bottled water.

'Hell, that's one of the neatest stories I've heard in a long time,' Patterson said when Fiona had brought him up to date. 'Murdered submariners, Nazi gold, in Connemara. That's cool.'

The food arrived, and Aisling steered the conversation around to Patterson's years in California and how he had ended up in Galway. When the table was cleared, they ordered coffee, and Aisling nodded at Fiona.

'We have a problem,' Fiona began. 'The guy who usually handles our research has been moved to Dublin temporarily. Because of the time that has elapsed since the murders, we can't follow our usual procedures of collecting evidence and interviewing possible witnesses.'

Patterson nodded.

'Since the murdered men had in their possession a considerable amount of gold and currency, the only real option is to follow the money. Three families left the area where the Germans most likely landed. We've cleared two of them and the third, the Gannons, had subsequently become very wealthy. We'd like to know how they got their start and did they have the ability to turn the gold into cash.'

'Do you mean the Gannon Group?' Patterson asked.

'Yes.'

Patterson lifted his coffee cup but didn't drink. 'Their chairman, Tim Gannon, spoke to our MBA class. He was nebulous about the beginnings of the business.' He sipped the coffee and replaced the cup. 'How soon do you need this information?'

'Immediately, the investigation is dying on its feet. If I don't produce something like concrete evidence soon, we'll be terminated.'

'We have a subject called Business History where we look at the paths followed by successful businesses as lessons for young entrepreneurs. I've got two MBA candidates who are looking for businesses to analyse. The Gannon Group has been successful, so I could put them on it for a couple of days. They're go-getters, so they'll do a good job. Pity we don't have more time.'

'I don't know how useful this is,' Aisling said. 'But the Gannons regularly appear in the glossy magazines. They have a high profile locally and they're active on the charity front. If you're going to point the finger at them, you better have a very good case. The chairman's second son is Conor Gannon, the former Minister for Justice.'

'I have Tracy combing social media for anything on the family,' Fiona said. 'Where we need help is on the business, particularly how they started and how they were funded.'

'Ok.' Patterson said. 'I've got a lecture at two. We have a deal. I'll put two of my guys looking at the genesis of the business with a concentration on where the seed money came from.'

Fiona took a card from her pocket and handed it to Patterson, who was already standing. 'Call me any time. And I'm very grateful for your assistance.'

'It's wicked working with the cops. Thanks for lunch, gotta rush.' Patterson was out the door.

'What do you think?' Fiona asked Aisling.

'The business guys are a law unto themselves. Tom will do his best, but you're asking for something that should take weeks. By the way, how's your friend Hindrichson?'

'He'll be out of hospital tomorrow.'

'Are you sure you're telling me everything?'

'You heard me with Patterson.' Fiona called for the bill.

'Hindrichson being mugged. You and Tracy being followed. Your bike being destroyed.'

'I told you it was probably an ignition problem.'

The bill arrived. Fiona was pleasantly surprised and settled with her credit card.

Aisling leaned forward. 'I asked one of the guys in the engineering lab. No way it was an ignition failure.'

'The insurance will check it out.'

'Forewarned is forearmed, Fiona. Are you sure that you're telling me everything? The Gannons are rich and powerful. They could turn out to be dangerous adversaries.'

Fiona was about to cross her heart and swear but changed her mind. 'If anything comes up, you'll know.'

CHAPTER FORTY-ONE

'Where to?' Tracy turned the ignition and they rolled out onto Mill Street.

'The Coast Road. Then on to Letter Mullen.'

'How did the lunch with the professor go?'

'We've got a couple of students for two or three days. They're going to research the Gannons from a business perspective. Meanwhile, you and I are going to dig into their lives from every other aspect.'

'I already started on the Internet.' Tracy turned onto Presentation Road and headed toward Newcastle Road. There was less traffic than usual and they were soon on the Coast Road and a direct run to Letter Mullen. 'I think the black car behind might be tailing us.'

'Ignore them.'

'You know there are more than forty pages of news stories on the Internet relating to the Gannons.' He nodded at the rear of the car. 'I printed out the first five pages and they're in the file on the back seat if you want to start reading.'

Fiona ignored the file and sat back. Her anger had cooled during the morning, but she was still committed to retaliating. The question was how and then where and when. She already knew the how and she wanted the when to be as soon as possible. It was the where that exercised her brain. The target had to be Darker himself and she needed to get him alone. 'How many in the car behind?' she asked, almost absentmindedly.

Tracy adjusted his rear mirror. 'Two in the front. I can't see anyone in the rear.'

She doubted that Darker was among them.

'What are we doing in Trabane?' Tracy asked.

'It's Trá Bán meaning White Beach in Gaelic but Trabane for you Anglophones.'

'Cliona has been getting me to practice my Irish more.'

'That's good because the woman we're going to see doesn't speak much English.'

'You're sure that the Gannons are responsible for killing the two Germans?'

'You know what they say? The only thing that's sure in life is death and taxes. They're the prime suspects, but as usual with us, there isn't a whole lot of proof. That's why we're on this jaunt. We need more information on them, both professional and private.'

'My genetic tests have come back.'

'I should have asked, but this bloody investigation has got to me. What's the story?'

'I don't have the genetic marker. My dad doesn't need the operation. He's having a radioactive something or other installed down below. The doc says he has a normal life expectancy.'

'And you're not going to die tomorrow?'

'Apparently not. It did give me another perspective on mortality.'

'As in if you were dying, you'd quit the Garda Síochána immediately.'

'Did I say that?'

'That was the content of the message. People usually get a

focus when they fear they're dying. Maybe there's something you'd prefer to do with your life.'

'Trying to get rid of me?'

'Quite the contrary. But if you think you'd be happier elsewhere, you should think about it.'

'I get frustrated with people like Horgan, and this O'Brien character seems like a real creep.'

'You mean why can't everybody be like you and me?'

'Something like that.'

Fiona knew where Tracy was coming from. The only copper she'd got close to was Dom Geraghty. He accepted her for what she was, warts and all. But men like him were the exception rather than the rule. 'Even the Garden of Eden had a serpent hanging around. No organisation is perfect, and neither are the people employed there. O'Reilly would sell his grandmother for the next promotion. Horgan is just an incompetent yes man trying to get to pensionable age so he can go fishing or join the priesthood.'

Tracy laughed. 'I thought he was married with kids.'

'He is and he has, but he wouldn't be the first man who harboured thoughts of escaping real life while serving his Maker. So, you decided not to quit.'

'Not yet anyway.'

'Good, I've gotten used to you.' She turned towards Tracy. He was smiling broadly. She closed her eyes. And if I wasn't gay, there might be a chance for us. She decided to keep that thought to herself. She didn't think either Tracy or Aisling would appreciate it.

They had already passed Béal an Daingin and were headed for Letter Mullen. When they crossed the bridge, she directed Tracy towards the left and pointed out their ultimate destination.

CHAPTER FORTY-TWO

'Cé caoi bhfuil tu, a stór' *How are you darling?* Brid Josie opened the door wide for Fiona and Tracy.

Fiona hugged the old woman. 'This is Detective Garda Tracy, he doesn't have much Irish but he's a nice man all the same.'

Brid sat in the easy chair beside the open fire where four large sods of turf smouldered. 'Three visits. You're spoiling me. My nieces and nephews don't visit me this much.'

Fiona sat at the dining table and motioned Tracy to do the same. 'Can I make us a cup of tea?'

'That would be lovely. I still have a bit of the cake you brought the last time.'

Fiona took the kettle from off the crook over the fire. The water inside might not be boiling to the level of an electric kettle, but it would do. She put four spoons of tea into the teapot and filled it from the kettle. She laid the table and fetched the cake from the fridge.

'I didn't realise that you were so domesticated,' Tracy said under his breath.

Fiona poured the tea and handed Brid the first cup. There

was only a sliver of cake remaining and Fiona presented it to the old woman.

'Remember the last time I visited I asked you about the families that left in the 1940s?'

'Of course, I remember.' Bríd made a sucking noise as she drank her tea. 'A man came after you'd left and asked me what we'd talked about. He had no Irish and I let on I had no English. I sent him away with a flea in his ear.' She chuckled and spilt some of her tea.

'Do you remember the Gannons?' Fiona asked.

'Of course I do.' Bríd reached into her skirt, took out false teeth and put them into her mouth before starting on the cake. 'They moved to Galway and made something of themselves. I used to read about them in the Connaght Tribune. But I haven't read that paper in years. The father, Peadar, was a cute one. He knew the value of a schilling even though, like everyone about, he didn't have many of them. His wife died and left him to bring up four children. I heard he was the one that started the business that made them wealthy. I wasn't surprised.'

'What about the children?'

'The young boy, Tim, was a clever one. The schoolteacher said he was the cleverest child he'd ever taught. He was twelve when they left. I played with him a few times.' She slurped some more tea and munched the last of the cake, then sat back and smiled. 'They were a good-looking family. They all had black curly hair and sallow skin. The pick of them was Áine. If she'd gone to Hollywood, she would have been a film star. I heard one of the boys died young in a car accident.'

'Did they own land?'

Bríd leaned forward with her cup and Tracy rushed to take it from her hand. She smiled and looked at Fiona. 'What did you say his name was?'

'Garda Tracy.'

'He's a handsome boy himself. You make a handsome pair.'

Fiona looked at Tracy and from the blank look on his face, she reasoned that he hadn't understood. 'The land, did they own much?'

'They did, maybe fifteen or so acres.'

'Do you remember, did they sell it?'

'My parents talked about it. They said they left with the clothes on their backs. The land was taken over by other families ten or so years later.'

'Do you remember anything about them leaving?'

'I think I was about eight. I remember they had a big van and a car. We'd never seen anything like that around here. They didn't tell anyone they were leaving. They just left.' She held out her hand to Fiona. 'I think I have an old photo from them times.'

Fiona took her hand and helped her out of the chair.

She crossed to the trunk and took out her photo album. She returned to her chair and Fiona squatted at her side. The first photo showed a family standing beside an old stone cottage. The parents stood in the middle and were surrounded by eight children of varying age. The woman held a baby in her arms. 'My family, all dead now,' Bríd said. She flicked through the pages. She stopped at another photo. A similar family group. 'I don't know why we had this photo.' The man in the centre of the photo was tall and well-built, with a thatch of grey hair, but was handsome enough to be a film star himself. He was surrounded by four children, two boys and two girls. They were a very handsome family. One girl in the photo outshone the others. She must have been fourteen or fifteen and growing into a woman.

'Is that Áine?' Fiona said.

The smile on Bríd's face said it all. 'She was an angel.'

'What sort of man was the father?'

'I knew him only as a child. He was a big, smiling, hardworking man who was totally committed to his children. The old ones who knew him said he was a gentleman who never said a bad word about anyone.'

Fiona looked at the photo again. Peadar Gannon was smiling at the photographer. He was big bodied but had a soft face. He reminded her of her own grandfather. 'Can I take the photo?' she said. 'I'll bring it back along with the other one I took.'

Bríd removed it gently and handed it to Fiona. 'It was a hard life then, but we knew no better. I remember it was always cold.'

Fiona put the photo away carefully in her jacket.

Tracy collected the cups and the teapot and cleaned them in the sink.

Fiona bent and kissed Bríd on the forehead. Just like she's done to her grandmother.

'You'll come back again,' the old woman said.

'I certainly will. And the next time I'll remember to bring a nice cake.'

They sat into the car.

Tracy put the key in the ignition. 'Nice lady.'

'She shouldn't be living on her own.'

'I didn't quite get the bit about the guy visiting her after you left.'

'He wanted to know what we talked about. She let on she didn't understand English.'

'Back to Galway?'

'Drop me off in Furbo.'

'I have a bicycle I could lend you.'

She punched him in the shoulder. 'It was no bloody joke.'

CHAPTER FORTY-THREE

Fiona sat at the table with the file that Tracy had made from the articles on the Gannons he'd downloaded from the Internet. There were more than one hundred pages in the file and that was only a fraction of what was available. It appeared that the Gannons were one of the wealthiest families in Ireland and, without doubt, the wealthiest in the west of Ireland. They were preeminent in two areas: business and charity. She flicked through the pages until she came to a family portrait. There were three generations of the family in the photo. At the centre were eighty-nine-year-old Tim Gannon and his sister Áine. Around them were Tim's sons, Minister of State Conor and the Group CEO Peter, with their wives and children. The occasion was a fundraiser for the family Foundation. She stared at Conor Gannon and wondered where she had seen him before. Then it clicked. The photos Brophy found of Darker. Gannon was in the forefront of the photo. Darker standing behind in his role as protection officer. Fiona could see two major problems ahead. Peadar Gannon was dead. If he had murdered the Germans, the investigation was over. Proving that he did it would be impossible and she would have to concentrate on the fact that after the murder, he had stolen the gold and currency that the Germans were carrying. That part of the story might become clearer when Patterson reported back. The second problem was taking on the Gannons as a family. They had held the family secret for over seventy years and they wouldn't give it up easily. They had money and power, and those attributes had proved impregnable in the past. She didn't like giving up, but the deck was stacked against her. She could go after the family as accessories after the fact, but they were children at the time and would have bowed to parental control. If it was all on Peadar Gannon, she might have solved the crime, but she couldn't get the perpetrator. But why had the mild-mannered, quiet man shot two men in the head and possibly murdered another? It was completely out of character. It had to be the money. She thought about the photo Bríd had given her. There were hundreds of poor families, just like the Gannons in Connemara at the time. The money would have been a big temptation. She felt a presence and turned to see Aisling standing behind her. She hadn't heard her enter.

'Someone has been busy on the Internet.' Aisling dropped her satchel and sat down beside Fiona. 'You're like that Columbo fellow on TV. You decide who the murderer is and you peck away at them until you build a case.'

'I wish. There's a very good chance that the murderer might have already shaken hands with the victims on another plane.' She took the photo of the Gannon family from her jacket and handed it to Aisling. 'The Gannon family circa 1943. That's the patriarch Peadar Gannon in the centre. At the moment, he's my prime suspect.'

Aisling stared at the photo. 'He doesn't look like a murderer.'

'Murderers seldom look like murderers.' Except that some did. John Wayne Gacy looked the picture of evil, as did Ian Brady and Myra Hindley. 'Anyway, he's dead, whether he was a murderer or not. That means that the investigation is at an end and we can all go home.'

Aisling looked up from the photo. 'Does that mean whoever firebombed the Kawasaki last night will leave us alone?'

'Who said that anyone firebombed the Kawasaki?'

'I saw the shards of glass that were removed by morning. I may live in an ivory tower, but I know what a Molotov cocktail is.'

'I don't think there'll be a repeat.'

'And you intend to let it go?'

'Yes,' Fiona lied.

'Okay, let's start at the beginning and please don't leave anything out and don't lie to me.'

Fiona stood and went to the kitchen. 'I need a glass of white wine first.'

'Get one for me,' Aisling called after her. 'And don't try to duck out like an errant child.'

'You REALLY PUT your foot in it this time.' Aisling refilled their glasses. 'These people don't mess around.'

Fiona sipped her wine. 'You could say that they went a tad too far.'

'You think they tried to kill us?'

'No, they just showed how bloody incompetent they are. It was all about me being scared enough to drop the investigation. I have five days left and I intend to use them all. I was hoping to convince you to visit your parents, but I suppose there's no chance of that now.'

'Absolutely none. I haven't any time off, anyway. So, what's the plan?'

Fiona didn't want to admit that there was no plan. 'I've thought from the beginning that we were scuppered. It was too long ago and the murderer was probably dead. And that's the way it turned out. We have some evidence, but not half enough. We have a motive, but I suppose we'll have the devil's job proving that the Gannons stole the gold and money. We're playing against a family that is rich and powerful. It's already past the time when we should just pack our traps and depart the stage.'

'That doesn't sound like you.'

'Maybe I know when I'm beaten.'

'That definitely doesn't sound like you.'

Aisling sifted through the articles from the Internet. 'I suppose there's no possibility of the direct approach. You could ask them straight out if their father murdered those two men.'

'I'd be on the dole the following day. There's no real evidence that the Gannons were involved.'

'Then you have to get some.'

Fiona laughed. 'Have you any idea where to look?'

'I'm the clinical psychologist. You're the detective.'

Fiona finished her wine. 'Let's have some dinner. I want to go to bed early tonight.'

'Are you expecting any interruptions?'

She shook her head. She wondered where Darker was this evening. She'd been screwed with once. She swore it wouldn't happen again.

CHAPTER FORTY-FOUR

Fiona woke early, after an uneventful night. It was Aisling's late morning at the university, so Fiona decided to catch the local bus into town. She couldn't remember when she had last used a bus and after speaking with her insurance and checking her bank balance, she determined that she should replace her ruined bike as soon as possible. She caught the bus at eight thirteen and was dropped off at Salthill Road sixteen minutes later. She walked the rest of the way to Mill Street, picked up two takeaway coffees and croissants on the way and left one on Tracy's desk when she arrived at eight fifty. She had spent her time on the bus reading as much of the Internet file as she could, although more than half the articles were still unread. She had only broken the surface of the Gannons. In the next few days, she would try to penetrate further into their secrets. She had received a text from Patterson that his students were enthusiastic about the research and that he hoped to have a result the next day.

Tracy entered the squad room just before nine. 'You're a lifesaver,' he said when he saw the coffee cup and the paper bag on his desk. He took a plastic box out of his pocket and tossed it onto Fiona's desk. 'Present from Cliona.'

She picked the box up and looked at it. It contained an unmarked DVD. 'What's on it?'

'A programme about Tim Gannon made by TG4. The rise of the Gannon empire and the family's road from rags to riches. It's in Irish, so I thought I'd leave it to you.'

She tossed it into her desk drawer. 'I'm still ploughing through this stuff from the Internet.'

Tracy bit into his croissant. 'Well, that's the recent stuff. There's probably the same amount again. Cliona said she thought there was a guy who was writing a book about the Gannons, but nothing came of it. She going to ask around at TG4.'

'Doesn't that girl ever make you breakfast?'

'She claims that she can't boil an egg, although she has a couple of dishes that don't taste half bad. We rarely have dinner at home. There's always something happening or we get invited to dinner at her friends. What do you make of the stuff you've already read?' The rest of the croissant disappeared. He pointed at the paper bag on Fiona's desk. 'Are you going to eat that?'

'Yes, I am, and don't be so greedy. We know they're rich and powerful. One of Tim's sons is a minister in the Government. We can assume he and the Commissioner are acquainted which explains O'Brian's visit.' She had been mulling over Aisling's remarks about the risks she was running in going up against a family as rich and powerful as the Gannons. If she screwed up, they would squash her like a bug. Tracy might also end up in the firing line. Given the low chance of success, maybe she should forget the Gannons and the German seamen. It was time to let sleeping dogs lie.

'Where does that put us?'

'Up shit creek without a paddle.'

'So, what do we do?'

'Keep drifting until someone hands us a paddle.' She tossed her paper bag onto his desk.

. . .

Fiona continued with her reading, gaining some more insights into the history of the Gannons. Of the original four children, only two were alive, Tim Gannon and his sister Áine. Tim was a widower with four children, the boys Peter and Conor, Kathleen was the Gannon Groups' accountant and Cora was married to a Swiss Bank executive. They lived the lives of high-fliers. The Gannon Group had been a family-owned enterprise for nearly twenty years before they went public on Peadar Gannon's death. She read article after article but never got a read on the personalities. The family appeared ready to speak about the company, their holidays in their chalet in San Moritz or their villa in Sandy Lane in Barbados. But there was nothing about who they really were. Tim was the spokesman for the family, and he appeared in ninety percent of the articles. Conor was a working politician, and his only outside affiliation was as a director of the Gannon Group. Cora lived in Switzerland and was also a director of the Group. When she finished the first stack of articles, Tracy had another file ready for her. The whole exercise was getting her nowhere. There was lots of family history, but nothing having any bearing on their investigation. The Gannons were close mouthed about each other and their antecedents. She had been reading all morning when her phone rang.

'The Super's office, now.' Horgan's voice had a trace of tension in it.

She knocked on O'Reilly's door and heard a brusque, 'Come in' from inside.

Horgan was already seated, facing O'Reilly. Fiona remained standing until O'Reilly pointed at the empty chair beside Horgan.

O'Reilly opened a file that was set before him on his desk. 'DS Madden,' his voice was deep and serious. 'I have been reviewing your case load. The DPP appears dissatisfied with the cooperation from this station on the Charles Grealish investigation. Since this might reflect on my management, I would like to see this situation rectified.' He locked eyes with her. 'Any comment.'

'We have just completed a package of papers for the DPP, which covers the outstanding issues. In the cover letter on this package, we requested the DPP to issue a final assessment of the documents that are required to continue the judicial process. I think you understand that considering the issues that process might bring to light, there is a certain reticence on the part of the DPP to advance the case. There's nothing more we can do until the DPP responds.'

O'Reilly closed the file and picked one from beneath it.

Fiona watched him hesitate before opening it.

'The German sailors,' O'Reilly said. 'Where are we on that?'

Fiona didn't reply immediately. She looked at Horgan in the hope that he would take the ball, but he looked straight ahead. It was under-the-bus time again. 'We should be able to wrap it up in four or five days.'

O'Reilly looked surprised. 'Satisfactorily?'

'I hope so.'

'Bring me up to date on the investigation,' O'Reilly said.

Fiona began at her father's funeral and went through every step of the investigation but left out the latest developments concerning the Gannons.

Throughout the briefing, O'Reilly sat with his fingers clasped in front of him and his eyes down as though in prayer. 'Your investigations normally leave a lot of cleaning up,' he said when she had finished. 'Will there be a lot of cleaning up to do on this one?'

'I take what comes my way,' Fiona said. 'And yes, there will probably be a lot of cleaning up to do when it's over. I would prefer to have a case where X kills Y and is still standing over the body with a bloody knife in his hand. But nothing like that has come my way.'

O'Reilly cast an accusatory look at Horgan. 'Perhaps we should have given you a few weeks off to grieve.'

There was a pregnant silence in the room.

O'Reilly cleared his throat. 'Certain important people have made representations to the Commissioner concerning this investigation. There are concerns about the fall-out.'

'Two men were murdered.' Fiona stared into O'Reilly's little piggy eyes. 'There's a possibility that a third man was also murdered. A considerable sum of money that I suppose belongs to the German government was stolen. The only satisfactory conclusion would be to identify the murderer and establish a plan of restitution. I think that might satisfy the German Ambassador but might make some important people unhappy.'

O'Reilly slumped in his chair. 'The German Ambassador is up to date on the investigation?'

'Not fully,' Fiona said. 'But he has the essential details.'

O'Reilly looked at the ceiling. 'That's all, Madden, you can go. I want this investigation closed as soon as possible and I want to be kept informed of progress.'

Fiona stood up and so did Horgan.

O'Reilly leaned forward. 'Not you Horgan. I want to have a word with you.'

Fiona turned to leave. Horgan retook his seat and looked uncomfortable.

CHAPTER FORTY-FIVE

Fiona had done enough reading for one day. She didn't need to read about another function they had attended or another building project they had broken ground on or another speech the family politician had given. Back at her desk in the squad room, she stared blankly at the computer screen. Her screen saver was a picture of her cottage taken on a beautiful sunny day with the blue waters of Galway Bay as the backdrop. The scene was peaceful and serene. She thought of Brid sitting beside the fire in a similar cottage. It was a life spent on the border of a splendid white sand beach in a place as remote as you could find. The old woman had never married, never bore a child, never had a nine-to-five job and lived alone. There were times when Fiona would have envied her. But she had learned that under all that peacefulness and serenity, there was evil. She wondered what Brid would think of her little ideal if she knew that her next-door neighbour had murdered three men and dumped their bodies in a bog.

'Another reaming from the man upstairs?' Tracy said.

'Not as bad as expected,' Fiona smiled. 'I think he finds himself between a rock and a hard place. A not very comfortable position for a man looking forward to a promotion.'

'I haven't seen him lately.'

'He's put on weight.'

'Have you watched the TG4 programme?'

Fiona opened her drawer and took out the plastic box, removed the DVD and put it into the tray in the centre of the computer. 'Care to join me for the show?'

Tracy slid his chair across. 'It's in Irish, so I probably won't understand all of it.'

The media player on the computer had opened automatically and Fiona pressed the start button. 'I think that you'll find that in deference to those like yourself, with a distinct lack of facility in the language, TG4 will provide subtitles.'

The programme opened with an aerial shot of the driveway leading up to the Gannon mansion of the western outskirts of Galway. The tree-lined driveway led through a well-tended parkland and terminated in an imposing former Victorian residence that had been renovated and added to over the years. The camera then followed the interviewer through the open double doors into a spacious library where Tim Gannon sat, right leg over left, in a leather-studded wing-backed chair. The first part of the programme was a one-on-one interview with the Chairman of the Gannon Group, who gave a potted history of the business and concentrated on the charitable foundation that had been set up by his father. After the commercial break, Gannon gave the interviewer a tour of the residence and gardens, pointing out the history of the building dating back to Cromwellian times and the loving restoration that was carried out. The programme ended with a tour of the gardens, which had contained a maze that had been renewed.

Fiona ejected the DVD. She'd learned nothing that she didn't already know. 'What did you think?'

'The usual crap. I was a little put out by the subtitles at the bottom. I think I missed out on some of the visuals as they rambled around the house.'

Fiona put the DVD back in the box and dropped it into her desk drawer. 'Tell Cliona thanks for thinking of us.'

'Do I continue with the Internet search?'

Fiona shook her head. 'I don't think it's useful.'

'No sign of a paddle, then.'

'Not so far. Hindrichson is out of hospital and I'm meeting him for lunch. He's heading back to Germany this afternoon.'

'Sorry, as they say in polite circles, I'm otherwise engaged.'

THEY SAT in a booth at the Hyde Bar close to the coach station. Fiona filled in the young German on the latest stage of the investigation, including her conclusion that the man who murdered his grandfather was himself dead.

'And the gold and currency?' Hindrichson asked when she finished. He picked up his pint of beer and took a swallow. He had turned down the offer of lunch. His bus left in half an hour.

'No sign,' she said. Hindrichson was still looking pale after his ordeal. She was more convinced than ever that Darker was behind the mugging. The Gannons needed to know that their secret was safe, which meant that they needed to know what Hindrichson had learned. When they saw that his research was concentrated on Germany, they would have breathed a sigh of relief. It was another example of using a sledgehammer to crack a hazel nut. They didn't need to give the young man a fractured skull. She would never associate Darker with subtilty.

'Your investigation will be terminated?'

'It looks that way. And what about your research?'

'I wanted to give my mother closure. I'm not sure that hearing the murderer of her father is himself dead will do that. However, as they say in the movies, it is what it is.'

'I'm sorry it didn't turn out better for you and your mother.'

'We got to bury my grandfather.' He glanced at his watch. 'I better leave. This evening I will be back in Germany and I will tell my mother what you have done.' He stood, picked up his bag, and held out his hand. 'Thank you for everything. If there's anything I can do for you in Germany, just ask.'

Fiona thought for a second. "There is something you could do. Baum disappeared, never to be seen again. There's a possibility that he returned to Germany. Is there any way that you can find out whether he did?'

'I have some contacts in the Bundesministerium für Arbeit und Sociales. I'll contact them on the coach and start the investigation. I'll call you with the result, if any.'

They shook hands and Fiona saw him to the door. His shoulders sagged as he made his way to the coach station. She thought he would never forget his trip to Galway.

CHAPTER FORTY-SIX

Fiona walked across Eyre Square and on to Shop Street. There was no need to rush back to Mill Street. There was nothing there for her. They had done their best and run down every lead, but they had come up short. It wasn't their fault. The crime was nearly a century old. The participants, and whatever witnesses there had been, were already in their graves. The money had been laundered or squandered and she didn't really give a damn. The good news was that the Commissioner would be able to put a solid investigation in front of the German Ambassador. Then O'Brien could decide what to do with her. A nice little station is some remote spot was her best guess. Back to her beginnings. She hadn't contacted her mother recently because she'd had been so caught up in the investigation. She thought about taking the afternoon off and going to Glenmore to visit her. But Darker had put paid to that thought when he destroyed her bike. She had spent years in the dojo learning techniques to control her baser emotions, but she failed to suppress the wave of anger that flowed through her. She didn't like lying, but she had done so when she told Aisling that there would be no repercussion for Darker. She was trapped in Galway for the afternoon and the investigation into the deaths of Eich and Muller was in the toilet. So far, she had read about the Gannons and had watched a TV programme about them. She realised she had never met one. Maybe she should rectify that.

THE VOICE on the other end of the line was officious. 'What's the purpose of your request? The Chairman has a solicitor so if there is any legal matter you should make a request through him.' She then reeled off the name and phone number of the most prominent solicitor in Galway.

Fiona knew that getting to meet Tim Gannon wasn't going to be easy. But she didn't think that she would be required to pass through the heavily guarded door of a busy solicitor. 'I'm reviewing an old case concerning the disappearance of a German professor who was a lodger with the Gannon family when they live in Letter Mullen.'

'Please call the Chairman's solicitor.' The line went dead.

Fiona slammed down the phone. 'We're the police, you arsehole, not some randomer who calls up looking for an interview. Who the hell does that woman think she is?'

'She the first gatekeeper,' Tracy looked over from his chair. 'And her job is to keep the gate closed to the likes of you and me. We don't count in Gannon's world.'

Fiona had written the solicitor's name and number in her notebook. She was going to stand in the same room as Tim Gannon by hook or by crook. She dialled the number.

'Mr Garvey office.'

My God, it's the same woman, Fiona thought. But, of course, it wasn't. It was simply a clone. 'Detective Sergeant Madden, I'd like to speak with Mr Garvey.'

'On what matter.'

She explained she wanted an interview with Tim Gannon and had been referred by his office to Garvey. She was investigating the disappearance of a German professor who had stayed with the Gannon family in Letter Mullen.

'Hold the line.'

Fiona listened to elevator music for over five minutes.

'DS Madden, Sean Garvey, please excuse the delay, I was on another line.' Garvey had the kind of smooth voice that could melt chocolate at ten feet. 'I fail to see how Mr Gannon can help with your investigation.'

'We are reviewing the original investigation into the disappearance and it appears that Professor Baum was living with the Gannon family in Letter Mullen at the time. The case has never been closed and we want to get it off the books.'

There was silence on the line. 'You will be interviewing Mr Gannon simply as a witness in this old missing persons investigation?'

'Absolutely.'

'How can I reach you?'

She gave him her mobile and the station number.

'Leave it with me.'

She was about to thank him, but the line was dead.

Fiona looked over at Tracy. 'What does Wikipedia say about Tim Gannon?'

Tracy hit a few keys. 'Timothy Gannon, born 1933, the only school mentioned is Presentation College, which he entered in 1945. Then First Class Honours Economics, Galway University followed by a Masters in Business Administration from Harvard. Took over as CEO of the Gannon Group in 1958 and became Chairman ten years later. List of board memberships as long as your arm mostly banks and blue chip Irish companies. Lots of photos with the great and the good.'

'Tim is no bunny,' Fiona said. She was beginning to have second thoughts on her plan.

'What good is talking to him about Baum going to do?'

Tracy said. 'To them, you're an irritating fly that won't go away.'

'Until we hear back from Patterson, I've nothing better to do. And like I told you before, sometimes you have to shake the tree to see what falls out.' There was something nagging at the back of her mind, but like all good ideas, it wouldn't come to the fore. She convinced herself that it would come back sooner or later and got down to clearing the mass of paper on her desk. By half-past-four, she'd finished. She called Aisling and arranged to be picked up so that they could go together to visit her mother. She had no idea why the thought came to her, but she had to accept that she was worried about her.

CHAPTER FORTY-SEVEN

Fiona was standing outside Mill Street when Aisling arrived to pick her up. 'What's the big smile for?' Fiona asked as she took her seat.

Aisling turned into Dominick Street. 'Normally I have to kidnap you and drag you in chains to see your mother. This is a real breakthrough.'

'Maybe it's just the result of boredom.'

Aisling headed for the Coast Road. 'Or maybe you're wondering how your mother is getting on. You father has just died. You've buried yourself in your work by taking on an investigation that probably never should have happened. Down the road, you're going to have to deal with the grief.'

'Just because some guy wrote a book about the seven stages of grief doesn't mean that everyone follows the same path.'

'I think you've already passed some of the stages. Right now, I think you're angry.'

'Damn right I'm angry, but just not at my father's death. I'm angry that someone has gotten away with murdering two, maybe three, men and stolen enough lucre to set his family up for generations. I'm angry that I can't get the bugger because he's already dead. I'm angry that I sent a young German home today, unable to give his mother the closure she deserves. And I'm bloody angry that someone, for no good reason, trashed my perfectly good bike.' She turned to Aisling. 'And you know what? Aside from all the psychological bullshit, I think I have a bloody good right to be angry.'

'You don't think that this obsession with the investigation has anything to do with the grief you feel for your father's death?'

'No, I don't. How many times have I told you that for me he died twenty years ago?'

'There's research that shows that people who are grieving become obsessed with work and sometimes behave irresponsibly. It's a condition that resembles post-partum for women who have just delivered. Are you behaving responsibly?'

'You bet I am.'

'What are you going to do now that the investigation has finally blown up?'

'Who said it's blown up? We're simply stalled.'

'Okay, you're stalled and the first person you thought of to contact was your mother.'

Fiona didn't bother to deny it. It was the truth. She leaned her head against the window. It felt cool. She didn't like to think that Aisling might be right. It was all about justice for the dead, wasn't it?

They continued the journey in silence.

WHEN MAIRE MADDEN opened the door of her small house, Fiona could see that she had been crying. She moved forward and hugged the older woman. It was only days since they had buried her errant husband, but her mother looked like she'd aged five years. Her back was bent and Fiona was certain that she was still wearing the dressing gown she had put on when she had wakened. Fiona led her mother into the living room while Aisling disappeared into the kitchen.

'Are you all right?' Fiona asked after she had seated her mother in her favourite chair.

Maire took a paper handkerchief from a box and dabbed at her eyes. 'I haven't been sleeping well. I keep seeing Conor in my dreams. Not as he was over the past few months, but as he was when we first married.'

Aisling walked in, carrying a pot of tea and three cups. She returned to the kitchen and fetched milk and sugar before sitting down and pouring tea for the three of them.

Maire took a cup from Aisling. 'I can't believe that he's gone. Even when he left, I had a husband. He didn't live here, but he was always my husband. I never thought of myself as a widow. When I saw him in the coffin, I didn't think it was him.'

Fiona took a cup and held it in her hand. 'You knew he was going to die when he contacted you.'

Aisling leaned forward and held Maire's hand. 'Feelings of shock and denial are inevitable in almost every situation where a loved one dies, even if the death is expected. Grief is a process. You'll get angry, you'll feel depressed and lonely, but eventually, through our help, you'll learn acceptance. The one thing you have to do is to start reconstructing your life. It looks like you've been in that dressing gown all day. Every morning, you get up and put on your normal clothes. You make breakfast just the way you always did. The house could do with a good clean. You should visit your friends in the village and have tea with them. Don't hide yourself away.'

Fiona looked at Aisling and scarcely recognised her. Her face had softened, and so had her voice. She was the professional clinical psychologist dealing with a client. Fiona was impressed. Her mother had already straightened her posture. She didn't appear as old anymore.

'Why don't you go now and put your clothes on?' Aisling squeezed Maire's hand and let it go.

'Okay.' Maire left the room.

'Thanks,' Fiona said. 'That was an impressive performance.' She noticed the teacup in her hand and drank.

'Your mother is displaying all the symptoms of grief. We're going to help her get through. You're the one I'm worried about. You're still in denial.'

'I already told you, I grieved when I was much younger.'

'If you say so.'

Maire came back dressed in a Paisley skirt and a brown pullover. She had combed her hair. 'I'll do what you say,' she said when she had taken her seat.

'Good,' Aisling said. 'Fiona and I will call every few days and see how you're getting on.' She picked up her cup and took Fiona's from her hand. 'I'll give these a wash.'

Maire stood up and took the cups from Aisling. 'I'll do it. It's about time I shook myself out of the lethargy.'

Fiona's phone rang, indicating the arrival of a message. She would be meeting Tim Gannon at his home at ten o'clock the following morning.

CHAPTER FORTY-EIGHT

Fiona woke early, caught the bus into Galway and arrived at the door of the dojo five minutes after it opened. She changed into her dogi and spent an hour working out. The previous evening, her mind had been concentrated on her approaching meeting with Tim Gannon. During the workout, she thought of nothing aside from perfecting the movements that any watcher would have considered already perfect. She showered, breakfasted in a small restaurant across the road from Roches Stores that specialised in organic food and waited until a quarter to nine before walking to Mill Street. She didn't know why she felt apprehensive, but she did. It was an unnatural feeling for her. She liked to meet her adversary head on. The Tim Gannon she would meet was the ninety-year old incarnation of the twelve-year old boy who must have known what was going on in the Gannon cottage in Letter Mullen. They were as uneven in power as David had been to Goliath. She was a Garda minion and Gannon was a business titan. What the hell had she been thinking about when she decided to get in his face? Had she suddenly developed death wish?

Tracy entered the squad room at ten past nine.

'We're meeting Tim Gannon at ten o'clock,' she said when he was seated at his desk.

'You never give up.'

Maybe this investigation was the time to break with the habit of a lifetime. 'It's one of my most endearing qualities.' She knew that not everyone would agree with her.

'Am I invited?'

'I don't know, but I need someone to drive me.' And you don't want to go alone, she told herself.

They left the station at twenty minutes to ten. The Gannon mansion was situated close to the village of Moycullen and bordered onto Lough Corrib. They arrived at the imposing gates to the property and were instructed by the guard to stick to the driveway and go directly to the main house. They followed instruction and parked in front of the red-bricked building. The guards had obviously rung ahead because there was a well-dressed young lady standing outside the front door when they arrived. Tracy pulled in beside her.

She pointed to her left. 'Mr Tim is in the barn. Go around the house. You'll see a large structure on the right.'

Tracy nodded and drove on around the house to the left and stopped outside a door of a large galvanised shed. They alighted from the car.

Fiona entered the barn and blinked while her eyes adjusted to the low lighting. She found herself surrounded by the most extraordinary collection of motor cars and motorcycles. She recognised Mercedes models from the 1950s and other British cars of much older vintage. A small man stood examining one of the cars. He turned as soon as they entered and walked towards them with the aid of a stick.

'Impressive, isn't it?' He held out his hand. 'Tim Gannon, pleased to meet you.'

Fiona took a hand that was bony and strong. The back of his hand was wrinkled and covered with liver spots, as was the receding area at the top of his head. She had to remember that he was ninety-two-years-old. The TG4 interview must have been made five or ten years previously, because Gannon had certainly aged in the meantime. 'Detective sergeant Madden,' she said. 'This is detective Garda Tracy.'

Gannon nodded at Tracy, but there was no handshake. Natural with Tracy being a Garda minion's minion.

Gannon examined Fiona. 'I understand you're an enthusiast.'

Fiona felt the power of Gannon's stare. She knew that humans have no facility to look into one another's soul but in Gannon's case she wasn't sure. 'My grandfather left me his old bike, but I've never seen a collection like this.'

Gannon smiled but continued to stare. 'I've been collecting for over sixty years and I rebuilt several from rusted old bodies and engines. They mean more to me than anything I've achieved in business.' He looked down at his hand. 'I had to give up working on them ten or so years ago, arthritis. My solicitor tells me that you wish to speak to me about Professor Baum.'

Gannon took her arm gently and walked her to the section where the motorcycles were stored. 'I noticed you staring at the motor bikes.'

Fiona stood gazing at a perfect Vincent Black Shadow and was hit with a wave of nostalgia. She had once owned a bike like this. It had been rebuilt from scratch by her grandfather and left to her in his will. She'd loved that bike and she wondered where it might be today. 'I had one of those,' she said, more to herself than Gannon.

'Great bike, but I prefer the Harley.' He pointed to three Harley Davidsons. 'The one in the middle is a XR750. The fellow who sold it to me swore it was the same one that Evel Knievel used until his final jump in 1977. I don't know whether I believe him or not.'

Fiona looked around the barn. It was an Aladdin's cave for

a motor enthusiast. 'There must be a million euros worth of cars and bikes here.'

'Possibly more. I'd heard that you lost your bike recently.'

She tried to remain emotionless. She could feel him watching closely for a reaction. 'It was firebombed by some miscreants.'

'Have you found them?'

'No, but I've a good idea who they are.'

'About Baum?' Gannon leaned on his stick.

Fiona saw Tracy idling among the motor cars and nodded at him to join them. 'There has been a missing-persons report on him since late 1944. This was brought to light by the recent discovery of two bodies in a bog outside Béal an Daingin. We know that Professor Heinrich Baum was studying Irish and stayed with several families in Letter Mullen. He disappeared without a trace. Local history has it that he didn't even take his clothes with him. I understand that he stayed in your family home.'

Gannon had his head tilted to the side like a bird watching its prey. 'I remember him vaguely. It must be more than seventy years ago. A large man with a goatee. Very particular about his appearance. He spoke good Irish as far as I remember, liked wandering off along the cliffs at the south of the island. I don't remember anything about him disappearing. We all supposed he went back to Germany.'

'We're looking into that at the moment. I'm impressed by your memory. You were only a boy at the time. There's a possibility that he was involved in the murder of the men we found buried in the bog.'

Gannon walked slowly in the direction of the door. 'Then I'm afraid that I can't help you. I remember he moved around the area and stayed with several families. I really don't think that he was staying with us when he disappeared. I do remember going for a walk with him along the cliffs. The weather was brutal, but he still insisted on walking along the edge. A fall there would have been fatal.' Gannon reached the door of the barn.

Fiona came level with him. You arrogant bastard. You've just told me how you murdered Baum and you know there's absolutely nothing I can do about it. He'd pushed Baum off the cliff. The German would have been killed instantly on the rocks below and been swept into the Atlantic Ocean. His skeleton would end up as part of the beach on the island. She breathed deeply before speaking. 'The case was abandoned at the time. I suppose it will be one of those cases where no solution will be found. Pity about his family in Germany.'

He bent his head 'Yes, I'll say a prayer for them.' He raised his head and looked serious. 'Good luck with your investigation and I do hope you find the rascals that torched your bike.' He extended his hand and Fiona took it.

'I think you can count on that. I don't think they knew who they were dealing with.'

Tracy led the way to the car.

Fiona looked up as the ignition caught and saw Gannon standing in the doorway of the barn. She was working on the hypothesis that the Gannon family murdered Eich and Muller. Now she knew they had. Tim Gannon might be well-educated and erudite. But he had murdered a man before he was a teenager. And there was nothing she could do about it. He had teased her with the story about the walk along the cliffs in stormy weather. She wondered why Gannon had agreed to the interview. He was a businessman and he liked to get the measure of the opposition. She hoped he was bothered by what he saw.

They drove in silence for a while. 'What did we learn?' Tracy asked.

'Very little, but there were a few interesting points.'

'Such as?'

'He could have held the interview in his solicitor's office, but I'd say he likes to choose his own ground. He'd read his brief on me and he knew I'd be impressed by his motor bike collection.' And he was right. 'We weren't invited into the house. Possibly because the tradesmen's entrance was in use. He's sure that we're not going to find Baum. My guess is Baum went off a cliff during one of his walks around the island. His body may, or may not, have washed up along the coast. We'll never know. And he knew about what happened to my bike. I assumed that the Minister had contacted his old protection officer, Sam Darker, to handle relations with us and I thought the old man would have been kept out of the loop. But having met him, I don't think that he's out of the loop on anything. I'd discounted the possibility that a twelve-year-old boy could have shot two professional soldiers and bumped off the professor, but now I'm not so sure.' She had a mental picture of the old professor and the young boy walking the cliffs. Baum wouldn't have feared the child. Maybe he'd made a mistake.

They arrived at the station and Tracy parked the car. 'Back to square one.'

'Not quite.'

CHAPTER FORTY-NINE

The call from Aisling came just as they took their seats in the squad room. Patterson and his students were ready and would make a presentation of their research at noon in the conference room of the School of Business and Economics. They had an hour to fill and Fiona spent the time writing a short note of the meeting with Gannon, mentioning her conclusion that Baum's body would never be found and consequently his disappearance would never be solved.

They entered the conference room at twelve o'clock on the dot. Patterson and his students were already there. The students were not what Fiona expected. Greg Thompson and Dougie Adams looked older than Tracy and she estimated that they were in their late-twenties or early thirties. Neither was Irish and during the introductions she gleaned that Thompson was Australian and Adams Scottish. Both had considerable business experience. Thompson handed around coffee in cardboard cups and all five sat at the top of the table where Adams was manning a laptop. A screen at the end of the room projected the laptop's desktop.

'Okay,' Patterson said. 'Let's get to it. I think the guys have done a swell job so Dougie will start.'

Adams brought up the first screen, which was the object of the research and their brief from Patterson. Then he moved on to the first slide, which gave a potted history of the Gannon Group. The Gannon family had arrived in Galway in 1945 and immediately bought an unloved large property outside Galway that was currently Tim Gannon's home. Thompson and Adams had researched the purchase and found that there was nothing on file. The deed had simply been transferred to Peadar Gannon, who had bequeathed it to his son Tim. They could find no details of the price paid or of a mortgage. Where did Gannon get the money to buy such a large property outright? The first sign of the Gannon's in business didn't surface until 1949 when Gannon bought a plot in the Newcastle area of Galway and build houses speculatively. He would have needed finance for the initial investment before the houses were sold, but since the initial company, Gannon Limited, was private, there were no accounts which would have shown the sources and uses of funds. Peadar Gannon had found money somewhere, but Thompson and Adams could not locate where it had come from. The company had joined the 1950s housing boom and had managed to buy good plots and obtain planning permissions where others had failed. Peadar had become a member of Fianna Fail political party and was listed as a donor. Towards the end of the 1950s, the family bought a six-bed chalet in Switzerland. Again, Thompson and Adams could find no details of the purchase. Around this time, the family got into bed with a small bank called the Canton Savings Bank located in Zurich. Adam changed the slide and the history of the Canton Savings Bank appeared on the screen. It had started life as a credit union type of organisation, taking deposits from local clients and making small loans. The picture changed after the Gannons got involved. The bank suddenly received an inflow of cash and became a more aggressive lender. The bank was a private institution and the secrecy laws associated with Swiss banking prevented Thompson and Adams from viewing the accounts.

Patterson tossed his empty cup into a waste basket. 'The source of the funds is what we call inherently non-transparent which means you'll never discover where they came from.'

'How much have you told Greg and Dougie about our investigation?'

Patterson smiled. 'Everything you told me, but don't worry, I've sworn them both to secrecy.'

'Could this be a valid way to launder gold and currency?'

Thompson took the question. 'We don't know how they travelled to the chalet for holidays or how often they travelled but if they used a car, they could have transferred gold and currency on every trip, stashed it in the chalet while they looked around for a small financial institution that could launder the money for them. By the early 1960s, the Canton Bank's principle customer was the Gannon organisation.'

Adams flashed up another slide. 'The 1960s and 70s was the major growth period for the Gannon Group. With the influx of money from their bankers, Gannons bought cinemas, farms, opened a clothing factory in Galway, took a large position in commercial property. This is the period when Tim Gannon took over the business and the father took a back seat. He died in 1969 from lung cancer. Then in 1975, Gannon Group went public, and the family took $120m off the table and they still own 51% of the shares. Let's say that they started with $1 million in 1945. That's a pretty healthy return on investment.'

'I think that covers the brief you gave me,' Patterson said.

Fiona tried to hide her disappointment. 'Thanks, we really appreciate your efforts.'

Patterson shrugged. 'But we didn't give you what you wanted.'

'No,' she decided to be honest. 'I was looking for proof that they had laundered one hundred and fifty kilos of gold bars and God knows how many US dollars.'

'Tim Gannon is one smart cookie,' Patterson said. 'They kept the company private until they'd grown enough to go public. They still own the company because they can out vote the other investors and they gave themselves a bonus of $120 million. We should all have a Harvard MBA.'

'Although there's no proof,' Adams said. 'We think they probably own the Canton Bank. The CEO is a member of the family and Tim Gannon's daughter is a director.'

Fiona stood. 'You guys did a great job.'

Adams handed her a folder. 'That's the complete presentation.'

Fiona took it. She would add it to the file on the investigation. 'Thanks.'

It was a fine day and when they exited the Business School building, students were eating lunch on the grass areas between buildings. Fiona thought about contacting Aisling, but in her present mental state, she wouldn't be a good lunch companion.

'I suppose that means we're done,' Tracy said. 'We followed the money and it brought up to the same place every other line of enquiry took us, a brick wall.'

Fiona forced a smile. 'The fat lady hasn't sung yet.'

'Don't you know when it's time to give up?'

That was the problem with being a maverick. You never do the expected. She'd never been one to play ball. People kept telling her that in the police to get ahead you had to have two qualities; ambition and the ability to get along. She had one but not the other because for a woman, getting along had a different meaning than for a man. If what Darker said was true, the only reason she'd made sergeant was because her mentor had sacrificed his gold watch. At least one person she respected had faith in her. There were still a couple of days before O'Reilly pulled the plug on the investigation. She told

Tracy to take the car. She wanted to be alone. He reluctantly agreed and they split up when they reached the car park. She exited the front gate along with a large group of bustling students. They didn't appear to have a care in the world, although she knew that the opposite was probably true. They scrimped and saved for their education while the kleptocrats ripped the system off from the outside and the inside. Don Quixote had some chance against the windmill. She had no chance against the might of a family like the Gannons. They'd be laughing up the sleeves at her pathetic attempt to solve a seventy-five-year-old double murder. She was at the top of William Street when she caught sight of Darker turning into Eyre Square. She slipped quickly into the doorway of a shoe shop and then came out as soon as he had disappeared down one side of Eyre Square. Fiona turned the corner. Darker was at the bottom of the square and about to turn left and she hurried along after him. She turned the corner at the bottom just in time to see him entering the Hardiman Hotel. She waited two minutes, followed him inside, and went straight to the reception. Taking out her warrant card, she showed it to the female clerk. 'A man entered here two minutes ago.' She described Darker. 'Where did he go?'

'The dining room.' The receptionist pointed her finger to the right.

Fiona walked to the restaurant and stood at the small table requesting guests to wait to be seated. When the maître d' arrived, she asked for a secluded table. She saw Darker seated at one of the tables facing Eyre Square. His back was to her. She indicated to the maître d' that she would prefer a table at the end of the room opposite to Darker. She found a spot where she could observe Darker, but where there was a wooden abutment she could slip behind if necessary. She wasn't surprised when Tim Gannon entered the room and went straight to Darker's table. Gannon sat in a chair at ninety degrees from Darker. The two men were soon deep in conversation and Gannon appeared to be telling a story. Then they let out a peel of laughter.

Fiona could feel her insides twisting. They were laughing at her. It was a celebration lunch. Gannon had out-played her, and, like many of his adversaries in business, she had been sent from the field with her tail between her legs. The dumb cop had been shown up.

A waiter arrived and asked for her order. She glanced at the menu. The soup of the day was the cheapest option, so she ordered it.

A waiter carried a tray with a bottle of champagne and two glasses to Gannon and Darker's table. He made a show of displaying the label and opening the bottle. After he poured each a glass, they toasted each other, drank, and laughed.

Fiona's soup arrived but she ignored it. Don't celebrate too soon, you bastards. She might have been prepared to throw the towel in, but not now. She had already decided that Darker was going to pay a price for torching her bike. Gannon was a different matter. One of Horgan's homilies concerned the fact that as police officers, they were involved only in examining the evidence and arresting the culprits. The justice end of the business had to be handled by the DPP and the courts. To hell with that. Two men sitting in the same room as her had committed crimes that they would never serve a day's prison time for. Where was the justice in that? She had seen the way the DPP had handled the Charlie Grealish case. There was an Irish politician who had been shown to be corrupt by a tribunal that had cost the Irish taxpayer sixty-five million euros. The man was still walking the streets free and he would be until he died, then those responsible for pursuing the fraud case could breathe a sigh of relief. Perhaps this time justice might need a helping hand.

She'd had enough of watching the celebration at the other end of the restaurant. She dropped a ten euro note beside the untasted soup and left.

CHAPTER FIFTY

Tracy looked up from his desk when Fiona slumped into her chair. 'Oh, oh. I don't like the look on your face. You're harbouring some dark and evil thoughts.'

'I am.' She told him about following Darker to the Hardiman and the scene in the Oyster restaurant. 'Those two arrogant bastards are laughing at us.'

'You're paranoid. They could have been celebrating something else.'

'They could be, but they weren't. They think we're whipped. And maybe we are, but we still have a little time to waste on them.' She was putting up a brave front for Tracy. They were running out of doors to open.

'Following the money didn't produce the goods.'

'Tim learned his lesson well and he had the perfect opportunity to implement them. The bastard probably invented money laundering. The chalet in St. Moritz, the skiing holidays, the Canton Bank, they were all parts of the grand plan. The gold was shipped piecemeal and the paper money used to buy assets. There were no company audited accounts. It was all done with mirrors. What did Patterson call it? Inherently non-transparent.' She looked at the squad room clock. It was too early to go for a drink. She wanted to get sloshed. She knew it wouldn't do any good and she would probably lose tomorrow. But right now, she needed oblivion.

'Where do we go from here?' Tracy asked.

It was the question that Fiona hoped he wouldn't ask. What would Dom Geraghty say? 'Go back to the beginning. There's something that we've missed.'

'I've been over that bloody file five times at least.'

'And you'll have to go over it five times more. We have maybe one more throw of the dice before we're kicked off the investigation.'

'What are you going to do?'

Another good question. The quick answer was head for Taaffes and a dozen pints. She opened the desk drawer and took out the TG4 interview with Gannon. 'I'm going to watch this DVD again and I'm going to read all the bumf you downloaded from the Internet. Tim Gannon told me how Baum died and hinted at his part in that death. He didn't say it outright but he's proud of the part he played. The man is a murderer plain and simple.' She removed the DVD from the box, inserted it in her computer, and pressed the play button when the media player loaded. She watched the opening shot as the drone flew over the driveway from the gate to the front of the Gannon mansion. Half an hour later, the credits ran up on the end. She wrote down the names of the producer and the director. She picked up the phone and called TG4 and asked for the producer.

'Liam Quinn.'

'Detective sergeant Fiona Madden from Mill Street Station. Ba mhaith liom ceist a chur ort.' *I'd like to ask you a question.*

'You have good Irish,' Quinn replied in Irish. 'Ask away.'

Fiona continued in Irish. She liked speaking her native language. 'I've just been watching a film of an interview you did with Tim Gannon of the Gannon Group. Do you normally shoot more footage that doesn't make it into the film?'

'Normally yes, sometimes we have bloopers that we have to cover up. Sometimes we shoot additional footage as fillers.'

'Do you still have the unused footage?'

'The interview was some time ago. Do you need it urgently?'

'Yes.'

'I'll have a look and call you back in ten minutes.'

Fiona paced the space in front of her desk. Once or twice she glanced at the whiteboard and realised how naïve they were. What little chance they had of success. How silly the whole enterprise was. When the phone rang, she snatched it up.

'We have about another forty minutes of tape,' Quinn said.

'Can you put it on a DVD?'

'I can, but it might be better if you view it here.'

'We're on the way.' She put the phone down and looked at Tracy. 'Get the car keys.'

He closed the file he was reading. 'Where are we going?'

'Baile na hAbhann.'

CHAPTER FIFTY-ONE

The offices of TG4 are situated just off the main Connemara Coast Road in the townland of Baile na hAbhann, which means river settlement in English. Tracy pulled into the car park in front of a modern elongated two-story building dominated by a large communication mast at the rear. They went to the reception and asked for Liam Quinn, who came presently and led Fiona and Tracy into a room that contained a series of monitors and a large old style tape recorder. Quinn turned out to be a middle-aged man with a developed beard and long hair who would have passed as a Beatnik in the 1970s. He explained that the interview had taken place six years previously, when TG4 was still using magnetic tape. However, it had been stored on a digital medium.

'I've already set up the monitors and the source.' He spoke in Irish. 'Do you want to use the machine yourself or do you need one of the technical staff to help you?'

Fiona watched the look of fear on Tracy's face. 'We'll take the technician.'

Quinn disappeared and returned with a younger man, who he introduced as Joe Burke and who sat facing the largest of the monitors. 'What do you want? We've archived all the footage, so you can have the complete shoot, a rough cut, and the final edit.'

'The complete shoot.' Fiona pulled up a chair and sat beside Burke.

Tracy followed her example and sat on Burke's other side.

Burke pulled the keyboard towards him. 'Do you want to just watch, or do you need a commentary on what's happening?'

'Let's just watch. This is just like a normal DVD? You can rewind and zoom?'

'We can do anything.' Burke hit the play key.

On the screen, people were moving around in the Gannon living room. Fiona recognised Tim Gannon in close conversation with the young woman who had directed them to the barn. The interviewer was arranging the chairs and the camera was moving around the room doing a check. Then the interviewer joined Gannon and gestured to the chair. The secretary brushed Gannon's dark blue suit and he took his place. They were about to start when a well-dressed elderly woman entered and went to talk to Gannon. It was his sister Áine. She looked up towards the camera. She was older than in the photos Fiona had seen and frail-looking, but there was no doubt that she had been an attractive woman in her youth. The Gannons put their heads together before the woman moved out of the shot and the interviewer turned towards the camera and began the introduction to the show. Fiona kept her eye on the clock that was running at the top of the screen and the next twelve minutes had appeared in the final edit that Fiona and Tracy had already viewed. The interview wound down at fourteen minutes. The camera kept rolling and the cameraman moved to a position behind and took a shot of Gannon nodding his head sagely. He then moved to the other side of the room and took a shot of the interviewer asking one of her questions. Then he moved around the room while the camera continued to roll.

'Stop,' Fiona shouted. 'Replay it slowly.'

Burke hit a key and the picture froze, then the picture started to rewind a frame at a time.

'Stop,' Fiona said. 'Can you zoom in to that wooden frame that's on the wall at the corner of the chimney breast?' Her voice was nervous.

Burke hit a few keys and the camera zoomed in on a wooden frame that contained a gun and a medal.

She smiled and turned to Tracy. 'There is a God. Take out your phone and show me the picture of the Mauser HSc.'

Tracy's hand shook slightly as he brought up the image of the gun he had saved. He turned the picture around towards Fiona.

Fiona stared at the image on the phone and then looked at the screen. 'He's not just an arrogant bastard. His arrogance knows no bounds.'

'It definitely looks like a Mauser HSc,' Tracy said. 'But is it **the** gun?'

'There's only one way to find out.' She turned to Burke. 'Can you print that frame?'

'Did I help solve a crime?' Burke's fingers flashed over the keyboard.

'Maybe,' Fiona said. 'But don't go around telling everybody in case Tracy and I have screwed up.'

Burke looked at Fiona. 'There's a colour print on the machine in the next room. Are we done?'

She stood up. 'We certainly are. Thanks for your help.'

Burke hit a combination of keys and the screen went blank.

Tracy picked up the print in the room outside and they made their way to the entrance.

Fiona wanted to scream, got you, you bastard, but restrained herself. 'We need to go somewhere where we can get a drink and I can make a phone call.'

CHAPTER FIFTY-TWO

The Potín Stil in Inverin was the closest watering hole and Fiona entered the establishment as though she was walking on air. It was amazing how an investigation can change with one small piece of evidence. Any old lag would have told Gannon that the first thing to do after a murder was to get rid of the murder weapon. But Gannon was as different from an old lag as an airplane is from a child's glider. Gannon wanted to relive one of the seminal moments of his life and that meant he couldn't bear to get rid of the murder weapon. But was it really the murder weapon? That could only be established when the Technical Bureau ran a test and compared the result to the bullets taken from Eich and Muller. They were close, but not there yet.

The interior of the pub had been renovated since her last visit, which she'd have to admit was probably twenty years previously. She had stopped by with her parent and had sat rapt at the table as they had reminisced about how they had met in this very spot for the first time. There had been a dance hall associated with the pub but that had disappeared eons ago and was a tarmacked over as a car park.

Tracy was sent for the drinks and returned with a pint of Guinness and an orange juice.

Fiona took the Guinness and toasted him. 'We were holed but not sunk.' She took a large swallow. 'We now only need one piece of information to go our way.' She took out her phone, checked her contacts and placed a call.

'Hindrichson.'

'Berthold, it's Fiona Madden in Galway. We've had a break in the case, but we need one further piece of help from you.'

'Anything, if I can.'

She told him about the Mauser HSc on the wall in Gannon's living room. 'Do you have the serial number of the gun that was issued to your grandfather or Muller?'

'No, but I think it will probably be in the *Bundesarchiv*. I'll be on to them first thing in the morning. I have a contact there who is an expert on the period and he will know where to look.'

'Please text me tomorrow with the information.'

'You seem excited, Fiona.'

'I thought we were going to fail, but now there's a chance we can get justice for your grandfather.'

'My mother and I are very grateful. I have one further piece of news for you. There's no evidence that Baum returned to Germany after the war. His wife is dead, but his two sons confirmed that he had never contacted them after early December 1944. In the Abwehr files he's listed as having perished during the war.'

'That confirms something that I already thought. Baum never left Ireland. The information on the serial numbers is important. I need it as soon as possible.' She didn't want to go over the top and say how badly she needed it.

'Tomorrow morning.'

Fiona returned to her pint while the frown on Tracy's face deepened. 'Okay, I've forgotten something, spill it.'

'Have you figured out how we're going to get our hands on the gun?'

'The last time I looked, it was illegal in this country to possess a firearm without a licence. I doubt very much if Mr Gannon has procured a licence. And if he has, it's for a shotgun.'

'But that doesn't answer the question, how are we going to get it?'

'We're going to take it off him.'

'How?'

'We're going to present a request for a warrant to confiscate an illegally-held firearm to our superiors. They won't dare reject such a request because if they do it will be the end of their careers. You'll get the warrant signed and I'll be sitting outside Gannon's mansion waiting for you to email me a copy.'

'That has a chance.' Tracy drank some orange juice and screwed up his face. 'How does Aisling drink so much of this stuff?'

'She's a serious lady and my designated driver.'

'I thought for a minute that you might go for a search warrant.'

Fiona finished her pint and asked for another. 'I have no desire to go through Mr Tim's drawers. Do you want another juice?'

Tracy shook his head.

Fiona took out her phone. 'I'll call Horgan and give him a head's up.'

'But he won't get the whole story until tomorrow.'

Fiona took the fresh pint from the barman. 'You're really getting to know me.'

CHAPTER FIFTY-THREE

'You're squiffy,' Aisling announced when Fiona almost fell over when she entered the living room.

'You're kidding I've only had two pints.' She pointed at the offending area on the floor. 'That carpet wasn't there yesterday.'

'That carpet has been there for years. Celebrating or drowning your sorrows?'

'Celebrating, I think we might have a chance to nab Tim Gannon.' She crumpled into an easy chair.

Aisling sat beside her. 'Do tell.'

Fiona told her about the extra footage shot for the TG4 interview. 'It's there in plain sight. It's like he's giving us the two fingers. Glass of wine?'

'Not yet. Tim Gannon thinks he's safe. You've rattled his cage and you saw what happened to your bike. What do you think will happen after you arrive at his house to remove vital evidence against him. The man is dangerous. I thought you were thinking of closing the investigation.'

'That was when I thought I had no chance of nailing him.'

'And now that you do, you're going to ignore the risks. You'd better be ready to plant a stake in his heart because if you don't he'll turn his attention on you and God knows what he'll do.'

'Don't worry. The trap is set. We just need to spring it. Once I get him into Mill Street he'll sing like a canary.' At least that was the plan. Fiona was wondering whether the euphoria mixed with Guinness was affecting her rationality. It was never going to be that easy. Aisling had a nasty habit of unsettling her by making her doubt herself. At the very least, she'd have him on possession of an illegally-held firearm and then she'd go for the gold ring, the murders of Eich and Muller.

'I think you should proceed cautiously. I know you, Fiona. When you get the bit between your teeth to tend to throw vigilance out the window. That would be the wrong strategy for dealing with someone like Gannon.'

Fiona struggled out of the chair and made for the kitchen. 'You sure know how to bring a girl down.'

Aisling followed her. 'I'm trying to tell you to be careful.'

Fiona removed a bottle of white wine from the fridge, opened it and poured two glasses. She handed Aisling a glass. 'The investigation has proved to me that Horgan's policy of leaving justice to others is horseshit. Gannon doesn't need to be treated with kid gloves. He needs to be exposed. Like the people who enabled that pederast Mangan need to be exposed.'

Aisling took the glass. 'We should bring back the pillory and let the people throw rotten fruit at the miscreants. Or perhaps the criminals should be stoned to death. This isn't like you.'

Fiona went back into the living room and sat down. 'Maybe being almost burned to death has given me a new prospective on criminal justice.'

'Come on, we weren't almost burned to death.' Aisling sat across from her.

'The bike was parked directly outside the door. If the tank had been full of petrol and it exploded, it would have shot flaming petrol over the cottage. It was an act of terrorism. What if we'd been off our heads and slept through it.' She told Aisling about Gannon and Darker celebrating in the Hardiman Hotel. 'I'm following police procedure at the moment but only until I get Gannon.' She went over and sat on the arm of Aisling's chair. 'Now let's forget about Gannon and have a nice evening. Tomorrow promises to be a very difficult day.'

'I think you're acting out grief for your father's death.'

Fiona went to the kitchen and returned with the bottle of wine. 'If you say so.' She refilled their glasses. 'I'll handle Gannon carefully. Now, no more shop talk.'

CHAPTER FIFTY-FOUR

Fiona's eyes opened and she swivelled to look at the bedside clock. It was exactly three o'clock. Her cheeks were wet and she realised that she had been crying in her sleep. She'd slept for four hours and knew that would be it for the night. She slipped out of bed, left the bedroom and sat at the dining table. Before she woke she had been dreaming about her father. The dream was so vivid and she had been so happy that she didn't want it to end. She and her father had been wandering on the beach holding hands and laughing. Her father was young and happy, not the haggard creature that had been put into the earth. As they walked along, her hand slipped from his and he gradually moved away from her. Eventually she found herself alone and started to cry. She turned and started for home but she failed to recognise the path she should take. She walked back along the beach and found it was unending. She was lost. That was when her eyes popped open. She sometimes forgot that Aisling's job was to understand people's minds. Living with someone like that has a downside. People tended to have a part of them that they wanted to keep secret. A part only they knew and understood. In Fiona's case there were many secrets and she sometimes felt Aisling was opening doors in her mind that she would prefer remained closed. She continually worked to suppress the anger and the anxieties that raged within her. The red mist enveloped her as she remembered the scene in the Hardiman Hotel. She turned on the TV and found a rerun of a comedy especially chosen for insomniacs. She was still watching the flickering screen when Aisling exited the bedroom shaking her head.

CHAPTER FIFTY-FIVE

Horgan was pacing around the top of the squad room when Fiona arrived. He looked like he'd had even less sleep than her. She bought a takeaway coffee for Tracy, but she took pity on Horgan and handed it to him. 'It's got milk and sugar.'

Horgan took it from her and looked at it as though he'd never seen a takeaway coffee before.

'Sit down, boss. You look tired.' She kicked Tracy's chair over to him and sat at her desk.

'What was that phone call about last night?' He saw the chair and sat in it, still holding the coffee in his hand. 'You're ready to make an arrest?'

Fiona removed the cap from her coffee cup and set it on the desk. 'I'm ready to interview a prime suspect and I expect to have a vital piece of evidence today. But I'll also be arresting him on another charge.'

'Would you like to tell me who the prime suspect is?'

She sipped her coffee; it burned her lips. 'Tim Gannon. Careful with the coffee, it's hot.'

'The businessman?' Horgan finally saw the coffee in his hand and he set it on Tracy's desk.

'The same.' Fiona blew air over the surface of the coffee.

'You've gone too far this time, Madden. O'Brien wants your blood, which means the Commissioner is on to you. Try to take down Gannon and you're finished.'

'I suppose if they fire me, I'll be able to tell everything I know about the Jesuits turning a blind eye to a pederast. The German Ambassador would probably like to know that the Garda Commissioner tried to stop the investigation into the murder of two German nationals. And I have Ginny Hinds' number somewhere.'

Horgan stood up. 'I wouldn't try blackmail if I were you.'

Fiona smiled and leaned back. 'What time does O'Reilly get in?'

'What's this got to do with O'Reilly?'

The smell of fear was present in the room. 'I need him to sign a warrant.'

'To search Gannon's house? Are you fucking mad?'

Fiona did a mock frown. 'Not for a search. The warrant is necessary to recover an illegally-held weapon. And I wouldn't like to be responsible for blocking such a warrant.'

Horgan looked like his world had just imploded. 'This is career-ending shit, Madden. Tim Gannon's son is a former Minister of Justice.' Horgan had turned white and sat down heavily.

Fiona rarely pitied him, but right now he looked like he needed a comforting cuddle. But there was no way she would provide it. 'You have to play the cards as they fall, boss. But I assure you we've done everything by the book.'

Tracy entered the room and walked to Fiona's desk. He looked at Horgan. 'What the hell did you do to him?'

Fiona shrugged. 'I told him who our prime suspect is and that we'd be requiring a warrant to recover an illegally-held weapon. He didn't take it too well.'

Tracy saw the coffee on his desk, picked it up and drank. 'I suppose you broke it to him gently.'

She smiled. 'Of course.'

'O'Reilly will shit a brick,' Horgan said, more to himself than Fiona or Tracy. He looked at Tracy. 'Tell me she's joking about Gannon.'

Tracy shook his head. 'She's not joking, boss. There is a serious offensive weapon on the loose and it needs to be taken into police custody.'

'O'Reilly won't go for it,' Horgan said.

'You're going to have to convince him,' Fiona said. 'He's a politician, but you're a real copper. And recovering a lethal weapon is real policework.' It hurt her to put Horgan in the same bracket as Tracy, Brophy, and herself.

Horgan nodded but didn't look convinced.

Fiona had gone too far to back out. One way or another, he would have to play ball. 'What time does O'Reilly get in?'

'Ten o'clock.'

She looked at the office clock. She had forty-five minutes to receive a call from Hindrichson.

CHAPTER FIFTY-SIX

Thankfully, O'Reilly was running late. Hindrichson called at a quarter past ten and provided her with the serial numbers of the guns held by Eich and Muller. He even faxed over the official requisition form issued by the *Kriegsmarine*. You had to love the Germans. In Ireland, requisition forms, even for weapons, tended to get lost. Everything was now in place except for the warrant. Fiona was certain that if she presented the request, O'Reilly would at least delay the process. There was also a distinct possibility that he would inform Gannon and the gun would disappear. Tracy was the ideal candidate. O'Reilly was aware that Tracy was on the hierarchy's radar. And he was a man. Therefore, he was more trustworthy than some hormonal woman. It was better for her to stay out of the way and let the testosterone boys make all the decisions. She had already organised for a couple of uniforms to accompany her to Gannon's mansion.

As soon as O'Reilly arrived, she left for Moycullen. Her nerves were as taut as an overstrung guitar as she drove the fifteen kilometres from Galway. She had her mobile phone on the passenger seat, and she cast glances at it for the whole journey. Tracy had prepared the warrant before she left and all it required was O'Reilly's signature. Why was it taking so long? Tracy was smarter than Horgan and O'Reilly together and she prayed that his cool manner would convince the chief to put pen to paper. She parked in a layby two hundred metres from the mansion and waited impatiently for the phone to ring.

When it came, she jumped at the sound and snatched at the phone. She took the call without checking the caller ID.

'That was like pulling teeth,' Tracy said.

'Did you get it?'

'I just texted it to you. There are two very unhappy men in the station at the moment. O'Reilly was insisting that he needed instructions from the Park, but I reminded him of the gravity of the situation and the possibility that the gun had been used in a more serious crime. It took some convincing, but I got there in the end. I'm on my way to you with the signed paper.'

Fiona checked her messages. The warrant was there. She started the car and drove to the gate. She had her warrant card out to override any objection from the local employee manning the entrance.

Gannon was standing on the steps when she arrived at the parking area in front of the house.

'Detective sergeant,' he said as soon as she alighted from the car. 'Back to make an offer on the Vincent Black Shadow. I saw you looking enviously at it.'

Fiona walked forward, her mobile in hand. 'Out of my price range, I'm afraid. I'm still waiting for the insurance check to replace my last bike.'

There was a smirk on Gannon's face 'I hear vandalism is on the rise in Galway.'

Fiona held up her phone 'Criminality certainly is. I have just been messaged a warrant from Mill Street that permits me to enter your house and take possession of a Mauser HSc which is illegally held by you.' She pushed past Gannon, entered the house, and went immediately to the living room. She smiled when she saw that the gun was still on the wall.

Gannon entered the room behind her. His face had lost all colour. 'Show me that warrant.' He held out his hand.

She handed him the phone and he scrolled through the page, searching for the signature.

'Someone is going to lose their job over this warrant and I sincerely hope it's going to be you. Get out before I have you thrown out.'

The secretary entered the living room.

'Call Garvey,' Gannon shouted. 'I want him here now.' He pointed at Fiona. 'And get that bitch out of here.'

Fiona took an old silver whistle from her pocket and held it up. 'I took this from the station this morning. You're old enough to recognise it as a police whistle. There are two uniformed officers outside and were I to blow this whistle, they would come rushing in here.' She walked to the frame on the wall and yanked it free. 'I'm taking possession of this firearm. If you can produce a licence, I'll return it.'

Gannon swung his cane at her and she easily avoided the stroke.

She held the frame under her arm. 'Try that again and I'll have to restrain you. Pity you don't have Sam Darker around today to do your dirty work. I suppose after your little celebration at the Hardiman yesterday, you told him he could return to Dublin.'

Gannon wobbled and his secretary rushed to help him into a chair.

Tracy entered the living room with the original of the warrant in his hand.

He was closely followed by another young lady who looked around at the assembly and handed Gannon a phone. 'Superintendent O'Reilly on the line.'

'Yes,' Gannon said into the phone. 'They're here and they

already served the warrant.' He threw the phone into the fireplace.

'Detective Tracy,' Fiona said. 'Would you please do the necessary?'

'Timothy Gannon, I am arresting you for contravening the provisions of the Criminal Justice Act 2009 by having an illegally-held handgun. You do not have to say anything when questioned, but anything you do say will be taken down and used in court.'

The two uniforms came forward, handcuffed Gannon, and took him out to the car.

Fiona watched him go. Eich and Muller had been waiting seventy-five years for justice. She was happy that she was the one who was going to give it to them.

CHAPTER FIFTY-SEVEN

Fiona looked through the two-way mirror at Gannon sitting peacefully in the interview room at Mill Street. He'd been signed in, charged, and his fingerprints taken. The serial number on the Mauser had proven to be the same as that on the gun issued to Eich in 1940. The gun itself was already on its way to the Technical Bureau for ballistics testing and fingerprinting. Gannon's fingerprints had been sent ahead over the wire. His solicitor had been called and was on his way. The interview would begin as soon as he arrived.

DI Horgan stood at her side. 'This better stick.'

She thought she smelled whiskey on his breath. He must have a bottle hidden somewhere in his office. Fiona continued staring at the man in the interview room. 'The ballistics test will show that the gun was used to murder Eich and Muller and that Gannon's fingerprints are on the gun.'

'You're always so bloody sure, Madden.' Horgan shifted uneasily. 'It might take more than that to convict him. He'll have the best brief in the country and they'll go over your case with a fine-tooth comb.'

She already knew that. That would be if he ever got to

court. Given the evidence of previous high visibility cases, there was a better than even chance that Gannon would never see a courtroom. The Irish justice system had a habit of waiting until the individual charged died before saying they were just about to bring the case. Gannon was an old man and couldn't be expected to defy the laws of nature by living far into the future. The case would be delayed until the accused shuffled off this mortal coil. 'I think you should worry about the court case when it actually happens. Like you always say, boss, we're only here to do the evidence collecting and charging. Justice happens further down the line.' Fiona watched as a tall, grey-haired, corpulent man in a black pin-striped suit enter the room, put a leather briefcase on the table and shook hands with Gannon.

'Fucking Sean Garvey,' Horgan muttered under his breath.

'Show time,' Fiona said.

FIONA AND TRACY enjoyed a coffee while the solicitor held a conference with his client. Eventually, they were invited to join the two men already seated in the interview room. Fiona introduced herself and Tracy and the solicitor introduced himself as Sean Garvey BL and handed Fiona his card. The two police officers sat facing Gannon and Garvey. Tracy turned on the recording and did the preamble.

'This is a piffling charge,' Garvey said in a blustering tone.

Fiona imagined that Garvey, with his height and size, had gotten used to bullying people since he was the star of the school rugby team. It was a fact that people were unduly impressed by an individual who was larger than them. She smiled. 'I might not agree. As you are no doubt aware, the Criminal Justice Act of 2006 introduced some of the toughest penalties for firearm offences. I think that your client, if convicted, may be facing a custodial sentence. I wouldn't call such a situation piffling.'

Garvey drew himself up to his full height. 'Then I am asking you to release my client immediately on police bail.'

'I can't do that,' Fiona stared back. 'We might be adding a more serious change in the near future.'

She put a photo of the Mauser on the table. She raised her eyes and stared at Gannon. 'How did you come by this handgun?'

Gannon looked at his solicitor. 'No comment.'

She placed the *Kriegsmarine* requisition order on the table. 'This is an official German document that states the Mauser found at your home has the serial number of a weapon issued to a German U-boat captain called Gunter Eich. Have you ever met Mr Eich?'

'No comment.'

She took out a photograph of the bodies taken from the bog. 'This is what the body of Gunter Eich looked like when it was taken from the bog at Béal an Daingin. Have you any idea of how Mr Eich ended up in that bog?'

'Where are we going with these questions, detective sergeant?' Garvey interjected. 'We are discussing an infraction of the rules pertaining to an illegally-held handgun. My client neglected to apply for a licence. Big deal. Let's stick to the charge and get my client out of here as soon as possible.'

'I'm trying to establish how a gun issued to a member of the German Armed Forces made its way into Mr Gannon's possession.'

'Mr Gannon may well have bought the weapon as a decoration for the wall.'

'Then he no doubt has a bill of sale. That might establish the provenance of the gun and it would allow us to broaden our enquiries.' She looked at Gannon. 'Did you buy the gun?'

'No comment.'

Fiona collected up the papers on the table. It was the conclusion she had hoped for. O'Donnell had promised to rush the gun through testing so that she could get on to the more serious charge of murder. She needed to be able to hold Gannon until the results came through. 'We don't appear to be making much progress here.' She nodded at Tracy, who terminated the interview.

'We'll give this another try this afternoon.' Fiona stood. 'We'll send in lunch and a beverage.'

'Don't bother,' Gannon said. 'My staff will attend to my needs.'

Tracy handed a cassette to Garvey before standing and opening the door for Fiona.

'Not going so well,' Tracy said as they walked back along the corridor in the direction of the squad room.

'What did you think was going to happen? You said yourself that people like Gannon think that the likes of us are just fleas on the backside of the world. We don't count. This is only round one and he's going to fight us with everything he's got and that's going to turn out to be plenty. I wouldn't like to be the prosecutor if this reaches court.'

'We may not get him.'

'We may not indeed. Just like I won't get Darker and his mob for beating the shit out of Hindrichson and torching my bike. If this were a sport, we'd be the team with one hand tied behind our backs. We have to follow the rules. The criminals don't have a rule book and if they did, they'd break every rule in it.'

They took their seats in the squad room.

Tracy sat and frowned.

'What's the problem?' she asked.

'If we don't nail him, what'll they do to us?'

Fiona laughed. 'They'll probably promote you. You should have worked out by now that you can be promoted in the Garda Síochána if they want to get you out of the way. Horgan and O'Reilly will agree that I have somehow infected you.'

Tracy glanced at the clock. 'Might be a good time to grab lunch.'

Fiona stood and started for the door. 'Never fight on an empty stomach.'

'Who said that?'

'I did.'

CHAPTER FIFTY-EIGHT

There was no rush on when they got back to the station. But Fiona knew that there were lots of things happening in the background. Judges were being called, government ministers were being contacted, the whole system of elitism that surrounded Gannon was being brought into play. And possibly Fiona's superiors were trying to find a way to subvert her and that wouldn't land them in jail. This was the lull before the storm. They couldn't hold Gannon much longer. That would be more than O'Reilly's job was worth. She figured that at most she had another hour and if O'Donnell didn't come through, then she might be doomed. Once Gannon walked out of Mill Street, there was a good chance she wouldn't get him inside again. The writs were already being written and they would begin to fly if Gannon remained in the station one minute longer than the legal limit. She spent an hour drumming on her desk and when the phone finally rang, she snatched it.

'You've got him.'

O'Donnell's broad Donegal accent was music to her ears. 'Gun and prints?' she asked.

'The gun fired the bullets that killed Eich and Muller and

Gannon's prints are on it. I'll send the details to your computer.'

Relief was coursing through her body. They had Gannon. 'I owe you one.'

'Next time I'm in Galway.'

'Done.' She killed the call and turned to Tracy. 'Round two.'

GANNON LOOKED up from the table when Fiona and Tracy entered the room. Fiona wasn't sure, but she thought a little of his confidence had drained.

She put her file on the table and sat down. 'Your solicitor has been informed and despite a busy schedule, he'll be here in ten minutes. Must be nice to be one of the great and the good.'

Gannon sat back and appraised her. 'It has its advantages. Do you hate me so much for making something of my life?'

'Who said I hated you? We're both from Connemara and I like to see a local doing well.'

Gannon smiled. 'I hear that your father didn't do particularly well in America. Maybe he should have come and worked for me.'

Fiona had sighed at the mention of her father. She should have known that Gannon had read the file on her that Darker had prepared. 'Let's keep our personal lives out of this. He's dead now so there's no chance of that. Anyway, he has no relevance to what we're doing here.'

Gannon was more talkative. 'Of course it has. Your whole life has relevance to what's going on here. You're a begrudger, you hate me because I have the power to snap my fingers and the most eminent solicitor drops everything and rushes to my side. If I were a poor fisherman, you'd be a lot kinder.'

Was there any truth in what Gannon said? Fiona wondered. Was the investigation about justice or class envy? Was she kinder towards the Connors and the other traveller families? She didn't think so. Her musing was cut short when the door was flung open, and Garvey exploded into the room.

He looked at Gannon. 'You haven't said anything?'

Gannon shook his head.

Garvey sighed audibly and sat down.

Tracy started the recording and did the preamble.

'Detective Garda Tracy,' Fiona said.

'Please stand up, Mr Gannon.'

Gannon stood.

'You are about to be questioned about the unlawful deaths of Gunter Eich and Dieter Muller on or before the end of 1945 in the parish of Letter Mullen. You do not have to say anything when questioned, but anything you do say will be taken down and used against you in court of law. You may sit.'

Fiona looked at Garvey and for a second she thought that he might have a heart attack. His mouth hung open and he appeared to have difficulty breathing. The writs he'd been preparing since he left earlier were destined for the shredder. Gannon, on the other hand, showed no emotion.

'Would you like some water?' she asked Garvey.

He was fanning himself with a file cover. 'Please.'

Tracy told the recording he was leaving the room and returned several moments later with a bottle of water and a glass which he placed in front of Garvey.

Garvey filled a glass and drank. 'Thank you.'

'Mr Gannon,' Fiona began. 'Earlier I asked you whether you had ever met a Gunter Eich and I showed you a photo of a man taken from a bog.' She put the photo Hindrichson had given her of his father at Willemshaven on the table. 'Would you please look at this photo and tell me if you recognise the man facing the camera.'

Gannon examined the photo and said, 'No comment.'

Fiona looked at Garvey. 'Would you please tell your client that proceeding like this is not beneficial to his interests.'

'Shall we get to the meat of your allegations. Can we please see some concrete evidence?'

Fiona removed a plastic bag from her file and laid it on the table. 'This medal is an Iron Cross and was in the frame containing the Mauser HSc.' She turned the medal over, exposing the inscription on the rear. This medal was awarded to Gunter Eich for his service as a submarine commander. If you haven't met Eich, how do you have his most prized possession?'

'No comment.'

Fiona sighed. She would have preferred if Gannon had confessed and told his story, but that was the perfect solution and he wasn't going to play ball. She took another photo from her file and put it on the table. 'These are the two bullets that were removed from the heads of the two murdered Germans. They have been identified as coming from a Mauser HSc. The same type of gun that we confiscated today.' She laid the ballistics report that O'Donnell had sent on the table. 'That gun was rushed to Dublin, where it has been examined by the Garda Technical Bureau and has been identified as the murder weapon. The fingerprints on the gun have been examined and there is a match with your prints taken at this station this morning. We have now linked the gun to the murders and the gun to you.' She looked at Garvey. 'I think that constitutes enough evidence to justify a charge. Now I would appreciate a comment.'

'No comment,' Gannon said.

Fiona leaned forward. 'You were only twelve years old at the time. If you confess, you'd be treated as a minor and this whole business will go away. There are extenuating circumstances.'

Gannon didn't look at his solicitor before shaking his head.

'With the evidence from the gun, we have pretty much the whole story. We know from Eich's grandson, who was mugged in Galway for papers which we already had in our possession, that Gunter Eich and Dieter Muller were the crew of a mini-submarine tasked with transporting gold and currency from Germany to the Canary Islands at the end of the war. The money was to be used to set up a Fourth Reich in Argentina. For some reason, possibly to repair their craft or to take on fuel, they had to stop in Connemara. A German agent calling himself Professor Baum was a lodger with the Gannon family in Letter Mullen. We don't know the exact motive for the murders, but we assume the money played a role. The bodies were dumped in the bog, and I think Baum went off a cliff into the Atlantic. The Gannon family left Letter Mullen for Galway and miraculously came into money, which they used to finance their first foray into business. I think Tim Gannon carefully laundered the gold and currency. All was well until Eich's hand came out of the bog and we began investigating.'

Garvey's mouth was flapping open as she spoke. He looked at his client, who was examining the ceiling.

Fiona looked at Gannon. 'Tell us the real story. I know that you pushed Baum to his death, but I'll never be able to prove it. You had balls for a twelve-year-old brought up on a tiny island in Connemara. You almost got away with it.'

Gannon didn't take his eyes from the ceiling.

Fiona turned to Tracy, who terminated the interview. 'Please put Mr Gannon is the cells. We'll try this again tomorrow when he's had more time to reflect and take advice from his solicitor.' She put her documents in her file and left the room.

'HE'S A COOL CUSTOMER,' Tracy said when he joined Fiona in the squad room.

'We'll hold him until noon tomorrow.' Fiona rubbed her eyes. 'O'Reilly won't agree to keep him a second longer than necessary.'

Tracy shrugged. 'Maybe a night in the cells.'

'He's not the type to crack. The DPP is going to have a heart attack when we put this to him. The gun evidence is solid but there's no way we can put it in Gannon's hand when the murders were committed. We tell a convincing story but that's what it is, a story. I know he killed Baum. I can see a twelve-year-old pushing an older man off a cliff especially if he felt he was a threat but a twelve-year-old executing two grown men. That's a stretch.'

Tracy smiled. 'Maybe this time we should have listened to Horgan.'

She stretched. 'I'm bushed. I didn't sleep too well last night. This investigation has gotten to me. I don't like the whole idea of listening to Horgan, but you might be right. I think we deserve a drink after a day like that.'

IT WAS LASHING RAIN OUTSIDE, but Taffees was toasty and there were a couple of decent musicians belting out jigs and reels. Fiona and Tracy sat in the snug and cradled their drinks both lost in their own thoughts. Their wet coats hung on a hook beside them and gave off a musty smell. The patrons burst into spontaneous applause when the group finished a set of reels.

'I'm really enjoying Galway,' Tracy said. 'Do you think they might move me?'

Fiona looked at his handsome face. He should be in the movies. Maybe if he'd been around in the 1950s he would have been. It might be good for him to get away from her. She was ruining his career by degrees. 'Maybe, I learned never to second guess the boys in the Park. They're a law unto themselves.' Whatever they decided probably wouldn't be good. The former Minister of Justice would see to that.

Aisling burst through the door and started shaking her umbrella. 'Filthy evening.' She sat down beside Fiona. 'Oh, I see the Glums are in town. Tough day?'

'You could say so.' Fiona told her about picking up Gannon and the subsequent interviews.

Aisling asked the barman for an orange juice. 'What did you expect? He's the CEO of a business that employs a lot of people in Galway and a Foundation that does a lot of good work for the poor and uneducated. He's well educated, erudite and has friends in high places.'

'Don't worry, Tracy had already given me the lecture on where we stood in comparison to Tim Gannon. But he's definitely murdered one man and stolen a fortune. That doesn't make him a paragon of virtue.'

Tracy finished his pint. 'One more?'

Fiona nodded.

Tracy placed the order. 'But, unfortunately, we have no evidence to prove either of those allegations.'

Aisling reached across the bar and took her juice. 'End of term is in two weeks, and I want to go somewhere warm where I can lie by a pool and drink piña coladas. I stopped by a travel agent at lunchtime and picked up a couple of brochures.'

Fiona took a pint from Tracy. 'The sun, the pool, and the drinks sound wonderful. Unfortunately, the insurance company haven't coughed up for the Kawasaki. And I'm financially embarrassed at the moment.'

'My treat,' Aisling said. 'I already booked. Two weeks in Denia.'

Fiona toasted. 'I can't wait.' She took a swallow of her Guinness. If O'Brien managed to sack her, maybe she'd stay on there.

CHAPTER FIFTY-NINE

The evening with Aisling was the perfect antidote to the day trying to get Gannon to confess. The rain hammering down as they perused the holiday company brochures and planned their upcoming holiday to the Costa Blanca. Despite the excitement generated by the upcoming holiday, every now and then Fiona's mind wandered back to Tim Gannon and the murdered German seamen.

She woke early, although her sleep hadn't been interrupted by nightmares. She contemplated taking the bus, but decided instead on a leisurely shower and preparing breakfast for Aisling. She didn't need to rush to the station for another frustrating encounter with Gannon. In her experience, most criminals are only too ready to tell their stories, which were generally nothing but a pack of lies. It was her job to sift through the nonsense and pick out the pearls of truth. Even those who continually repeated the no comment refrain eventually wanted to talk. Tim Gannon wasn't your usual criminal. He'd decided on his strategy and he was going to stick to it. If they wanted to put him away, they would have to work for it.

She was already on her way to the squad room when she heard her name being called by the duty sergeant. She turned, expecting to see him pointing upstairs, but found his finger crooked in the come here fashion.

He pointed to his right. 'The lady has been here for an hour. She asked for you in particular.'

Fiona followed his finger. Áine Gannon was sitting on the hard bench in the reception area reserved for visitors.

'Is Tracy here yet?' she asked.

'Five minutes ahead of you.'

'Get him down here and rustle up a cup of coffee for the lady and a bottle of water.' Fiona walked over to where Áine Gannon sat. 'I'm sorry for keeping you waiting. If I'd known you were here, I would have come earlier.' She turned as Tracy came into the reception area. 'Let's find somewhere more comfortable where we can talk.' Áine had to be Ninety-three-years-old but you would never believe it to look at her. Her grey hair was cut fashionably short, and the pale facial skin hadn't a wrinkle. She was slim and wore a long black skirt and a matching pullover. Even in old age she was a fine looking woman.

Áine tried to push herself up. 'Bloody knees.'

Fiona helped her stand and they walked together to the interview area and into the room that her brother had recently vacated.

Fiona led the older woman to a seat and sat down on the other side of the table. Tracy joined her.

'How can we help you?' Fiona asked.

Áine placed two gnarled hands on the table. 'I understand that you've arrested Tim for the murder of the two German seamen.'

'I'm afraid so.'

'Does that mean that he'll be tried for that crime?'

'That's not our decision. We'll prepare a file for the DPP and he'll have to decide.'

'I'd like to make a statement. I believe that's the right expression.'

Fiona could see the light at the end of the tunnel. Áine Gannon was going to skewer her brother. She nodded at Tracy, who set up his mobile phone on the table. 'Okay, we're ready, go ahead.'

'I shot those men.'

Fiona and Tracy looked at each other. 'What!' they said together.

'I said I shot both those men in the head.'

'Let's begin at the beginning,' Fiona said. Her head was spinning. She never for one second thought that Áine Gannon was the culprit, but she was anxious to hear the story. 'How did you meet Eich and Muller?'

'It was all because of Professor Baum, a German who was studying Irish. He was staying with us at the time.'

There was a knock on the door and a uniform entered carry a tray supporting a cup of coffee, a milk jug and some sachets of sugar. He put the tray on the table, handed Áine a bottle of water and left.

Gannon continued. 'We all knew that Baum wasn't there just to learn the language, although he had excellent command of Irish. He spent the evening with headphones on, listening to the radio. We guessed he was a spy, but Ireland was neutral. In fact, we thought it was bloody stupid sending a spy to Letter Mullen. One day, he became very excited and spent the entire day on the shore scouting the horizon with a large pair of binoculars. Two days later, he arrived at our cottage with Eich and Muller. They had docked their craft in a cove close to the house. My father greeted them as guests and we fed them whatever we had, which wasn't much. To be honest, from the outset I didn't like either of the men. They had no Irish and we didn't have any English or German so Baum translated for them, but I think he didn't give us the full picture. The three Germans spent a lot of time together and I heard them arguing once or twice. On the third day Baum asked me to show them the beach close to our house. I tried to get out of it, but Baum said I should go with them and come straight home.' She stopped and drank some water.

'Would you like to rest?' Fiona could see where the story was going, and she wasn't happy to be dredging up long dead memories.

'No, I prefer to continue. They brought along a bottle of poteen and were already drinking before we left. When we got to the beach, I tried to go home but they grabbed me.'

'They raped you,' Fiona said.

Áine's head dropped. 'Repeatedly. While one drank, the other took me, again and again. Eventually, I collapsed and fell into a sort of sleep. When I woke, they were both lying on the sand asleep. I took Eich's gun from his holster and shot him in the head, then I did the same to Muller. Then I collapsed again. I woke when I heard my father crying. He brought me into the sea and washed me.'

'It was your father who dumped the bodies in the bog.' The old woman was about to break down and Fiona tried to help her out. They could fill in the details later.

'Baum went crazy. He said we had messed up a German operation. He started shouting about the Führer's money. What was to be done? My father and Tim went back with him to the boat. That's all I want to talk about. Tim is innocent. You can let him go now.'

'You never married,' Fiona said. She was internally debating whether the story she had just heard was the truth or just a ruse to get Tim Gannon off. Because of the resonance with her own case, she was inclined to believe Áine. There would be no closure for Baum and the money. She had been totally wrong on the motive for the murders.

Tears streamed down Áine's cheeks. 'I became withdrawn. It turned out I had been damaged internally by the rapists. I could never have a family.'

Fiona looked at Tracy. His eyes were glassy. She hadn't just hit a bump in the road, she'd reached the terminus.

'Am I going to jail? Do I need to call our solicitor?'

'You're not going to jail and detective Garda Tracy will call your solicitor.'

'Can Tim go home now?'

'I think that can be arranged.' Fiona stood. 'Detective Garda Tracy and I are going to leave for a few moments. Will you be okay on your own?'

'You're very kind.'

Fiona went to the door. 'We won't be long.'

CHAPTER SIXTY

Horgan looked at Tracy. 'Get Gannon out of here pronto and don't forget to apologise to him for your and DS Madden's stupidity. He'll receive a letter of apology in due course from the Superintendent.'

Tracy looked sheepish and stopped before the door. 'What about his sister?'

'She stays here for the moment.'

Tracy left.

Fiona looked up from the desk and into Horgan's eyes. 'We'll take her statement and let her go. The DPP will have to decide what to do with her and we all know what that will be. The woman is ninety-three and had lived for most of her life with the trauma of being gang-raped and shooting her rapists.'

'Do you still believe you were right to pursue this one?' Horgan held her stare.

'A murder is still a murder, despite the circumstances.' It was a simplistic answer. She had intended to seek justice for the men who had been murdered, but in the end the person that should have had justice was the woman in the interview room. Nobody was a winner. The investigation was over, but she had no joy in finding Eich's and Muller's murderer. She wouldn't tell Hindrichson that his grandfather was a rapist. There was no point in bursting his bubble. She had already decided to lie that Baum had killed the seamen and disappeared with the money. There was nobody to contradict her.

Horgan sighed. 'We'll be lucky if Tim Gannon doesn't bring a case against us for wrongful arrest.'

'I don't think he'll want to expose the circumstances of the investigation.' He had gotten away with murder, theft, and money laundering. He should be happy not to be in jail. 'We'll drop the firearm change as a quid pro quo.'

'Some day, you'll do for us. Madden.'

'Hosting a drink this evening, boss?'

'Fuck off.'

They took Áine Gannon's statement and seated her carefully in the rear of the Mercedes 750 that her brother had sent to the station to pick her up. Fiona had explained to her that given the time elapsed and the circumstances surrounding the deaths, it was unlikely that the DPP would proceed against her. Áine thanked Fiona and Tracy for being so kind before the driver closed the door and the Mercedes pulled out of the station car park.

'Satisfied?' Tracy asked as the car disappeared down Lr. Dominick Street.

'We did our job and we can be proud of that.' She walked back to the station entrance.

'What are you going to tell the German Embassy?'

'Above my pay grade talking to ambassadors and the like. O'Reilly will handle that. He has a diploma in obsequiousness.'

Tracy laughed. 'You're a closet academic. That was a four syllable word. What about your pal Von Ludwig?'

Fiona stood at the entrance to the station but didn't cross the threshold. 'The next time I'm in Dublin, I'll look him up and run through a redacted version of the truth. By the way, Horgan has decided that our efforts don't justify a drink with our colleagues. When I broached the subject with him, he told me to fuck off. I suppose that's the end of the tradition.'

'I don't know about you, but I want to get royally pissed.'

'Strange, I don't really want to be in this station for the rest of the day. So, a nice warn snug in our favourite hostelry for the afternoon sound very appealing.'

Tracy was about to put his arm around her and lead her off to Taaffes, but he stopped himself at the last minute.

They looked at each other and laughed.

'We're a fine pair.' Fiona linked his arm and led him down Dominick Street and off to Taaffes.

EPILOGUE

Fiona stood pressed against the wall in Fitzwilliam Lane. She had followed Darker earlier in the evening and watched him enter his office. When darkness fell she disabled the lights that illuminated the portion of the lane that joined Fitzwilliam Street. She wore a black pullover and black trousers and a balaclava left only her eyes exposed. On her feet she wore a pair of Doc Martens.

The lane was pitch black when Darker exited his office and locked the outer door. He looked around. Like an animal he sniffed the air.

Fiona watched and waited.

Darker hesitated before moving off in the direction of Fitzwilliam Street.

Fiona stood away from the wall as he approached and barred his path.

Darker stopped. 'Not very smart, young fella. I'm a former copper and I'm trained in Krav Maga. That's an Israeli martial art for your information. Now get out of my fucking way before something very hasty happens to you.'

Fiona didn't move.

'Your funeral,' Darker said.

He immediately closed the distance between them and launched a punch at Fiona's head. She stepped to the side and at the same avoided the kick that accompanied the punch. The surprised look on Darker's face was priceless. She smiled behind her balaclava. He had been off balance and she could have ended it then but it would have been over too soon to satisfy her. She was pleased when Darker decided to continue. He was more circumspect this time. He approached carefully. Fiona stumbled on purpose and Darker rushed into the attack. His kick narrowly missed and the knife hand that followed cut through the air without finding its target.

Fiona had already formulated her response. She kicked hard at Darker's left knee. The noise of the bones shattering reverberated around the walls of the narrow lane. As he fell forward she smashed a punch into his open mouth that broke most of his teeth. The reconstruction of his knee would take more than one operation and the dental bill would put a dent in the fee he had made on the Gannon job. He would walk with a limp for the rest of his life.

She walked away, removed her balaclava, shook out her hair and had reversed her jacket before she reached Fitzwilliam Street. Some lout had sprayed two CCTV cameras with black paint earlier in the evening. She waited until a group of girls on a night out passed before joining them.

DID YOU ENJOY THIS BOOK?

If so and you'd like To try my Wilson series go to my website, https://www.derekfee.com and sign up to receive the first two books in the series FREE.

Thank you for your support.

EXHORTATION

Author's Plea

I hope that you enjoyed this book. As an indie author, I very much depend on your feedback to see where my writing is going. I would be very grateful if you would take the time to pen a short review. This will not only help me but will also indicate to others your feelings, positive or negative, on the work. Writing is a lonely profession, and this is especially true for indie authors who don't have the backup of traditional publishers.

Please check out my other books , and if you have time visit my web site (derekfee.com) and sign up to receive additional materials, competitions for signed books and announcements of new book launches.

You can contact me at derekfee.com

ABOUT THE AUTHOR

Derek Fee is a former oil company executive and EU Ambassador. He is the author of seven non-fiction books and twenty-two novels. Derek can be contacted at https://www.derekfee.com or on email at derek@derekfee.com

ALSO BY DEREK FEE

The Wilson Series
Nothing but Memories
Shadow Sins
Death to Pay
Dark Circles
Boxful of Darkness
Yield up the Dead
Death on the Line
A Licence to Murder
Dead Rat
Cold in the Soul
Border Badlands
Mortal Blow
Moira McElvaney
The Marlboro Man
A Convenient Death
Standalone
Cartel
Saudi Takedown
The Monsignor's Son

ALSO BY DEREK FEE

Crash Course
Galway Murder Mysteries
Connemara Girl
Murder in Clifden
The Druid's Dagger

Printed in Great Britain
by Amazon